RELEASED FROM THE SHADOWS

RELEASED FROM THE SHADOWS

Donna Cantor

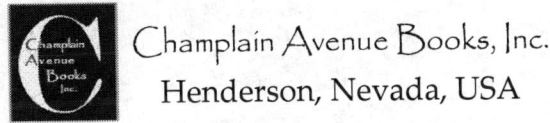 Champlain Avenue Books, Inc.
Henderson, Nevada, USA

Published by Champlain Avenue Books, Inc.,
Henderson, Nevada

ISBN-13: 978-0-9908256-9-2
Library of Congress Control Number: 2015930279

Cover Artwork by LAWRENCE

FIRST EDITION
2015

Printed in the United States of America

For my mother, who always encouraged me to read good books. And in memory of my father, who actively cultivated my sense of humor.

Chapter One

On Christmas Eve, hands seeking warmth in the flannel pockets of a thermal sweatshirt, Robert Zarro leans against the hood of his five year old blue Camaro, and watches the flames sear Maggie Ocampo's building in Bushwick, Brooklyn. Flashing red lights illuminate the street, courtesy of Engine 277, Ladder 112 and the ambulances that sit double-parked awaiting passengers. A covey of neighbors huddle, steamy wisps of breath rising from their mouths, sending unreadable smoke signals out into the cold. Zarro's dark eyes scan the scene, but he is numb to the drama playing out before him. He has been anesthetized since his stint in prison for selling drugs out of his college dorm and his release six months ago did little to revive his dormant senses. His eyes seek out his co-worker Maggie Ocampo, and he sees her slowly inching through the crowd as close to the burning row house as the FDNY barricades will permit. She is looking toward the flames, her eyes large and liquid. But Maggie is positioned too far back to see faces. The faces of her friends and roommates. He sees her forming silent words, over and over. *Dios Mio. Dios Mio.*

Stretchers are hoisted onto ambulances whose sirens wail as they tear away from the curb. Torrents of water pummel the flames, as grey smoke curls upward into the frigid air. Zarro can taste the ashes in the back of his throat. He notices a few snowflakes and momentarily becomes nostalgic for a white Christmas, but they are just cinders, swirling in the night. As he glances at the crowd of onlookers, Zarro spots a short man in a leather jacket talking to Maggie. The more the man says, the more upset Maggie becomes, but Zarro remains unmoved. Not his problem.

It is his own damned fault that he's spending Christmas Eve at an inferno in Brooklyn when he could have been seated before a boatload of seafood with his family in Revere, Massachusetts. Zarro did drop some hints that he'd be home in time for Christmas Eve. If he could leave his new job. If his boss Rick Schwab could spare him. He piled on the excuses to reduce expectations, but in reality Schwab's Uniform shut down altogether between Christmas and New Years. Zarro never mentioned that to his parents as he had no intention of actually visiting and dealing with that extra helping of guilt, for the last three of Robert Zarro's Christmases were spent as a guest of the warden at Old Bay Correctional. That meant two slices of overcooked turkey swimming in a moat of glutinous brown gravy and a solitary scoop of cold mashed potatoes. Busted in his junior year for running an on-campus drug operation. A very successful on-campus drug operation that specialized in but was not limited to the delivery of Adderall. As he shivers in the cold, Zarro realizes that his life is on a downward trajectory. Scholarship. Bentley University. Betrayal. Prison. Dead end job in Queens, New York. And now this—standing in the cold at a Christmas Eve fire. The icing on the cake. When had it all gone to shit? Once upon a time, he had wicked smarts. Majored in

Business, minored in good times. Maintained a 3.67 GPA even with his on campus pharmaceutical business. Ancient history, all of it. But he no longer knows the Robert Zarro with a future, except as a vague historical reference, a starred footnote at the bottom of a well-worn page, the person once inhabiting his skin having fled so long ago.

Maggie rejoins him at his car, cutting through his inner monologue. Tears streak her pretty face. "My house is burn, Roberto."

"You know those girls they carried out?"

She fishes out a tissue from her coat pocket and dries her face. "We live there. In the basement. I can't see who they bring. What hospital they go? I want to go with them."

Zarro takes a moment to process her hapless situation. "The hospital doesn't make sense, now. You'll just be in the way. So where can I take you now, Maggie? You have family here? Friends? Someone you can stay with tonight?"

"My family live in Nicaragua. And everything is in the apartment. My clothes. My bed. My toothbrush. My moneys. All I have is the twenty-five dollars bonus Marilyn Friedman the bookkeeper lady give me today."

Zarro frowns. How did this become *his* problem? All he did was drive Maggie home from Schwab's Uniform where they worked. After the party, he was supposed to drop her off and then drive back to his apartment in Queens. That's all he signed up for. The End. "Get back in the car. We'll figure this out."

"You can take me to the big church we pass. Father Benedicto will know what to do.

Maybe he put me with the sisters."

"Father Benedicto will be busy tonight. It's Christmas Eve. Any other ideas?"

"Don't put me on the street, Roberto. *Por favor*. I am nobody in this country."

Zarro starts the engine, turns up the heater, and pulls out of the spot. He hadn't dressed for an extended stay outdoors and he's frozen solid. Another ambulance speeds away from the burning house, its flashing lights etching a headache directly onto his retinas. "Who's the guy in the leather coat, walking around like he owns the street?"

"Rafael Guzman. He is very bad man."

Zarro doesn't press her. He got to know plenty of Rafael Guzmans in prison. "You'll come home with me," he hears himself say.

"Yes, but first I need stop at Good Wheel."

"What's that, some automotive place?"

"No 'berto. Good Wheel to buy some jeams. I leave my working clothes in Schwab's. But I need some nightgown, the toothbrush."

"Jeans with an 'n'. Oh, I get it. You mean Good Will."

"That's what I say. Buy the jeans with the 'en-nay', the sweater."

"Closed. Everything will be closed tonight and tomorrow. I'll ring my landlady's bell. Rose is nice. She'll lend you some things for tonight. And I'll open up Schwab's in the morning and you'll get your stuff." He is a warehouse manager at Schwab's Uniform. Zarro is aware he has a twentieth century job in the twenty-first century. He is a living, breathing anachronism, he who was supposed to have been a supply-chain wizard. That's where he was headed, before prison tripped up his big plans.

* * * * *

4

As he drives back to Queens, Zarro revisits the day and tries to make some sense out of it. It had started like any other day, so why hadn't it ended like any other day? He had left his hole in the wall apartment, crossed the street and was at Schwab's Uniform, distributor of military insignia to the Armed Forces by7:30 that morning. An overly decorated eight foot tall plastic Christmas tree stood at attention in the middle of the warehouse. Seventy-two year old Mel Lieb, all five foot four of him, sat at his front office with an electric menorah propped up on a shelf that faced the Plexiglas window into Rick Schwab's office. Zarro sat on the other side of Mel's desk with an iPad on his lap, ready to take down the last minute thoughts and instructions of Mel Lieb, future retiree. After New Years, Zarro would have Mel Lieb's job as warehouse supervisor. Lucky him.

"The boss positively hates this," Mel Lieb said pointing at the menorah, "which is why I insist on putting it up. You probably don't even know what it is."

"Never assume, Mel. One of my neighbor's has one, the one and only Mrs. Selma Feinberg of Revere, Massachusetts."

"Feinberg is not exactly an Italian sounding name."

"We can't all be perfect. Anyway. I would think Schwab probably figured out you're one of the chosen by now."

"He's none too happy to have it shoved in his face. Good country club WASP that he is."

"Why in all hell are you wasting time on *this* bullshit? I don't give a flying fuck if he's a virgin-sacrificing cannibal. There are a hundred and five other things I need to know — this being your last day. So give me a break. The Christmas party starts at noon and when that's over you and that oversized Lincoln of yours are heading for greener pastures."

5

"What I'm heading into is the largest honey-do list known to mankind. Respect where you've come from. That's all."

Why do old people always go off on some tangent? Zarro wondered. "Did it ever dawn on you that I'm not sitting here with a pad and a pen looking for homilies? So spare me the world according to Mel Lieb, and tell me why the inventory isn't on a goddamn computer." Mel Lieb's two age-speckled hands shot into the air. "Stop worrying. You'll do your learning on the job, just like everyone else. They're walking the food in. Let's go."

"I'll be sitting right here."

"That's what *you* think. Only two people stay in the office. Rick Schwab and that idiot of a son-in-law, and that's because they feel they're too good to mingle with the common folk. Even Marilyn Friedman, the crankiest bookkeeper on earth, comes out and makes herself a sandwich."

"That's because she feels like she personally paid for it."

"Never mind. You're going to be supervising these people. Don't tell me you're too good to party with them."

"No Mel, that's not it. You don't understand." Nobody understood. Nobody here knew what he had been through. Respect his past? His past consisted of time served.

"I understand. You're scared to death. Some of them know more than you do. And some of them are resentful that you're going to be over them. Look, you'll have to prove yourself—there's no getting around it. But you're all they have, Zarro and don't you ever forget that. You're what stands between them and that fancy manicured, Porsche-driving lunatic Rick Schwab, who'd sell them down the river in a heartbeat just to save a lousy ten cents an hour."

6

Zarro stood up and unzipped his sweatshirt, casually tossing it across the chair. Then he bent down and tightened the laces on his work boots. "I'm as ready as I'm ever going to be."

"God almighty, that's how guys dress for parties, these days? Even an old fart like me knew enough to wear a collared shirt. Here, at least splash on some after-shave. It's Brut, Zarro. Women positively go nuts for this stuff." Then Mel smoothed a wayward shock of white hair around his two elfin ears and began to croon, "Oh, how we danced on the night we were wed. We danced, and we danced — 'cause we didn't have a bed."

Zarro couldn't help but smile. "Since when did you start keeping after-shave in your drawer?" Zarro asked as he uncapped the bottle, took in a good whiff, and passed the bottle back in a hurry.

"Since I reached puberty a hundred years ago. This is a *party*, Zarro. Has it ever occurred to you that any one of those girls out back might want to dance with a tall, strong, handsome blonde guy like you? Don't you know I'd give my left nut to trade places with you? Twenty-five years old, world on a string."

But Zarro didn't have the world on a string. He was six months out of prison and he would have to socialize. He might have to touch people and resist the urge to knock them to the ground. Halfheartedly, he tried convincing himself that he had made progress. Old Bay was history. Maybe he could pull this off. Maybe. *Shit* on maybe. He would have to do this.

Mel slid open a desk drawer. "Take a look at this Hess truck, Zarro. It's for my grandson. Six years old and smart as a whip. Think he'll like it?"

"It's a good looking truck. I was always happy to see one of those under the tree."

7

Rick Schwab's voice traveled across the loudspeaker into the warehouse. "Okay, people. It's past twelve o'clock. We wish you and yours a Merry Christmas and a Happy New Year. It's been a good year and hopefully next year will be even better."

"Yeah, maybe World War Three will break out," Zarro muttered under his breath.

Mel Lieb smiled. "You're going to have yourself a great time here, Zarro."

He followed Mel into the warehouse, both of them finding their way to a huge tray of baked ziti. He observed an attack on the food from every corner. He saw two order-pullers produce a roll of aluminum foil and slip an extra sandwich or two into their purses. He marveled as two sewing machine operators divvied up an entire tray of sausage and peppers and quickly shoveled it into industrial sized Ziplock bags.

"Unbelievable," Mel remarked. "Darwin would call that survival of the fastest."

"Hurry yourself up, Matty. Bust a rhyme white boy," Suzie Q, one of the order pickers instructed loudly. Suzanne Quentin: Suzie Q, Fat Suzie, Black Suzie. Crazy Ass Suzie. Everyone had nicknames at Schwab's Uniform.

Then Matty McClellan, a pug-faced, permanently buzzed toothpick-sucking moron who drove the company van and his sidekick Weeds (or Rupert Byron as he was officially known on Marilyn Friedman's payroll), a scrappy Jamaican guy whose dreadlocks weighed more than he did, hooked up two huge speakers to the old boom box and began to feed it CD's. They alternated between Latin and hip-hop, blasting music decibels above and beyond the usual racket. The three Spanish guys from shipping, Manuel, Israel, and Junior, jumped up onto the long tables and started singing above the music. The sound was loud enough to rouse Elmo-the-cleaning-guy from his siesta and he

8

cursed loud and clear, saying he was convinced no one thought to save him a sandwich.

"Don't worry Elmo," Maggie reassured him. "I get for you." She produced a bulging napkin wrapped around a turkey sandwich. *"Mira."*

Elmo kissed the top of Maggie's head, put the sandwich into the large blue denim apron that he wore, and started dancing with Lygia, one of the young girls who sewed medal sets at Schwab's. "Careful Elmo," Matty McClellan shouted to him, "You might rupture an artery."

Others followed Elmo and Lygia. Within fifteen minutes, the floor was covered with dancers. The younger ones climbed up onto the long tables and danced up there. Suzie Q, now dressed in a Santa suit, had taken Elmo's hand and together they climbed up on a table and began to dance. .

Zarro's dark eyes recorded all that was around him, pulling slowly on his beer. This is his world now, he thought. Instead of working quietly at a desk with his app-laden up-to-the minute tablet, he would have to manage this dysfunctional circus. "They're going to kill themselves," Zarro said to nobody in particular.

"You no dance, Roberto?" Maggie asked, her husky voice startling him.

Zarro allowed himself to take a quick peek at her. Large olive green eyes, shoulder length light brown hair. She had a good body. Who could have predicted that? Her baggy grey sweatpants were gone, replaced by a gray knit dress and a pair of black high-heeled shoes.

"I used to," he said.

She took the beer out of his hand and pulled him to the makeshift dance floor. *Please God, let me do this. Please God, let me be a human being for a little while.* He put his left hand across her back and with his right he gingerly reached for her hand. When he was able to excavate the old Robert Zarro, the partying college boy Robert Zarro the frat nicknamed Kicker because he could always kick the party up a notch or two, he let his hips swivel and she smiled up at him. He really wasn't ready for human contact. Then Rick Schwab paged him into his office and that ended Zarro's uneasiness.

"Lock up," his boss said. "I'm out of here. Don't let the party go past five. They'll be fall down drunk by then. The older ones will leave as soon as Marilyn hands out the bonuses. The younger ones will party until midnight if you let them. And don't you let them."

"I hear you."

Mel Lieb appeared in Rick Schwab's doorway. "I'm heading home."

Rick extended his hand. "Mel, don't be a stranger."

"Don't forget the Hess truck," Zarro said to Mel Lieb.

"Ooh yeah. Got a mind like a steel trap this one has," Mel said, winking at Zarro.

"Listen Zarro, I put your phone number down as first contact for the alarm company," Rick said.

"I won't need a call, Zarro said to his boss. "I live facing the garage. If it goes off, I'll hear it loud and clear. Hey, Merry Christmas to you."

"Don't start with that happy holiday horseshit," Rick said. "I'll see you a day after New Years."

"Well," Mel said gathering his belongings. "I guess this is goodbye."

"Happy holidays Mel," Zarro said sticking out his right hand.

"That's it? I grunt and sweat next to you for three months, impart to you all the wisdom I possess on a silver

10

platter, and all I get from you is a handshake? I thought all you Italians were emotional. You know, all tears and hugs and kisses. Wait Zarro, my Italian fantasy is cranking up. Me and a gorgeous Italian babe. We're in Disney World. I'm dressed as Mickey Mouse and that magnificent chest of hers is falling out of her blouse. My wife is busy in the souvenir shop."

"Not to interrupt your Italian fantasy, but I'll be calling you six times a day so it's not like this is any great departure."

Mel Lieb shut his light and made his way up the hill, past shipping and into the space set aside for a garage. It took him nearly an hour, as he said goodbye to each and every one of the people he had worked alongside over the years. Suzie Q shouted, "Speech, speech," but the old man declined, and after he said his last goodbye, Zarro watched as he climbed into his Town car, and heard him locate the sweet voice of Bobby Darren. Then he pushed up his glasses, let out a good, long sigh, and drove off.

At five o'clock, Suzie Q removed her Santa suit and put an oversized Depends undergarment over a pair of pink spandex pants. For some reason she also added a curly blond wig to the ensemble. "Now I'm the New Year's baby," she announced with a smile, her round black face revealing three crater-sized dimples.

"Whatever you've been drinking, I want some of it," Zarro told her.

"I dress for all the holidays, Zarro. You should see my Saint Patrick's Day get up. Baby, it's mean and it's green."

"Looking forward to it," he answered. And with that, Zarro unplugged the music and the few people remaining found their coats. Then it registered that Elmo-the-Cleaning-Guy had left and Zarro swore softly under his breath when he realized that he would be the one to clean up a warehouse full of empty plates and trays.

"What a mess," he said, looking around and shaking his head.

"No worry. I help you Roberto," Maggie said, rolling up the sleeves on her dress and pulling her light brown hair into a high ponytail.

"Go home. I got it."

But Maggie Ocampo stayed, and helped him clean up the warehouse. So, Zarro felt obligated to give her a lift home. And that was how a twenty-five year old ex-con without a future got stuck bringing home a girl who was nobody in this country.

Maggie's tears reappear just about the time the Camaro's heater starts blowing hot air. "My friends. Myrna, Carmen, Linda. They are like my sisters. Oh 'berto, I feel sick in my heart."

He keeps driving. Not knowing how to offer comfort, he stays quiet. He glances at the clock on the dashboard. A little past eight. His family would be sitting down to shrimp, just about now. *The family I should be with for an Italian Christmas Eve in Revere. The family I shamed.*

The steady unblinking gaze of large, old-fashioned Christmas bulbs on Rose Petruzzi's three-family house lights up the deserted street. Zarro rents a dumpy one-bedroom here, across the street from the Schwab's Uniform warehouse on the 39th Street side. The ninety-year old house is the lone residential dwelling on an industrial strip that included C.J.'s Auto Body

12

and Ed's Corrugated Carton. He parks the car, enters the hallway, climbs a flight of worn out wooden stairs that for some reason always smell of raisins, and unlocks the door to the furnished apartment he's been living in since he moved to New York in September. He hopes the three small rooms are at least presentable, for he does not remember cleaning them or not cleaning them, making his bed this morning, or leaving it in a rumpled heap. The morning happened weeks ago. Since his stay at Old Bay, he no longer has a handle on time.

Maggie follows him and her eyes widen when he opens the door and switches on the light. "Oh Roberto, this is very nice. You live here all by yourself? Alone?" She tells him his apartment is the same size as her parent's little house near Leon, the little house that they all lived in with the dirt floors and the pretty cloths her mother had hung from the ceiling to make "rooms."

"Yes, all by myself. Alone." He goes into the bathroom and pulls a bottle of aspirin from the mirrored medicine chest, Maggie following him two steps behind.

"You have a big bathtub. *Mira,* your bathtub have the feet like a bird. You are lucky," Maggie says, apparently unaware she has entered his private space.

"I use the shower." He washes two aspirin down with a gulp of tap water.

"Are you hungry, Roberto? The lunch we have at Schwab's is a long time ago."

"I don't know what I am." And he doesn't know what he is capable of. Prison had swallowed the charming party boy and spat out an uncivilized brute.

Maggie unzips her purse and pulls out a can of Franco American beef ravioli.

"You have the hotplate and the can opener?"

13

He stares at the can as strangely as if she'd pulled a rabbit from her hat. "Give it to me. I'll dump it into a bowl and heat it in the microwave." In college he hung with girls who were all on special diets. Lactose intolerant locavore vegans who avoided gluten as if it were arsenic. Zarro pulls two bowls from the cabinet and poured some ravioli in each. He opens his refrigerator and finds two cans of beer. "*Salute,*" he says dryly, raising the can to his mouth.

"Eat, Roberto," Maggie said. "Is good. Yes?"

"No," he snaps, "is *not* good. Overcooked macaroni from a tin can is *not* good."

His mother made *fresh* raviolis. She bought it from her favorite *pastosa* in Revere. She ripped each piece on the perforated line, laid it out on a white bed sheet and boiled it twelve at a time, cooked to his father's taste. She served them in the blue ceramic pasta bowl in a light marinara sauce. His mother would be in her green and red Advent sweater. The house he grew up in would be aglow in candles and colored lights. Or maybe not. He couldn't remember if his parents fully lit up the house since his maternal grandparents died in an accident on a senior citizen bus trip to a Connecticut casino back when he was in college.

"You angry on me, Roberto?" Maggie asks, her voice bringing him back to his kitchen in Sunnyside, Queens.

"No, I'm not angry. I have a headache."

"I wash these bowls very good so the mouses don't come. We have so many mouses in Brooklyn. I see the mouses walking in Schwab's too and I tell Mel Lieb and he has Elmo put the green poisons on the floor. Then I see dead mouses."

"Well Maggie, what would you rather see, dead mouses or live mouses?"

14

"I like to see *no* mouses. Roberto, can I take a bath in the big bathtub with the feet like a bird? I get so close to the fire I am smelling of smoke."

"Yeah, knock yourself out." He gets up and rummages through the dresser in his bedroom. "Here, you can put this on when you get out." He hands her one of his old Bentley U sweatshirts and a pair of boxers that will be down to her ankles. "You might want to clean the tub before you get in. Rose, my landlady wiped it down before I moved in but it hasn't been used in God knows how long."

"*No problema.* I take the Ajax from the kitchen. A towel?"

He finds a towel in the linen closet and she closes the door and runs the water. She sings a sad Spanish song, her husky voice mingling with the cascading water. Zarro positions himself under his set of weights and begins to lift. He bench-presses until he no longer feels his arms. Then he towels off on a raggedy dishtowel and nearly jumps out of his skin when he hears a loud knock at his door.

"Rose?" he asks, opening the door.

"Merry Christmas Robert Zarro," his landlady says, squinting for a second before she slides her extra thick black glasses to the bridge of her nose. "And here I thought you'd be in Boston by now. I must say I was real surprised to see a light on."

"My plans changed."

"I brought you some fried *calamari* in sweet sauce. My daughter Louise, her husband Hector and my ten-year old grandson Frankie are with me. I wish I knew you were all by yourself. You could have joined us. I got plenty of food being that my sister-in-law and her kids were supposed to be here, but they're all sick with the flu." Rose picks up the empty can of ravioli that is still on his counter. "Now I don't know nothing

15

about your mother with the exception being she's Italian. And that's enough for me to know she would ab-so-lute-ly drop dead on the spot if she saw you eating *this* on Christmas Eve."

"You got that right," Zarro says, pulling at a piece of *calamari*. "Mmm. This is good stuff, Rose. Thanks."

"Robert Zarro, is that *singing* coming from your bathroom?"

"That's Maggie Ocampo. I work with her over at Schwab's. Her apartment burned down today and she needed a place to stay temporarily."

Rose shifts her weight to her good ankle and brushes back a dark pouf of hair. "Hey, what you do in your apartment is your business. If you want to invite naked girls into your bathtub, that is ab-so-lute-ly up to you. But as your landlady, I got only one concern."

"Yeah, what's that?"

"Young female persons on the premises can only mean sanitary napkins. And I can't begin to tell you what a sanitary napkin can do to this sensitive plumbing. I told you my grandfather built this house brick by brick. Anyway, my daughter Louise, Lou-Lou, the one who lives in the building, flushed one down when she was a teenager. Said it was an accident, but who knows with her. Anyways, thank God she's pregnant with her second, and I don't have to think about this problem for another four months. Unless *your* girl slips up, that is."

Robert Zarro falls into a chair laughing. Who would believe what his life had become?

"Is something funny here? Did I say something funny?" Rose asks, pushing her black-framed eyeglasses up over the bridge of her nose for the second time.

16

He tries to regain his composure. "Not at all. It's been a crazy day. Hey, you don't happen to have any leftover bread to mop up the sauce, Rose, now do you?"

"Get yourself downstairs. *Paysan* or no *paysan*, if you think I'm gonna make two trips on this lousy ankle, you're crazy. I got bread. I got eggplant. Take what you want. Ravioli from a can, what a sin. That stuff was invented for people from Wisconsin, people who don't know what fresh raviolis are supposed to taste like."

"I swear I'll never do it again. Rose, can I borrow a toothbrush, a set of clothes? Whatever you can spare. My friend lost everything in the fire."

"It's too bad. I just donated a big bag of clothes to St. Vincent de Paul."

"Why, are you two the same size?"

"Ab-so-lute wise guy, you are. Maybe my daughter has something to spare. How tall is she?"

"Five-four, thereabouts."

"What's her figure? Big boobs? Small boobs?" she asks as they descend the staircase to Rose's apartment.

"Jesus, Rose. I don't know. Most times we're fully dressed over at Schwab's Uniform. But let's assume just for argument's sake now, they're in the medium range." He tries his best not to notice these details, but he isn't completely dead. Only half-dead. *Mezzo morto* as his mother would say.

"Everybody, this is Robert Zarro from Schwab's," Rose says as they enter her apartment. "His girlfriend is taking a bath in the tub upstairs so if water comes dripping down the ceiling, we'll all know why. Lou-Lou, can he borrow some clothes for her? She set her apartment on fire and she got nothing to put on. She's five four and has medium boobs. You know, I didn't even think to ask about her coulie."

17

"Ma please, you're embarrassing the guy. I got plenty of clothes to spare," Louise says, her extended belly brushing up against the Christmas tree, causing pine needles to rain down on her mother's floor. When Louise re-emerges from across the hall, she tells Zarro, "She can keep all these things." Louise starts to put the stack of clothes into an Associated Supermarket bag. "Take a look at this sweater," she says to her family, holding up a skimpy striped knit. "It's in perfect condition, only thing is I'm sick of looking at it. After I have the baby, I'm getting me a brand new wardrobe. You hear that, Hector?"

"My wife is giving away all her clothes. She must have a rich husband somewhere I don't know about. That's our ten year old son Frankie and I'm Hector, her poor husband," he says extending a hand. "That's right, don't even think about saying it. I hear this every day. I sound just like Ricky Ricardo," he tells Zarro. "I will do this once and only once. Ready? Lu--cy, I'm ho--me."

"Not bad," Zarro admits.

"The only difference between me and Ricky is that I don't play the congas and I can't sing to save my life. I install windows for a living. In fact, as a Christmas gift to my mother-in-law, I am putting new windows on this old house because if we wait for Rose to pay for it, we got ourselves one long wait."

"Don't start with me, Hector," Rose protests. "You know I'm living on a fixed income."

"Except your fixed income is bigger than my unfixed income."

Rose waves a hand. "Don't mind him," she tells Zarro. "He don't know what he's talking about. With all the nice Italian boys in the borough of Queens, my one and only daughter has to go for Cuban Pete. And this good-for-nothing can't even sing Baba-Lou."

18

"You don't happen to have a spare toothbrush, would you?" Zarro asks.

"Of course I do," Rose says, squinting at him from behind her glasses. "My dentist gives them away like candy. You think your girl would like firm, soft, or medium?"

Louise shakes her head. "Ma, do you ever hear yourself talk?" Then when her mother is somewhat out of earshot, she tells Zarro, "Please don't mind her. In case you haven't figured it out yet, she's nuts. And I mean whacko with a vengeance."

"Let's go with the medium, Rose," Zarro says, trying his best to suppress a smile.

"Okay. You're all set. Bread. Eggplant. Medium toothbrush. Medium bra."

"Thank you. I really appreciate this. Merry Christmas." he tells Rose and her family.

"Merry Christmas Robert Zarro," Rose echoes. "And don't you forget to warn your girl about the sanitary napkins, okay?"

"Yeah, tomorrow over a couple of cocktails."

Arms laden, he climbs the stairs to his apartment. Overwrought from the day's events, Maggie is sound asleep, her body pulled up into a ball on the unopened sofa, her damp hair splayed across a throw pillow. He slides the eggplant and the calamari onto an empty shelf in the refrigerator and fetches a blanket out of the closet. He spreads the covers around her and after some initial hesitation, he allows himself a long look at the soft chestnut down at the nape of her neck. He pulls his cell out of his pocket and leaves a message on his family's answering machine, timing his call precisely for the block of time they'd be on their way to midnight Mass. Mission accomplished, Zarro goes into the bathroom and treats himself to the coldest shower he could tolerate, dousing his lust with a healthy dose of highly rated New York State reservoir water.

Then, he enters his bedroom, flips the news on, and watches Maggie's building burn again on the recap of the evening's top stories. Three girls dead, nineteen injured, of the nineteen—four in guarded condition, the wounded taken to Lutheran Hospital in Brooklyn. The well-coifed reporter at the scene expresses all types of disbelief at the crowded living conditions of these young women, presumably undocumented aliens, nameless, faceless women, some of them no more than girls, hankering for their piece of the American dream. People no different from you and me. And Zarro knows that by the time the reporter climbs into the Eyewitness News van and smoothes the designer skirt over her recently waxed legs, the plight of those young women will be all but forgotten. As soon as viewers get off their sofas, and slide under a warm blanket, those girls will fade from memory. In a week's time the entire incident will be expunged from the collective consciousness, as new tragedies tug at the public's worn-out heartstrings.

Zarro awakes the next morning to the aroma of coffee. He shows Maggie the toothbrush and the clothes that are sitting on the kitchen counter. She throws her arms around his neck and Zarro, promptly removes them.

"Thank you. These are so nice. Jeans with the 'en-nay' and the sweater. Socks. *Mira*, you ever see anything like this, Roberto? This bra is backwards, no?"

"This type of ladies' undergarment is not at all uncommon here in these United States. Believe it or not, the hooks go in the front. It's what's commonly referred to as a front loader. Lucky for you, I've come across this item once or twice in my travels," he replies.

"A front loa-der. You like? Yes?" She holds up her new bra, as pleased as a child with a new toy.

"I like, yes."

"Your lady upstairs, she give to you these things?"

"The clothes are from her daughter, Louise. And Louise said you don't ever have to return them. She lives here in the building, downstairs on the right side with her husband and her son."

"I thank her very much today, Louise. The front loa-der and the underwears she give to me is new. The tickets are still hanging."

Maggie takes the clothes into the bathroom and models them. "Oh, this is nice. Very soft," she says, patting the clingy front of a beige angora sweater.

Zarro takes a sip of his coffee. "This is not going to work out, you staying here."

"I know. Just for this week, okay? Then I talk to Lygia in sewing at Schwab's and maybe I can move into her apartment if there is room for me."

"I...I don't mean it's any rush or anything." Then he takes a deep breath. "Maggie, how many girls lived with you?" Zarro asks, dreading to tell her what he learned on last night's news.

"Twenty-one."

"Get out of here. In the basement of that building?" He pictures twenty-one Maggies trying to get up the smoky staircase.

"*Si.*"

"Why so many?"

"Because."

21

"Because is not an answer."

"You want some more coffee, 'berto?"

"Answer me."

"Because we no have green cards. We are nobody here."

"How do you get paid at Schwab's?"

"Marilyn Friedman the bookkeeper bring to me the cash."

"How much?"

She stares at him.

"Goddamn it Maggie, as of next Tuesday I am your supervisor."

"Five dollar and fifty cents an hour."

"That's way below minimum wage. Who else is making that?"

She rattles off a list of fourteen names.

"*None* of you are in the union?"

"No green card. When the union come, we hide in Matty's van or in the bathroom so we no have troubles."

"Five dollars and fifty cents an hour for the work you do? That's not right."

"Roberto, can I go to find my friends? I am so worry."

Zarro hesitates for a minute, hoping the right words will float to the top, realizing quickly there are no right words. "Three girls died. The rest are at Lutheran Hospital, and some of them are in pretty bad shape. If you want, we can take a ride over today."

"Three girls die. I have to find out who. My friends are hurt. This is terrible." She pronounces the last word as they do in Spanish—terr-ee-blay.

Zarro goes into his room and pulls a flannel shirt out of a drawer and puts it over his T-shirt. It's downright frigid in the apartment and he wonders where Rose is with the heat. "You

22

have an account at Citibank?" he asks, because that's where Schwab's Uniform did all of their banking.

"No bank. No social security number. I keep my moneys very safe inside the towel."

"Very safe inside a towel that got charcoal broiled. What did you do with the Bullshit Club money?" The Bullshit Club, Zarro learned when he started at Schwab's, is a rainy day fund for the company's underpaid workers. Every payday, workers added twenty dollars into the fund, and they'd wait for their week to collect the pile of money, and feel rich.

"I give that five hundred dollars to the lawyer, Mr. Quinones."

"For what?"

"He apply me for the visa so I can get the green card last year and he say he need more moneys now to process the paper."

"Jesus Christ. Are you that naive? Why in holy hell would you give him cash?"

"Please don't yell at me, Roberto. The cash is all I have."

Zarro nods. "I didn't mean to yell. You have an address on Mr. Quinones? A phone number?"

"He's in Brooklyn on the funny street called Flushing Avenue. He don't come to the phone when I call him from the telephone."

"Okay," he says, unaware at first that he is frowning. Finally, the heat comes clanging through the radiator, Rose's anvil chorus.

"What is that?"

"The heat coming up from the old pipes."

"The heat is very good," she says. "You are very lucky."

"Look Maggie, I know it's a long shot, but I'm going to walk down Queen's Boulevard, see if anything's open." He

23

needs some air. Some time to collect his thoughts. He needs space. "Okay. I clean for you."

"Leave it. I'll take care of it when I get home."

"No, no I used to clean for ladies. Just when I come from Nicaragua, I have to clean for Jackie's Cleaning Service in Staten Island. To pay off my trip. She give me thirty-five dollars a day."

"Yeah? And what did Jackie get?"

"Fifteen, because she bring me in the car. But she promise me visa to stay as live-in maid in the house. But I wait eight months but this job no happen. So I quit and then I find Rick Schwab's. But I still owe moneys. The man Rafael Guzman, you see yesterday in the leather coat, is working with Jackie. And Jackie is working with the mens who bring me to this country. He is very bad."

Zarro checks the time. Ten thirty-five. He wears a new watch now. The one that sat for years in the prison bin could not be resuscitated. It lay in a Massachusetts dump, correct in eternity twice per day, forever and ever 11:11. He throws on his jacket and walks downstairs. As a frigid wind blows across Queens Boulevard, bile rises in his throat when he thinks how she was taken advantage of at every turn. Zarro had been a witness to all kinds of victimization when he had been locked up. He had been a target, himself. Each day he'd put blinders on, and go about his prison business. Over time, scar tissue formed on his soul, a black crust he could not scrape off with a sharpened knife. But for some reason her plight stirs up some long buried feelings within him. And he just cannot make himself numb.

* * * * *

In the apartment, Zarro's cell phone sings out on the kitchen counter. Maggie hesitates before she answers it.

"*Hola*, I mean to say, hello."

"Sorry, I must have the wrong number," a female voice replies. "I'm looking for Robert Zarro."

"No, no. He live here. He go outside. Can I tell him who is this?"

There is a moment of silence. "Yes, this is his mother. And what is *your* name?"

"Magaly Ocampo. They call me Maggie. I work with Roberto at Schwab's. He is very good to me. I tell him you call, okay? Merry Christmas to you Mrs. Zarro."

Zarro finds a map of the five boroughs at the 99Cent store that is open on Christmas Day until noon. It will be good to keep it in the car. The GPS on his cell ate way too much battery and liked to send him on out of the way expeditions.

On his way back into his apartment, he smells cleanser as he enters and he halfheartedly scolds Maggie for cleaning.

"A very nice lady your mother call on the telephone."

"Shit," he says, slapping the map onto the counter. "Goddamn son of a bitch. I can't ever catch a fuckin' break, can I?" Involvement and explanations. Lies to cover lies. The ever-present guilt trip. He really doesn't need any of that now.

"Why you say this?"

"Forget it. It's a complicated family situation that I'm not going to get into. I just want to look at this for a minute. Are you ready to go to the hospital?"

"I am ready. You do not say Merry Christmas to me this morning, Roberto."

"Can we just get the hell out of here?"

He sits in the waiting room as she goes from room to room, a stack of work he brought from home occupying him for the first hour, games on his cell phone filling the second . Of the nineteen hospitalized girls, four are in intensive care. She'd gone to visit with the remaining fifteen, then emerges, drained and red-eyed. She lowers her head onto Zarro's chest and he taps her. "Come on," he says, gathering his papers and brushing her off. "Let's get in the car."

"They say the four in the special room are very bad. They no let me in to see them. And the rest they say are not so bad but they look so very bad to me."

"Do you ever think to yourself how lucky you were that you stayed late at Schwab's? That could have been you in there, you know. They were trapped on the smoky staircase, no way for all of them to get out."

"I am *not* lucky, Roberto. Three of my friends are dead. I have no place to live. My moneys are burned, except the twenty-five dollars. And I am very afraid."

"Afraid of what?"

"Afraid of everything."

They eat the remainder of Rose Petruzzi's food that night and Maggie asks Zarro for permission to watch the TV in the living room. Zarro lifts his weights and Maggie flips through the channels. "I never get to watch the show I want in the

26

apartment. We only have one TV for all of us. And my friends like the MTV."

"Don't even *think* of putting that crap on." The only thing that network does is remind him of the old party boy Robert Zarro. The half-naked bodies mock him, goad him, and trigger rage. He finds nothing beautiful in those images. He wouldn't let his younger brother Anthony watch it when he spent those two hellish summer months in Revere after his release. Two months, where he tried his best to avoid the neighbors. Two months, where he endured his mother's tears and his father's sullen disappointment. Why didn't he let them visit him in prison, they wanted to know. Why Robbie? Why? He ignored their questions. Feeling a burning need for distance, and plenty of it, at the end of the summer Zarro only applied for out of state jobs. When Schwab's Uniform called, he made his escape.

Maggie selects a Spanish soap opera on the *Telemundo*, channel 47. She becomes transfixed and Zarro watches her concentration as the male lead says something to the young woman on the screen.

"What's the guy saying to her?" he asks, grunting as he curls.

"He say he loves her, but everyone know he really loves the other girl, Rosa Salmaje."

He remembers his mother watching a soap opera when he was home sick from school. How she'd become so involved pieces of laundry would fall from her hands, floating onto the living room floor like frail petals from an October rose. Even as a kid, it all seemed so hokey to him back then, so contrived. But observing Maggie, he understands now. One can escape into the pretty faces, the perfect clothes, and the tastefully arranged furniture. Gone is the ugly warehouse, the hardscrabble existence. Gone is the monotonous housework. Willed away, one could become those people an hour at a time.

After a series of intense dramatic conflict, the music begins to play. Crescendo. The screen fills with empty beach. Horses appear out of nowhere, galloping across a blanket of sand, their black hooves kicking up a spray of sand and ocean water.

"Okay Maggie," Zarro teases when the show ends. "We tune in *manana* to find out what happens to our..." And then he pauses deliberately in the overwrought style of the Spanish announcer, "Ro--sa Sal--ma--je."

His impersonation makes Maggie laugh. "Tell me Roberto, why you lift those heavy things every night?"

"To make me big and strong."

"You *are* big and strong."

"You can never be strong enough." Zarro had learned that lesson the hard way, in Dawes Block at Old Bay Correctional.

Chapter Two

Her life changes once again, Maggie thinks. Yesterday, she lived in a basement in Bushwick, Brooklyn with twenty girls just like herself. Girls from Nicaragua, from Honduras, from Guatemala. Girls who ran away from poverty, or ran away from men, or from drugs, or from violence. Girls who heard it was better in the USA. At night, they'd sit on their cots all in a row and tell their stories. Stories of a cousin who has a dishwasher. An aunt who drives a car. A neighbor who made the trip and now works in an office with soft, thick rose-colored carpeting. And each one would all pay attention to the stories, hoping one day *she* would be the subject in the story. But "one day" might be far away, Maggie realizes. One day might be never.

She left Nicaragua this past June and did not arrive in New York until late July. Every month she paid the *mara*, the gang who had smuggled her into the country. Her first job was cleaning houses for Jackie's Cleaning Service. The *mara* had an arrangement with Jackie where they took their percentage right off the top. Jackie also took a percentage, leaving her with fifteen dollars for an eight-hour day. One of the girls Maggie lived with told her about Schwab's Uniform where they did not ask too many questions about green cards. She had been working there since the beginning of August. Picking orders. Sewing ribbon sets. Slowly, she is learning English. But Americans speak very fast.

She misses her mother and her brothers and sisters. She does not miss her father. No, there's a large, round dead spot on her heart where his words had wounded her. Her mother said nothing when her father threw her out of the house. Of course she kept quiet. Her mother had other children to feed. And Maggie could be sacrificed.

Her Aunt Karla made the arrangements to get her out of Nicaragua, to start a new life. Aunt Karla knew someone who knew someone. And there were people to pay. Her aunt took care of that. But what her aunt didn't know was that the last leg of the journey was run by the *mara*. And with the gang, paying is forever. And that is how she came to live in the Brooklyn basement with the other girls with similar stories. Every month the gang had to be paid. Otherwise she would be forced to sell drugs on the street or work as a prostitute or they would cut off a finger or an ear, or they would find and kill her family in Nicaragua. She can never walk away from her debt. She is her debt.

Although Maggie lives in this nice apartment now, she has to be careful because Roberto doesn't like being with her. Roberto turns his ten-minute errands into two-hour excursions in order to get away from her. So, she tries to make herself useful by cleaning. She irons the clothes. Makes everything neat. She makes herself tiny, too. She can shrink by staying in the corner of the room, not talking, keeping to herself. This way he would not notice her and throw her out into the streets, the way her father had. And just like her father, Roberto cannot even look at her, and that is not a good sign. Sometimes his dark eyes look so sad, and she wonders why. Maybe people had hurt him, people from the life he had before he came to Schwab's Uniform. She knows hurt. And she knows about keeping secrets, too.

Had it been a good decision to come to New York? You can start over, her Aunt Karla had told her. Nobody knows you in America. At work, she could put her sorrows up on a high shelf, and forget. But this week Schwab's is closed and she is not busy. And her sorrows jump off the shelf where she stores them and demand to keep her company. All the sadness of her trip to New York creeps in. It crawls over her, clamping its insistent hand over her throat. She remembers one of her poems, safe in her purse. *El Terremoto.* The Earthquake. Her personal earthquake. The day her world shook beneath her. *El dia del temblor debajo mis pies.*

Maggie gazes out the window onto 39th Street and looks at Schwab's Uniform, the rear of the building squat and ugly. Yesterday, she learned about snow. Snow is no longer a beautiful picture in a book. It is cold and wet and it stings the face. Snow becomes speckled with soot and gets into her shoes. And suddenly, she feels a ghost, a breeze—a warm breeze. She will tell Lygia at work about it after the holiday. But she will not tell Roberto. People in this country do not believe in spirits. The dead are supposed to disappear.

Chapter Three

On New Year's Day, the last afternoon before they would return to work, Zarro spots a tall, thin dark-haired man in gold wire framed glasses out his bedroom window. The man's large hand holds onto the red woolen mitten of a little girl, and they are smiling sunshine at each other. It takes Zarro a full minute before he realizes that the man is the brother of Matty, Detective Tommy McClellan, for in the presence of his daughter, that mocking look of his has completely vanished from his face.

Recalling the first awkward encounter with the obnoxious detective back in October, Zarro frowns. He had been in the warehouse office of Schwab's Uniform slicing a box open right after closing when this same man appeared at the Plexiglas, tapped out a Latin beat in time to the radio and strolled in. From Zarro's initial glance, the man looked to be in his early to mid-thirties, had slicked back dark hair, a pair of gold wire frames, and was dressed as sharply as Rick Schwab on a good day. "Funny," the man said to Zarro, "you don't look like Mel Lieb."

Zarro retracted the blade and stuck the box cutter into his pocket. Then he checked the contents of the box against the invoice. "Mel left for the day," he said not bothering to raise his eyes from the paper.

"You ever wonder how he reaches the pedals on that Town car?"

"Look, that postal meter is off," Zarro said, pointing in the direction of shipping. "So why don't you get to making it right so I can lock up?"

"Hey pally, do I look like I'm dressed to fix a fuckin' postal meter?"

"Aren't you from Pitney Bowes?"

"Negative. I'm Thomas Patrick McClellan, brother of Matthew Sean McClellan. And you are?"

"Robert Zarro, assistant to Mel Lieb."

"Zarro, huh? Well, it's about time Ricky Schwab found himself an Italian boy. The place was beginning to look like the Hebrew Home for the Aged."

Zarro raised his head and gave the man another once over Thomas McClellan looked nothing like his moronic brother. Matty was of average height, broad shouldered, and freckled, a pug face on a mastiff's body. This McClellan was tall, lanky, good looking. He had eyes that looked as dark as Zarro's, but a closer glance behind the glasses revealed they were navy blue. And Zarro could tell they were eyes that had seen everything. And this brother of Matty sported a constant smirk on his face.

"Don't go taking no offense. I feel no need to be politically correct being my wife is Jewish and I was always taught you're allowed to insult your own. Ain't that right?"

"So you're the cop," Zarro said.

"Detective. And from the way you're murdering the English language, I can tell that you're fresh out of Sox country.

34

Our PC's outta Boston. Visited me in the hospital when I took one in the gut for the great City of New York."

"He's famous. You actually got to meet him?"

"Yeah, but I had to get shot for the privilege. The commissioner talked just like you. He said he hoped the hospital was bringing me up "Hoodsies". That's what he said. A hero like you should have a couple of "Hoodsies." I didn't know what the fuck that man was talking about, but since he was high-level brass I didn't want to appear stupid. Not that I could talk too good anyhow, me laying there with a bunch of tubes shoved up my nose."

"It's ice cream. Comes in a small cup with a wooden stick. Hood is a New England dairy. Hood. Hoodsies."

"Thanks for clearing that up for me after all these years, Zarro. We call them Dixie cups in the rest of the civilized world."

"Hoodsies taste better."

Zarro pulled out the box cutter again and lifted another carton onto the metal desk.

"You know the box cutter is the weapon of choice in the New York City school system."

"Are you here for conversation, Detective?"

"Actually I'm here to check you out. My brother said you'd be his new supervisor once Mel Lieb retires."

"That's right and I'm not going to put up with his bullshit the way Mel does."

"I was afraid of that," the detective said, "but my brother needs this job. This job happens to be the only thing standing in the way of him drinking and gambling twenty-four-seven."

Zarro hoisted the carton onto the top of a filing cabinet. "That's not my problem now, is it?"

"You got yourself one lousy looking tattoo there," the detective said, eyeing Zarro's bicep. "Get yourself inked in the joint, did you?"

"College," Zarro said without skipping a beat. "Fraternity initiation rite."

The detective smirked. "A college boy, huh? Very commendable. My wife is into that quest for learning. Anyways, I'd better be going. Shouldn't be here at all, in fact, being that I'm officially banned from Schwab's for life."

"And why's that?"

"My wife's mother May Barron used to do embroidery here, back before she decided that life sucked enough for her to throw herself out a fourth-floor window. Worked here day in and day out for twenty-five years. After our daughter was born, my wife walked into Schwab's office and asked him if she could bring the baby back to show her off to the women her mother used to work with. And that hump you call your boss asked my wife just who May Barron was. Worse, he didn't even pretend to remember her."

"I still don't see why you're banned for life."

"After my wife's tearful return to our apartment, I waited until the place emptied out and I paid the almighty Rick Schwab a little social call. As it so happens, there's a shell casing still lodged in this very wall from our encounter." The detective paused for a second. "Let me tell you something Zarro, Mel Lieb is what makes this place human. And no offense, but I got me some serious doubts if some inked up Beantown guinea frat boy is up to the challenge."

Their eyes met for an uncomfortable second and then the detective pulled out a card from his breast pocket and jotted down something with Zarro's pen. "Now you got my work

36

number, my home number, and my cell. If my brother looks at you cross-eyed, I want to hear about it."

Zarro glanced at the detective's card and shoved it in his pocket.

"Rumor has it my mother gave you the heads up on an apartment over at Rose's place."

"Trudy's my favorite waitress. Guess I know the whole McClellan clan now."

"Now that's where you're wrong, Zarro. I got me a sister who's a hotshot corporate lawyer over in Manhattan, but it ain't real likely you'll be running into *her* anytime soon. Hoodsies, huh? Better than a Good Humor Dixie, my Irish ass."

After the detective was safely outside the back exit, Zarro worked on slowing his heartbeat down. Inked in the joint, the detective had said. Yeah, I was inked in the joint—but nobody needed to know that, Zarro thought. Nobody. He came to New York to start over. A do-over. A fresh start.

And now, three months later, the detective is outside his doorstep. Yet, despite the *agita* of their last meeting, Zarro runs down the stairs, wanting to feel the detective out about Maggie's situation, figuring that asshole brother of Matty McClellan would know the ins and outs of the legal system, if anyone would.

"Hey Detective, Happy New Year to you."

The sardonic look reappears instantly. "Likewise. Robert Zarro. This here's my daughter Agnes May McClellan."

"You two taking a walk?" Zarro asks the detective's little girl.

37

"Yes, I'm going to play with Frankie. We have a Christmas present for him even though it's New Years."

"Oh, I know Frankie," Zarro says, as she skips ahead of her father to get to the house. Rose's grandson."

"Me and the wife are pretty tight with Louise and Hector. In fact, I used to date her once upon a time. And I'm using the word date as a euphemism for banging her often during senior year of high school."

"Rose?" Zarro asks with a grin.

"Her daughter Louise, wiseass. Reminds me of this one night my grandmother caught the two of us doing the wild thing in the backseat of my stepfather's limo. I can still see Nana's pissed off face mashed up against the glass. And that had to be the best kind of birth control known to man, Nana Agnes Interuptus." He turns to his little girl. "Knock real hard on that door, Aggie. Put the present down on the step and give it all you got." And then quietly to Zarro, "That bell's been busted since Lou-Lou still had her cherry." He addresses Aggie again. "Sweetie, you tell Louise and Hector I'll be up in a minute. I'm gonna talk to Zarro here for a second."

"Have you seen Louise lately?" Zarro asks. "She's very pregnant you know," he mentions.

"Don't go looking at me, pally. These days I'm a happily married man. And I think the world of Louise. In fact I'm the one who introduced her to Hector, in the true spirit of friendship. And my buddy Hector was happier than a pig in shit to get a model that was already broke in real good by yours truly. Anyways, Lou-Lou's a good friend of my wife's, too. The four of us know each other just about forever."

"You know you keep saying 'your wife', but I haven't seen any evidence of a wife, none whatsoever. So just where is the elusive Mrs. Thomas McClellan?"

38

The detective looks momentarily pensive. "Home. Under the weather." Then he moves toward Rose's front door. He gazes up at Zarro's apartment and gets a brief glimpse of Maggie in the window. "Hot damn, you got yourself a *girl* up there, Zarro."

"You don't miss a fuckin' trick, do you?" he says. "That's Maggie Ocampo. Works at Schwab's. You hear about that house fire in Brooklyn on Christmas Eve?"

"In Bushwick. Basement apartment crammed full of Spanish girls without green cards. I seen it on the news."

"She's staying with me until she can make other arrangements."

"Cozy."

"She's sleeping on the couch. She had nowhere else to go."

McClellan grins. "Are you trying to tell me you got that beautiful *seniorita* squirreled away upstairs since Christmas and you haven't even *tried* to get in her pants? Give me a break. No offense, but what are you, some kind of fag?"

"I work at Schwab's Uniform, Detective. We are contracted to the United States military." Then Zarro lowers his voice. "And despite the change in the law, we at Schwab's still adhere to a strict don't ask, don't tell policy."

"You're a trip, Zarro. A fuckin' trip."

"You got a second to spare?" Zarro asks. "I need some advice. Law and order advice."

"You got it. Break any law you want only be smart enough not to get caught."

"That's very helpful. Seriously, some lawyer took five hundred dollars in cash from Maggie on top of whatever else she already gave him. Told her he's processing her visa but won't even answer her phone calls. Maybe if I pay him a visit and perhaps use the friendly art of persuasion," Zarro says holding up a clenched fist.

"Don't even think about it," the detective warns. "On account of he'll have you cuffed and in court before you can whistle the first verse of 'I Like to be in America.'"

"That's a very popular song over at Schwab's ever since we hired that new blister pack operator, America Diaz."

"You want me to handle it, Zarro?" the detective asks, ignoring Zarro's attempt at levity.

"No, I'll think of something."

"Oh, I get it. You want to come through as her knight in shining armor. Can't say I blame you. Even from down here I can see she's hot."

"Get off that already. She's been taken advantage of at every turn and I'm not going to be part of that. You know what she makes at Schwab's?"

"Not a hell of a lot. She got no papers on her. But, take it from me, pally. You can't change the world. Think about it, Zarro. When your people finally reached Beantown and stepped off the guinea banana boat, weren't they taken advantage of, too?"

Zarro shrugs. "Did I actually hear the words 'guinea banana boat' come out of your mouth? I thought all you cops had to be politically correct nowadays."

"I see no need to be politically correct here being my cousin Colleen married Italian—and the rule is you're allowed to insult your own. But you listen to me and don't even *think* of doing nothing stupid on that lawyer business. They're a crafty bunch, all of 'em. Like I told you, my sister Teresa Ann is a lawyer."

"To quote my landlady, she must be the ab-so-lute pick of the litter."

40

Tommy McClellan grins, extinguishes his cigarette, and pulls open the door to Rose Petruzzi's house. "Try and trap the lawyer," he advises before he enters the dark hallway. "Most of 'em will do anything to avoid bad publicity. No one wants their meal ticket disappearing on 'em."

"I'll keep that in mind. I'm pretty sure Maggie also has someone shaking her down for money every week. Payoff for her trip across the border."

"I know people. Would she be willing to talk?"

"No way in hell. She's scared to death."

"With good reason. Them guys will slice off a body part just to send a message. And they know illegals won't talk 'cause they don't want to rock the boat and risk being deported."

"So you're saying she should keep paying this bastard the rest of her life?"

"That's *not* what I'm saying. But she has to be willing to come forward."

Rose leans out the window above them. "Will you get that skinny coulie of yours in this house already and close the door?" she shouts at Tommy. "It's supposed to snow again tonight. I can feel it in this lousy ankle. More cold weather means more heat. More heat means big bills. Do you happen to know how much oil this house drinks in the winter?"

"Happy New Years to you Rosie," the detective replies, completely ignoring the admonishment.

"From one *paysan* to another, Robert Zarro," she shouts down to him, "don't you go making friends with *that one*. Where *that one* goes, trouble will ab-so-lute-ly follow."

"Don't pay her no mind, Zarro," Tommy says. "Rosie ab-so-lute-ly worships the ground I walk on, on account of I tricked this hardworking Cuban guy into making an honest woman out

41

of her daughter, run-around Lou." He motions to Zarro. "You coming in?"

He glances up at the second floor. Maggie is no longer visible from the street, but he has no trouble imagining her. "Not yet. I have some stuff to, uh, to take care of."

With his back to Zarro, the detective raises his shoulders and then pulls the door closed behind him. Zarro has no trouble at all imagining the smirk on the cop's face.

Chapter Four

On the second of January, the two of them return to work, Maggie going through the warehouse entrance on 39th Street and Zarro walking through the front door on 43rd Avenue on the office side. "Schwab's Uniform" in red block lettering announces the business directly over the main entrance and a caricature of a smiling soldier outfitted in an Eisenhower administration era Class A uniform hangs below the sign. Rick Schwab motions for Zarro as soon as he crosses the threshold.

"Afraid I'm the bearer of bad news."

"I heard all about it," Zarro interrupts. "The war on terrorism still hasn't reached epic proportions and the union's looking for a three cent raise."

"I'm not trying to be funny here, Zarro. Mel Lieb died two days after Christmas."

"What did you say?" *Mel is dead? Mel who had taught him whatever he knew about the business is dead? Mel who is supposed to be available for telephone consultations is dead? Goddamn it, he can't be dead.* The news washes over Zarro like a rogue wave. He lowers himself into a chair.

"You heard me. He suffered a massive heart attack. Went fast, no suffering. There are worse ways to go."

43

"Well that sucks. The poor guy never got to retire. Two days after Christmas. Jesus Rick, why the hell didn't you call me? I would have shown up at the funeral, you know. I really liked Mel. He was a good guy. Had the patience of a saint. You could ask the man a thousand dumb questions and he'd answer every single one and not make you feel like an idiot for asking them."

Rick Schwab leans forward, resting his elbows on the desk. "Don't you know anything? The Jews bury their dead in ten minutes. Plant them in the dirt before they're even cold. Besides, I assumed you were up in Boston."

"Plans change. Jesus Christ, how are you going to tell them?" Zarro asks, pointing over Schwab's head toward the warehouse. "They'll be devastated. He was like a father to all of them. They really loved the old guy."

"Actually, I wasn't planning on telling them. As far as they know, he's retired. Mel wouldn't have been here today anyway. So, let's just forget about it."

"Are you serious? They have a right to know. Maybe some of them would like to pay their respects to his wife. You really need to tell them."

"*Me* tell them? Hell no. I keep telling you it's great to be king. And a king doesn't have to do the dirty stuff. A king's job is to make money and leave behind a dynasty. If you're so keen on letting them know, why don't *you* tell them? And do it at a quarter to four so we get a full day's work out of them."

Zarro stands up. "You know something Rick? It's probably not in my best interest to say it, but I'll say it anyway. You are one hardhearted money-grubbing prick."

"That's right, Zarro. But I'm the one hardhearted money-grubbing prick whose signature is on your paycheck."

Zarro walks across to Mel Lieb's front office. It will be his office now. He picks up the plug from the menorah that sits on a shelf facing Rick Schwab's office. He jams the plug into the electrical socket, illuminating the nine orange candles. Fuck you, Rick Schwab.

The remainder of the morning Zarro spends up the hill in shipping with Matty McClellan and his boys. Together, they work side-by-side pulling in and slitting open huge cartons and getting the merchandise ready for blister pack. It is the most physically demanding job in the warehouse, but Zarro realized early on that if he were to gain any kind of respect, he had to be willing to work as hard as his strongest workers. And he approaches the job with panache, easily catching twenty and thirty-pound cartons to the ever-present salsa beat.

Matty McClellan doesn't say more than two words to him all morning, but Zarro feels flattered at lunchtime when they go outside and Matty offers him a toke from a skinny joint he keeps tucked in his back pocket. And although it is incredibly tempting to take the edge off in light of what faces him that afternoon, he declines the offer. It is too much a reminder of the old Robert Zarro. Instead, he leans against the yellow bricks and watches as Matty pulls the high into his lungs, Zarro trying his very best to experience the secondhand buzz. But after a couple of hits, Matty pinches the life out of the joint and returns the remainder to his pocket. Then he finds a football in the corner of the garage, and Zarro and the guys in shipping, dressed in thermal shirts and Schwab's U.S. Navy regulation watch caps, go out and toss the ball around a snowy 39th street.

45

"Yo, go deep," Zarro shouts, sending a gorgeous spiral over toward Weeds who is positioned at the base of Skillman Avenue, the Jamaican's skin blue-black against the pallid gray-white of urban winter.

For half an hour they play hard in traffic to the consternation of harried truckers trying to reach Manhattan, now forced to maneuver their great rigs around twelve boisterous guys and man-made mounds of black slush.

"Nice arm boss," Matty says to him when they were back inside. "You ever lace up the gloves?"

"No, never got into that." Still, he did kick the crap out of people barehanded back at Old Bay Correctional.

For the remainder of the afternoon, he checks inventory, goes over the shortlist, and makes a few phone calls to their suppliers. At a quarter to four, Zarro jumps up on one of the long tables and summons the entire warehouse with a, "Yo, I need everyone to come down here."

When he has all seventy-five of them at attention with the exception of Elmo-the-Cleaning-Guy, who is snoring away on an empty steel shelf, he announces the untimely death of Mel Lieb. With his eyes focused on the back wall and his hands thrust deep into his sweatshirt pockets, he says it in English and pauses while it is translated into other languages. Within minutes there is stunned silence followed by quiet weeping. Anxious to remove himself from this overflow of emotion, Zarro jumps down from the table. Once on the floor, he catches Maggie's eye.

"Say something more, Roberto," she says softly in that low, husky voice of hers that has the ability to drive him to

46

distraction if he lets it. "They look for you to tell them something more, okay?"

He stares at the wall, hoping some words will spring up from somewhere. Then he begins to speak from his position on the floor. "Look, Mel Lieb was not a large man, but he leaves a large empty space. And it will take many years, if ever, before I can fill his shoes. I hope we can work together and-and I promise to do my best for all of you." Again he waits until his words are translated. His heart races now, races because he has left himself open as he stands there pretending to be the same caring person as Mel Lieb. He knows he's a Mel Lieb imposter, an insult to the genuine article.

Stunned, the workers punch out and Zarro slumps into an old leather chair in Mel's small back warehouse office. It will be his office now. He routs around Mel's metal desk until he finds a piece of cardboard. With it, he stencils a sign with black marker and tapes it above the Plexiglas doorframe. MEL LIEB LANE. Then he walks up the hill toward Mel's mostly unused front office and unplugs the electric menorah and displays it unlit on the top of a file cabinet. A makeshift shrine to the late, great Mel Lieb. Zarro wonders if Mel Lieb's grandson ever got to see the Hess truck his grandfather had bought for him. He shuts down the warehouse lights and is about to set the alarm when a "Hey Zarro," stops him in his tracks.

Matty McClellan is seated in the Schwab van, a toothpick circling the inside of his mouth, his broad freckled nose red, his light eyes watery. "Why are you still here" Zarro asks. "I saw you punch out fifteen minutes ago."

"I'm just sitting in the van, thinking about Mel. He's the one who hired me. Been working here since I quit high school. I been at Schwab's since I'm seventeen, since I got this Turkish girl in trouble. He saved me my job, too. Lots of times."

"Get out of the van. I want to lock up. What do you think about you and me sending his wife a condolence card?"

"That's a good idea. You write it out though, and I'll sign my name to it." Matty says. "I can't spell to save my fuckin' life."

Then Matty climbs out of the van and slams the door shut. "Hey Zarro, want to grab a beer? You know, in memory of Mel?"

"Another time. I have some stuff to take care of." Maggie is probably shivering on the doorstep, he thinks.

But he is wrong. Zarro is surprised to find his lights on and Maggie heating soup for their supper. "How did you get in?"

"Miss Rose see me and she open the door. She very nice, Roberto. I meet her Friday. Such a tiny little person in such big, black glasses. She tell me a story about her daughter Louise the one who give me the clothes, and the sanitary napkin."

Zarro warms his hands over the pot of soup. "That Miss Rose is full of stories, most of them involving the plumbing. Maggie?"

"Yes?"

"I've been doing some thinking and I'd really like to get your money back from that lawyer of yours."

"Then I do not get the papers, Roberto."

"That shyster lawyer is not going to get you your papers. For Christ's sake, he won't even return your phone calls. He took your money. He ripped you off. He took advantage of you just like that cleaning service you slaved for, Jackie the Cleaning Pimp for Illegal Aliens."

48

Maggie ladles soup into two bowls. "What do I do?"

"The two of us are going to pay Mr. Quinones a little visit. You'll go in with my cell phone hidden in your purse. And you'll record every lie he feeds you. And when you're all done, I'll come in, all dressed up in a suit and tie. And I'll tell him I'm going to sell our story to Eyewitness News. The plight of immigrants is big headlines these days so I want to do it soon, while that Christmas Eve fire is fresh in everyone's mind. You up for this?"

"Yes. But how will I get the green card?"

Hungry, Zarro takes great sips of his soup, draining the bowl quickly. "I don't know about you, but I'm still hungry." Zarro gets up and peers into his refrigerator. He makes each of them a sandwich out of cold cuts and seeded semolina bread. "I'll look online. We'll just have to find a way."

"You make a nice speech today, Roberto."

"Yeah, it was great, wasn't it? Me standing there not knowing what the hell to say and everyone crying their eyes out."

"They like Mel. Me, I like him very much too. He is very good to me. His wife sent him with the extra food and he always share with me and the other girls. He love the Twinkies and those little chocolate puddings in a can."

Zarro nods. "I can never replace Mel. I don't have his heart." Then sensing rough waters, he changes the subject. "Your story is on later tonight. We have to find out what will happen to," and then he pauses, and spreads his hands. "America's sweetheart, Ro-sa Sal-ma-je."

"I ask about the apartment today. Lygia in embroidery say she will let me know. She has to ask the others."

"Another basement with twenty girls, a smoking space heater, and a blocked exit?"

"Is not so bad, 'berto."

"It's bad enough. Stay here for a while," he hears himself say. "Take the bed tonight. I'll open the sofa." He'd take a cold shower. He is getting used to them.

"Oh no. I stay on the sofa." And then she adds, "Lygia has to wait for the other girls to say yes for me to come. I will be away from here soon."

Zarro logs off the computer and picks up his weights. "I've heard all I want to hear about Lygia and her goddamn hellhole of an apartment. I don't have a gun at your head, you know."

"A gun?"

"It's just an expression. What I'm trying to tell you, is you can take your time on the apartment. No need to jump at the first thing that comes your way. Hey, go get comfortable. Your show's coming on." He watches her from behind his set of weights, as she goes to the couch, sits and slowly becomes transfixed.

Chapter Five

Not too far from the Brooklyn Navy yard, amidst the seedy looking bars that had once served more than a thousand hardworking thirsty men, between an abandoned four-story house and an old fashioned barbershop, is the storefront office of Mr. Quinones. The sign above the door says "Abogado de la Migracion." His office is a dingy affair in the as-of-yet-to-be gentrified part of the neighborhood. The doorway is littered with unanswered mail, the window smudged with the sweaty anticipation of many an undocumented nose.

Maggie is dressed in the gray knit dress she had worn to the Christmas party and Zarro, unhappily, had poured himself into his too tight suit, the one he wore to trial.

He hadn't counted on the forty-five minute wait in the unheated waiting room as other hopeful immigrants sit on uncomfortable folding chairs, waiting to see Mr. Quinones. Maggie strikes up a conversation with a young dark-skinned Spanish woman who bounces an even darker-skinned little boy on her lap as they converse. It occurs to Zarro just how much Maggie gave up when she crossed the border into the United States. In Spanish, her conversation flows effortlessly, every nuance, every inflection appreciated by the listener. A mixture of jealousy and envy curdle inside him as this woman and Maggie seem to have so much to say to one another. He admires people who still have their words. He used to have words, once upon a time. They used to flow from him no problem, splashing out of him like an overturned bucket. And now they are gone, lost for good. Uneasy, he fidgets with his tie. The knot is out to strangle him.

When it is Maggie's turn, Zarro points at her purse to remind her to switch on the cell phone recorder. For fifteen minutes he paces in the waiting room. He hopes Maggie remembers to ask the lawyer which particular visa he is preparing. He hopes Maggie remembers to ask how long this process is supposed to take. But most of all, he really wants to nail this bastard requesting additional money. Finally, he cannot take it anymore. He heads in.

The lawyer clearly knows something is amiss when Zarro enters the office sporting an ill-fitting suit and a thinly applied mask of controlled rage. "Okay Quinones," Zarro says to the short, fat man with a fringed black horseshoe around his shiny skull. "You danced her around enough already. She'd like her money back."

The ugly guy looks uncomfortable, and says, "Miss Ocampo and I have been discussing the procedure. I have made application under a student visa."

"Really now?" Zarro says. "Show me a copy of this."

"Unfortunately there has been a delay on the copies because our machine has broken. May I ask what is your relationship to my client?"

"I'm her supervisor at her place of employment. I'm also a journalism major at…at City University," Zarro says, thinking fast. "I didn't think you'd mind us recording the entire conversation. Since that terrible fire over Christmas Eve that

52

affected so many immigrant girls, I got to thinking that another story on how some ruthless, money-hungry lawyer who preys on his own people would also be of interest to the listening public." *Calm down. Stay cool. Be in control. This isn't Old Bay.*

"What are we saying here?"

"We are saying that any network would love an exclusive on this story right about now," he says. "Poor, immigrant girl gets fleeced by shady lawyer while seeking American Dream."

"You have nothing on me."

"I got you on my cell phone asking for more money. I got your fiction about a bogus student visa. Lies, all of it." *Take a breath. Control yourself, Kicker.*

"Our entire conversation was in Spanish."

"So I'll sell it to the Telemundo. They can run it before and after Rosa Salmaje."

"Ooh, my wife loves that show," the lawyer says, running a handkerchief across the top of his head. Then he reaches into his pocket and peels two hundred-dollar bills from a gold money clip. "Take this and erase our conversation. We'll call it even."

Zarro lunges across the lawyer's desk and clamps the lawyer by the shoulder. He tightens his grip and then he feels his right hand draw back into a hard fist. "Even? You call this even?" Zarro is breathing hard now, the adrenaline pumping fast and hot through his system. "Get up," he shouts, pulling the lawyer out of his chair. "I'm going to splatter your brains against the wall. You're a dead man, taking advantage of a girl like that. Now you'll pay, you fat piece of shit."

" 'berto, no," Maggie yells. "Let him go."

Far away, he hears her voice. As if on a seven-second delay, it penetrates him slowly in muted waves of sound. When the words register fully, Zarro releases his grip and unclenches his fist, each knuckle hard and stiff as a cudgel. "Take the money," he says quietly to Maggie, who doesn't react. "Take it I said." he repeats.

"Delete the conversation," the lawyer says, smoothing his collar in an exaggerated fashion. "That was part of the deal." But Zarro gives him a look that says all deals are off.

As they walk out, Zarro says to Maggie, "Tell the woman with the little boy what this scumbag is about."

"She is a *nica*," Maggie tells him.

"You're calling her names, now?" he asks. "You think you're better than she is because your skin is light? Wake the hell up, Maggie. You're all in the same goddamn boat. This country doesn't want *any* of you here, dark or light."

"Shh, 'berto. Do not yell *por favor*. You do not understand. What I try to say is she is a *nica*, a *nicaraguense*, just like me. She come from my country, Nicaragua." Then Maggie says something softly in Spanish. The woman scoops up her little boy and exits with them.

When they are in the car, Maggie says, "Roberto, what happen to you? You are very angry today. I am thinking you will *kill* Mr. Quinones."

"He took your hard earned money and money of others just like you. Ripping off his own people like that. You should have let me beat the shit out of him. That bastard deserved to catch a good beating." But they are words he says to camouflage his own fears. He realizes that he still belongs in a cage.

"No, Roberto. I will not let you do that."

"Well, at least you have part of it back now." He could have killed him. He could have killed him easy and she stopped him.

"And the recording?"

54

"Oh, that's going to any TV station that wants it. Did you remember to ask the right questions?"

"Yes."

"And he asked for more money?"

"Yes. How do you know this?"

"Because I know what this guy's about. And if this recorded conversation ever makes it to TV, he'll be embarrassed for all of ten minutes. Believe me, he won't be out of business anytime soon. He'll be ripping people off forever, piece of shit that he is."

"I still need a visa."

"I want to talk to the union's lawyer. Maybe we can finagle something with the union. I have to do some research. I'm not promising you anything, you understand?" He slows his breathing down. He is okay now.

Maggie looks out the car window. The two hundred dollars is safe in her purse. "Yes, I understand. You are a fine man." She looks away from him, out the car window. You took me into your house when I had nowhere to go, no one to turn to."

"No, Maggie," he says. "I'm *not* a fine man. I'm not Jesus Christ and I'm not Mel Lieb. And I don't want you ever thinking any different."

Maggie feels too happy to let Zarro's black mood overshadow her. "With all this money I can go to Good Wheel."

"Tell me, have you ever in your life been to a department store, Maggie? I mean a real department store, you know, like Lord and Taylor?"

"Lahd and Talah?" she asks, trying to mimic the strange sounding words.

"I never thought you of all people, would give me grief over my accent."

55

She looks puzzled. "I do not know Lod and Talah."

"How about Macy's? You ever been there?"

"Is too much moneys. I send moneys to my mother in Nicaragua."

"Put your money away. I want to buy you something. Something *not* from Good Will. If you had all the money in the world, what would you buy?"

"I always want to buy a sewing machine. My mother says to me a girl with a sewing machine will never go hungry."

Zarro nods. "I understand. I can talk to the guy that services the machines at Schwab's. Maybe he can give us a break on a used machine. Then you can put an ad in the paper for Maggie's Tailor Shop. 'All Alterations Are Done on Premises at Reasonable Rates. Pleated Skirts Can be Altered for an Additional charge.' How's that?"

"Yes Roberto, that is sound good."

"I'll talk to the guy when we're back at work. There must be something else you want. Something not so damned practical, something I can buy you today."

"I have the moneys. I buy for myself."

"No, you keep that. This one's on me. So Maggie girl, what will it be?"

"You laugh at me when I tell you."

"I won't laugh. I promise."

"I want to buy a blue dress like Rosa Salmaje is wearing last night."

He drives her to the Queens Center Mall. They walk through the lingerie department of Macys and she runs her hands over a velvet robe. And she pulls a satin nightgown off the hanger and rubs it against Zarro's cheek. "Feel this. Is so nice, 'berto." she says. "So smooth, *si*?"

"Put it back," he says, flinching. "Let's find the dresses. Go ask the lady where the Rosa Salmaje department is."

"I ask you not to laugh at me, Roberto."

"I'm not laughing."

They take the escalator and Maggie flits through each section of designers. "Who is Liz Claiborne? And who is Donna Karan and Anne Klein?"

"From what I hear, Liz Claiborne is the sister-in-law and Donna Karan is the aunt of Rosa Salmaje. And this Anne Klein is their hairdresser. Take a look. They have blue ones. Go find your size."

"I try on. They have the rooms here to try."

He leans against a rack of dresses, vaguely recalling being taken on the T to Macy's the day after Thanksgiving, and playing soldiers with Nee under a fortress of hanging winter coats. And then he remembers the time that has lapsed since his last call home. He shelves the image. He'll deal with his family later. His heart lurches when she emerges from the dressing room wearing a simple royal blue knit with two oversized black buttons at the front.

"You like?" she asks, twirling around in her bare feet.

Zarro can only summon the strength to nod. He slides a credit card out of his wallet and waits for her to come out of the dressing room.

She cannot stop talking for a minute on the short drive home from the mall. She loves Macy's and she loves the silky things and Liz Claiborne. "Thank you so very much."

"Why did you come to New York?" he asks her. He knew why *he* came. He had to get away from himself. Only *himself* is still shadowing him, tailing Zarro like his old dog Clem, the golden retriever who died while Zarro was locked up. The joy peels away from her face. "For a life that is new."

"Was there a war going on there?" Zarro had never given too much thought to Central America, or anyplace else that wasn't Boston for that matter. Those events appeared on someone else's radar screen. Still, he recalls reading about Sandinistas and Contras somewhere along the line, but he certainly can't tell those players without a scorecard.

"No…but it still no nice there sometimes. I don't want to talk."

He nods, wondering what he said to upset her. "How did you get here?"

"Car and then the vans. Nicaragua up to Honduras, from Honduras to Guatemala and then into Mexico. We sneak over the border in the night to Brownsville, Texas. And from this place to New York City."

"That sounds like one hell of a trip."

"*Si*. Very long trip. Very crowded. And I see such terrible things. Children, little children who sleep on the street in the city of Guatemala and smell the glue in a little jar and they walk like they are drunk. How you say this?"

"Glue sniffing. The poor man's high."

"These are not mens. They are children, 'berto. And people are walking over them. I never see nothing like that. But someone on the bus say the glue stop them from being so hungry. Is so sad. The bus stops for the fast lunch in McDonald's. And one little girl dress in the rags, two years old sharing the glue of her bigger brother, come to me and hugging on my legs and call me Mama. I want to take those children away from there but I have to get back on the bus. I leave for

58

them food. Sometimes I am dreaming of those little *Resistoleros* with their jars of glue."

Zarro cringes. After all, he had sold drugs, too. No, not to little kids, but he was no angel. "Tell me about Nicaragua. Tell me about your family." *Anything to change the subject. Anything.*

"Not today. Today is supposed to be a happy day. I have some of the moneys back. I have for me a beautiful dress like Rosa Salmaje."

She sounds melancholy for some reason, Zarro thinks. Some family reason. It makes Zarro uneasy. Despair is *his* territory.

Back in the apartment they are seated on the sofa, the Macy's bag beside Maggie's knees. "Can you a little bit hold me, Roberto?" she asks.

"Not a good idea," he says. A disaster. Carnage. No one can hold him. No one can touch him or take advantage of him or use him for his own pleasure and leave him on the floor like a spent candy wrapper. He's stronger than that now, way stronger.

"Why?"

"Because."

"Because is not an answer. You say it to me and now I say to you. I think you do not like when someone touch you, Roberto."

"This conversation is over. Go hang up your dress."

"Do I thank you enough for it?"

"Yeah, more than enough."

"I give to you some moneys for the rent so you are not always angry on me."

59

"I'm not angry and I don't want your money. When you get the sewing machine, you can sew me some curtains."

Maggie doesn't watch her *novela* that night. Instead, she cleans the apartment. Zarro watches as she loses herself in the rhythmic motion of the broom and the mop.

He sends a text to his Zarro brother Anthony, keeping it light and breezy.

Hey Nee, what up? I'm good. Getting used to Big App. Happy New Year. Sorry I missed Xmas, but a situation came up. Pres. Day weekend?

"Why you text and not talk?" Maggie asks him.

"Not talking is just easier."

Chapter Six

On the third Monday in February, Rick Schwab calls Zarro into his office. Maggie is hovering over Schwab's left side, sewing a loose button on the sleeve of his dress shirt.

"Hang on a second, Zarro. Maggie, my wife is going to put the housekeeper on the phone. She doesn't speak English worth a damn. Be a good girl and tell her I like my eggs cooked soft."

"Soft?"

"Yeah, soft. Mushy. Runny." Rick Schwab hands her the phone.

"What is her name?"

"How the hell should I know? The agency sent her last week. Eggs, Maggie. Just talk eggs."

Then Schwab turns his attention to Zarro. "Take a look at these logos. And after you finished perusing, I want you to tell me which one you think we should go with and why."

Zarro positions himself on Rick Schwab's other side and looks at each one. Maggie's husky voice discussing *huevos* distracts him, but he forces himself to focus. Schwab's Uniform in black, bold letters. Schwab's Uniform in blue script. Schwab's Uniform in red bubble letters surrounded by a semi-circle of gold stars. Schwab's Uniform in simple brown Helvetica type with a fierce eagle behind the name.

"The one with the eagle has been our logo since Marilyn Friedman started. I think both Marilyn and the logo have seen better days. What's your take on the others?" Rick asks.

"Makes no difference to me."

Maggie hangs up the phone, snips a loose thread from Rick's sleeve, and quietly leaves the office. Zarro's eyes follow her into the warehouse.

"Some help you turned out to be. It's time to shake things up around here. I'd like to change Schwab's logo."

Zarro turns his attention back to his boss. "That means every blister pack, every business card, and just about every piece of stationery would have to be changed."

"Goes without saying."

"You're talking big bucks, no?"

Schwab put his hands behind his head. "Times change. We have to keep up. By the way, are you portable, Zarro?"

"Portable? I have a set of wheels, if that's what you mean."

"That's *not* what I mean. One of the reasons I hired you was your complete willingness to relocate and start fresh. You're young, single. No ties to the area."

"I'm listening."

"I'm kicking around the idea of pulling up stakes and moving the firm to Charleston, South Carolina."

"You're shitting me."

"Think about it. I can remove the union from the picture while cutting the rent and tax load in half. All around, it's cheaper to do business in Charleston."

"Your workforce is here."

"You're worried about the great brain trust we're fostering in the back. Surely we will never find another Matty McClellan or another, what's his name? Weeds, that's it. And that's a sobriquet I'm fairly certain he earned not from his gardening ability. Wait, wait, we cannot forget that unholy trinity of PR hooligans up in shipping or the unique talent of Suzie Q. Did you get a load of her Valentine's Day getup? She spent the day pulling stock in the largest pair of heart-covered boxers I ever saw. You're right, Zarro. We could never replace these highly skilled employees."

"You got seventy-five people out back and at least ten up front who count on this job to eat. Besides, you got a good deal on this location. It's right smack in the middle between your wife on Long Island and your girlfriend in Manhattan. Who could have it better than you?"

Rick Schwab clucks his tongue. "Gee Zarro, why ever would you say something like that?"

"Because it's true."

"You don't hear me denying it, but let's assume a king always puts business ahead of pleasure."

"You set me up, didn't you? You had designs on moving long before I darkened your doorstep. But you needed someone to lay the blame on because kings don't get their hands dirty. I get it now. 'Hey Zarro, go out back and tell them they're all laid off. Sugarcoat it a little. We'll put a little something extra in their pay, a whole extra five dollars for every year of loyal service. Cheer up. Why are you looking so gloomy, guys? We have unemployment insurance in this great country of ours.' Zarro looks directly at his boss. "You waited Mel Lieb out, didn't you? You knew he'd never in a million years stab his own people in the back."

"You have me all figured out."

63

"Yeah? Well fuck you *and* the Porsche you road in on. I'm writing you another script. Change the way you do business, right here in Sunnyside, Queens."

"Well, well. Listen to you. You walked in the door ten minutes ago and now you want to *change* things."

"Hear me out, king of mine. I want to computerize the inventory, including purchasing. I want to set up a web page that doesn't look like it was done by your nephew and I want to market to other than the Army, Navy, Air Force and Marines. What about the airlines, Broadway, the Boy Scouts, and doormen? Why is this goddamn company married to the military?"

"This is a *military* business, Zarro, and has been since day one. If we had a mission statement, that would be mentioned at the top of paragraph one."

"Bullshit. A patch is a patch, whether you sew it on a general's shoulder or a dancer's ass. And we need to be on Facebook, Twitter, and anything else that gets us noticed. Make me your social media specialist." Rick Schwab shrugs. "Go for it. Improve the website. Do a mass mailing. Tweet your ass off. You need office help, come out front. You need a suit, a handshake and smile, I can put my son-in-law to work. Trust me, it's all nickel and dime stuff."

"What about the inventory system? The logo stuff is crap compared to what really matters. Don't you see this place is conducting business like it's still nineteen fifty-seven?"

"Not true. Our billing is computerized and our correspondence is all handled by fax and e-mail."

"Not enough. Not if you intend on staying in business that is."

"So get some bids. See what it costs. Look, I don't really want to move. I just see it as the only way out."

"I don't see that at your only option. But as long as we got everything out on the table, I want to put the entire warehouse in the union, including Elmo the narcoleptic Panamanian cleaning guy."

"Don't fuck with me, Zarro."

"Even *you* can see that this two-tier pay system is bad for morale, not to mention the height of cupidity."

"Don't you mean stupidity?"

"No, I mean cupidity. Look it the hell up."

"Hey, I didn't go looking for these people. Did I tell them to doggie-paddle across the Rio Grande? They knocked on *my* door and I gave them a job."

Schwab does have a point, Zarro thinks. But he keeps his thoughts to himself. "Stay with the eagle, Schwab's very own symbol of liberty for the fifteen workers who are busting their asses and earning five dollars and fifty cents an hour."

Rick Schwab laughs. "You're such a choir boy, Zarro."

"Yeah, that's me," Zarro mutters, as he walks through the door to his own office. He doesn't sit down at his desk, however. Instead, he peers through the Plexiglas window out at the warehouse floor. Work goes on as usual. Work is blissfully ignorant of the grand plans of Mr. Rick Schwab. Zarro's eyes wander up and down the aisles, but freeze in their sockets when they reach Suzie Q. A boy is at her side, a boy who couldn't have been much more than seven years old. He sat beside Suzie hooking green elastic boot bands around a card, work usually farmed out to local sheltered workshops. Next to him is a little Chinese girl who is also busy at the same task. The little girl looks away when she glances up and Zarro's eyes meet hers.

Zarro exits his office and finds Suzie Q. "Are you aware there are child labor laws in this country?"

"That's my grandbaby Quarnel," she says, as if that fact alone would clear the entire matter up.

"You're a grandmother? Jesus Suzie, how old are you?"

"Forty-two this September," Suzie replies. "Not that it's none of your business."

"It's *my* business when people bring their kids in here and put them to work. Who's the girl next to him?"

"That's Shirley Wong's little girl, Anastasia. Ain't she the cutest thing? Them Chinese girls look like baby dolls, don't they?"

"Tell me. Are we running a goddamn daycare center?"

"Schools have half a day, today. That means before and after-school is cancelled. So, just what are we supposed to do with these here kids? Shirley and me got no one to go pick them up at noon and no one home to mind them 'til school starts."

Zarro looks in the direction of the two children. The little boy is dressed in his Sunday suit and tie, giving him the dignified bearing of an executive in miniature. The little girl is in her Sunday best.

Zarro had no trouble picturing the pre-work conversations. *"Today's special because you get to come to work with me. Now, it's very important that you behave there. Act just like the little lady and gentleman that you are, so the boss doesn't throw all of us out the door — and then what would we do? We wouldn't have food on the table and no place to live."* Followed by, *"But Grandma, where's the nice old man at, the man from last time? He gave us cake."* Then, *"Oh, he up and left for a better place."* That's right little Quarnel and Anastasia, Zarro thinks. *He left for a far better place. Left us all in a fuckin' lurch is what he did.*

"Quarnel and Anastasia. Q. and A. Look, I don't want them within ten feet of any machinery, *capisce?*"

"We ain't stupid, Zarro."

66

"It's cold in here. I'm wearing a thermal and a ski vest and I'm still freezing my ass off. Put a space heater next to those kids. I'll bring one down from shipping." Absentmindedly, Zarro runs his hand through his hair. "Well Suzie, just what the hell are you going to say when Rick spots the two of them out back?"

"Nothin'."

"He's not blind and he's not stupid. You and Shirley had better come up with something."

"Schools have half days all the time. These children worked here before and Rick Schwab never said boo. And why should he? These here kids are working eight hours for free."

Zarro shakes his head. "You're killing me," he mutters under his breath as he heads back into the front office and enters Marilyn Friedman's cubicle.

"What do *you* want?"

"Twenty bucks out of petty cash. I have a C.O.D. waiting."

"What for?"

"A part for the blister pack machine."

"Show me the invoice."

"Come on Marilyn, I got a guy waiting out back with the engine running."

She looks Zarro up and down. "Don't you dare lie to me. You want that money to pay those children, don't you?"

"We got two kids back there today who are probably putting in a better day than half the adults. It isn't fair them sitting here stringing boot bands for eight hours and coming home with nothing. I'd like to hand them something at four o'clock."

"I'll give you fifty cents and you can buy them a lollipop each."

"Not good enough."

Marilyn Friedman grunts in disgust. She pulls out the key to her petty cash drawer and extracts two ten-dollar bills. "Here," she says, shoving the bills in his face. "But this sets a very bad precedence. Word gets out and they'll *all* be bringing their snotty-nosed brats to work."

"Thanks Marilyn. You're an angel."

"One of them gets hurt, and *you* fill out the paperwork."

Zarro tries his best to avoid eye contact with those two children. For each of them is a flesh and blood reminder of the burden that chose him, the first black-inked entry on the to-do list he had been handed. Hey kids, that well-dressed man Mr. Schwab is going to close the place down and put your mother and grandmother on the goddamn unemployment line. Zarro knows he is supposed to do jump in and do something about that, only he really isn't sure, what. His formal education had been cut off before he ran the final lap. Those kids, looking at him with those faces, those innocent little kid faces. Fuck it. He had paid his dues and then some. He hadn't been hired to save the world.

Chapter Seven

Spurred on by Rick Schwab's threat to pick up and leave Queens, Zarro has a basic bare-bones inventory system up and running by the end of March. As he predicted, Matty and his boys hate it. Instead of just tearing open a carton and checking the contents against the invoice, now they had to log in the stock, item by item, using a barcode. They balk at first, calling Zarro every name in the book — and some not in any book — their initial defiance eventually settling into a resigned reluctance. Still, Zarro gets the cold shoulder even if he spends three hours working beside them. But he knows he wasn't hired to win a popularity contest. And like it or not, the computerization of the inventory has to be done. In fact, if anyone was interested enough to ask, Zarro would have been the first to tell them it was long overdue. But no one asks. All he receives are the staff's loud complaints, to which he offers a deaf ear and a raised shoulder.

One afternoon, Zarro catches Matty all the way in the back where Rick Schwab parks his silver Porsche with "THE KING" vanity plates, doing lines of coke with Manny, Israel and Junior from shipping. He thinks about calling Matty's brother the detective, but after some consideration, he opts to handle it alone. He recalls a nasty prank somebody played on an inmate back at Old Bay, and he thinks that experience might prove useful to rein in the recalcitrant Matty, the self-appointed ringleader in shipping, as well as setting an example for the Spanish boys as well.

The next day Zarro scoops a couple of tablespoons of sugar from the office coffee service into a small poly bag they used to pack the ribbon attachments in. He cuts the sugar with a tiny amount of baking soda until the glint of the granules disappears and the texture could fool even his own knowing eye. Then he calls Maggie over. "I want you to give this to Matty when you see the van pull in from the post office."

Maggie stares back at him.

"Oh, don't look at me like that. It's not what you're thinking. I want you to tell him it's a present. A friend dropped it off and asked that you give it to him, didn't leave his name. Believe me, he won't be asking too many questions."

"You are sure?"

"It's just sugar. But darlin', stand back and watch 'cause sugar can teach one hell of a sweet lesson."

Zarro waits for the Schwab's van to pull in and he watches Maggie sneak him the poly bag. Matty McClellan is ear-to-ear grin. He doesn't even bother sneaking off to the far corner of the garage, so pleased he is with his luck. Matty glances around and lays the white powder on the shipping table. With a great snort, the entire two tablespoons of sugar goes right into his pug nose. Matty's yelping swears could be heard down in the office. His eyes water. Gasping for breath, he can't stop coughing. And when he is finally able to see straight, Matty catches Zarro's wave and broad grin from across the warehouse floor. "What's the matter there, Matty? Didn't care for the Domino treatment?"

*　*　*　*　*

A few days later Detective McClellan pays Zarro a visit. He is waiting for him at a quarter after four in the back office. The detective sits on Zarro's chair, propping his feet up on the desk, as if he owned the place.

"Detective, for someone banned from Schwab's for life, you certainly don't hesitate to barge in at any old time."

"Now, now at least I'm a good boy. I always wait for the king to leave. Hey, what you got there in that carton? Don't tell me Ricky boy is selling ladies' kerchiefs now."

"Ascots for the Blue Angels. They're the guys who fly in formation."

"Ascots, huh? I once got my ass-cot in a car door, hurt like a bastard."

"Hang onto that day job, Thomas. Anyway, I'm getting this feeling you must be here for some reason other than to entertain me."

"I'm here to take my hat off to you, Zarro. That sugar thing was very impressive, very creative. Couldn't have done it better myself. Ooh my brother was pissed. And then he got double-pissed 'cause I laughed my ass off when he was looking for sympathy. Tell me something, did you learn that hands-on management tool at that college of yours?"

"Bentley University's on the cutting edge when it comes to business problems and solutions."

The detective nods. "Oh, I'll bet." Then he continues, "Say, how did it go with the immigration lawyer?"

"*Menza-menza*. We got some of her money back. I really could have cleaned his clock but Maggie wouldn't hear of it. And the recording went off to a local Spanish cable station."

71

"Not bad for a day's work. Listen, I need a favor off you, Zarro. And indirectly, it would be a favor to my mother, your favorite waitress."

"Anything for Trudy." Trudy, who looks like an older version of his very own mother, his very own mother whom he hadn't seen since September.

"I was wondering if my step-father could maybe park his limo back here on a temporary basis. See, Billy's been in one hell of a jackpot since he decided to buy the limo off his boss. Hasn't been making the payments on a regular basis, if you hear me. Anyways, he'd bring it in at night and roll it out before eight."

"No skin off my back. Matty knows the alarm code. And he has a key so I don't see it being a problem."

"I appreciate it. I can't see it going on for more than a few weeks. Until the shit-for-brains wiggles himself out of this situation he got himself into."

Maggie knocks on the glass. "Excuse me. I go home, Roberto."

"Come in. Maggie, this is Matty's brother Detective Tommy McClellan."

Maggie's face falls. "*Policía*?"

The detective removes his feet from the desk, and smiles. "Not to worry. I'm the good *Policía*. Not the immigration *Policía*."

Maggie does not smile back. "Nice to meet you."

"Maggie, do you have something on your mind that you would like to tell the detective?" Zarro asks.

Maggie's face colors. "I don't know what you are talking about."

"Rafael Guzman, the man you are so scared of," Zarro reminds her. "The man who you pay every week. Sound

72

familiar?" The shakedown couldn't go on forever. Something had to be done.

"I don't know what you are talking about," she says angrily, heading toward the door. "And I not paying nobody every week."

The detective grins. "Well Zarro, you certainly have a way with the ladies. And don't even try and tell me you still haven't made any visits south of *that* border, Ro-ber-to."

"Don't let the door hit your Southy Irish ass on the way out."

Marilyn Friedman hands Zarro his paycheck on Friday. "Take a look. Rick gave you a raise."

"Rick didn't *give* me a damned thing. I earned it. After I put in a full day in the warehouse, I go home and transform myself into a social media specialist. And let me tell you, it's a stretch because I'm basically antisocial. But, it's important that customers can like us on Facebook, follow us on Twitter, yelp about us — ."

"Shut up already," the bookkeeper cuts him off mid-sentence. I overheard what you said to him that day, about putting everyone out back here into the union."

"He wasn't too keen on the idea."

The bookkeeper looks down and scribbles on a scrap of paper. "This is the number of the union rep from Local Twenty-one. And be smart and don't tell him who gave it to you. Maybe you can work something out."

Zarro is taken aback. Before him stands Marilyn Friedman, a woman who makes an injured worker show blood before she parts with a Band-Aid, a woman who wears the key to the supply closet around her neck like an amulet, a woman who has to have proof that pencils are down to nubs, every available space on a pad of paper covered with ink. The toner for the copy machine has to be on "E" before anyone can *dream* of asking for a replacement. Zarro recalls the day when an exasperated Matty McClellan threw down a cardboard toilet paper dowel on the bookkeeper's desk and requested permission for a roll of toilet paper so he could get down to the business of wiping his ass.

"You're surprised I'm giving this to you."

"Yeah, a little surprised." Shocked is more like it.

"You're right. It's not fair them being paid like that. Besides, I have to keep two sets of books."

"By the way Marilyn, how do you like that new receivables software I got for you?" Zarro asks, figuring hell had already frozen over.

"About as much as I like hemorrhoids. Now get the hell out of my office Mr. Social Media Specialist."

Chapter Eight

With the increase in take home pay, Zarro buys himself a suit that fits, and a new denim pullout sofa for the living room, donating the old one to Suzie Q. And it is from Suzie Q that he learns that Maggie's twenty-first birthday will be on Tuesday. It will be a treat for both of them to go into the city Saturday night. He realizes he likes being in Maggie's company. He likes her good common sense, her eagerness to learn new things. In his travels, he had bought her an English language CD, and she practices diligently each night. And she is gentle, easy to make laugh, and especially mindful of his privacy. There is only one drawback, one unavoidable frightening drawback. He is incredibly attracted to her in a way that he fears might end up being no good. But Maggie turning twenty-one warrants a Saturday night appointment in a restaurant. An appointment, not a date, no way a date, for he refuses to even think along those lines. Just a celebration, a birthday celebration for a good friend who happens to share his apartment. Besides, he wants to get back in her good graces after that conversation with Tommy McClellan. Maggie didn't talk to him for days after that. Evidently she's not a big believer in good *Policías*.

The very notion of Manhattan, however, makes Zarro somewhat ill at ease. He doesn't normally venture too far from home base. The borough of Queens provides him with everything he needs. But there are those rare times when he allows the Manhattan skyline to come sharply into focus, and he feels a painful tug. He knows for sure that *if* his situation were different, *if* he had finished college, *if* he hadn't spent the years in jail, certainly he too could have been a player in that Manhattan scene. The trendy lower East Side bars, the four digit cubbyhole rentals, hipster friends, the career with limitless potential. Yes, that could have been his world. That goddamn *should* have been his world. And when he permits himself that westward gaze out the second story window, his two dark hungry eyes dart from one unreachable skyscraper to another, filling Zarro with an intense longing for the door forever locked, an unsolicited reminder of what could have been and what would never be. Truncated dreams, plans severed, opportunities hacked off at the knees.

But he is determined to tuck his ambivalence away for Maggie's sake. Maggie deserves a night out in the city, some elegance in her life. And as much as he hates being beholden to his boss in any way whatsoever, he swallows his pride and asks Rick Schwab for a recommendation on a restaurant.

"A restaurant, Zarro?" his boss asks, leaning back in his chair, clasping his hands behind his head, thoroughly enjoying his position as bon vivant Rick Schwab, man about town. "What do you have in mind?"

"I don't know, something nice in Manhattan. My cousin's coming in from Boston and I'd like to show her a good time."

"A cousin, eh? Well, why don't we narrow it down a little? There's only about ten thousand nice restaurants to choose from. Do you and this alleged cousin of yours have a particular type of cuisine in mind? A certain ambience?"

"How about a good Italian restaurant with an extra heavy dose of ambience? Are you familiar with any of those?" His boss is enjoying this just a little too much. He should have just gone online so he wouldn't have to deal with this prick.

"And in what price range are we speaking, sir?"

"Whatever. Quit breaking my balls and give me a name, will you? I have tons of work to do. Israel and Manuel in shipping had the great goddamn luck to get shot at last night, so they both decided to take the day off."

"Doesn't that sound just a tad suspect to you, both of them getting shot on the very same night?"

"From what I can piece together, the same bullet winged Manuel in the shoulder and went on to hit Israel in the elbow. In order to keep my sanity, I really try not to get too caught up in the details."

"You can't make this stuff up, can you?" Rick remarks.

"Focus on the restaurant before I have cartons backed up to your office door."

"Okay, let's see if I've got this straight. We're talking a nice restaurant, Italian food, ambience out the wazoo, money no object. Do you mind wearing a jacket, Zarro?"

"Yeah I mind, but I'll wear one anyway."

"Well, then I hope your sartorial potential extends somewhat beyond that ill fitting garment you interviewed in," Rick says, unclasping his hands to brush a tiny fleck of lint off his sleeve.

"Ah, fuck you where you breathe. Sorry I asked."

Rick reaches for his cell phone. "Oh, don't *you* get sensitive on me now. It's bad enough I have to deal with my wife. I'll e-mail you a couple of websites with menus. And call ahead. You'll need a reservation at any of these places. I hope you and your Bostonian *cousin* have a love-ly time."

"Thanks, I appreciate it," Zarro says, exiting Rick's office from the back, eager to escape into the soothing repetition of warehouse routines.

"And for the percentage of your salary you're going to have to part with at any of these places, I sure hope this so-called cousin of yours puts out," Rick shouts after him.

But Zarro's retreat into the warehouse is a short-lived one. No sooner as he steps across the threshold, Maggie is by his side. "Roberto, there is a big problem."

"The Roach Coach ran out of Danish?"

"This is not to be funny. Suzie Q is crying in the ladies room."

"For any reason in particular?"

"Yes for a reason. She and Weeds from upstairs have a big fight."

"Jesus Maggie, I really don't have time for bullshit on a day we're two guys short."

"Forget I say something to you."

"Look, I'm sorry. I didn't mean to raise my voice at you. You stay with Suzie. I'll talk to Weeds."

He walks up the hill and separates Weeds from Matty and the Spanish boys. "So what's the deal with you and Suzie? Rumor has it she's crying her eyes out downstairs."

The Jamaican rolls his own eyes. "Well, that be women for you, Z. Laughing one minute, weeping an ocean full of tears the next. Maybe her period come down."

"Don't hand me that crap. What the hell happened between you two?"

"Moms come waddling up here with two trays. 'Pack this up now,' she say. 'This be a rush order,' she say. 'FedEx,' she say. And I tell her to march those trays out of here. It's not her job to bring up the trays. And I can certainly read when the order is marked FedEx."

"I was right there and that's just what happened boss," Matty adds. "Just like Weeds said it did."

"Yo, when I ask for toilet paper you can come rolling in," Zarro says. "Shh, listen. Do you hear it, Matty? There's a carton on the shipping table calling you. Why don't you go see what it wants?"

Matty shrugs and ambles over to the table.

Zarro turns his attention back to Weeds. "Yeah, you told her to put back the trays and then what happened?"

"The woman pretend to be deaf. Moms puts the trays on *my* shipping table and waddles herself down the hill. Why she crying, I don't know."

"Oh, you know all right. Maybe you're not telling, but you know. What did you call her?'

"Maybe I say she ignorant, but that only after she call me a coconut. Anyone from the islands be a coconut. Jealous they be, you know. All of them Americans. Jealous we come here and start businesses and they're still collecting welfare."

"Not this again. I don't need any Jamaican superiority bullshit today, especially not with Israel and Manuel on the disabled list. I'll talk to her, okay? But if Suzie walked the order up here herself, it must have been for a goddamn good reason. And there's no need to call her ignorant. And don't even *dream* of calling her Moms if you want to keep yourself employed."

"The bitch be ignorant. All of them ignorant as goats."

79

"Why don't you shut your fuckin' mouth and get back to work?"

Weeds looks at Zarro and nods. "You tell Moms not to come up here again."

"I'll *ask* Suzie why she came up here and if her reason was a good one, you will get your goddamn dreadlocks-wearing, Bob Marley-listening, ganja-smoking ass down there and apologize, *capisce?*"

Weeds snorts and Zarro heads down the hill. Maggie and Suzie Q are now standing in front of the water cooler and when Maggie spots him, she slips away.

"Talk to me Suzie darlin'."

"If this ain't made right, I'm quitting. A body can only take so much, Zarro. Only so much. I just can't cope no more. Can't cope..."

"Calm down and let's see if we can get to the bottom of this. First of all, why did you bring the order up the hill?"

"I took it there, because the son-in-law told me it was very important. 'See it gets picked right and shipped pronto,' he says. 'I'm holding you personally responsible.' And that uppity Jamaican calls me ignorant in front of all of them upstairs. It's either him or me, Zarro. Him or me. I can't take none of this no more. My youngest daughter stuck me with two kids from her boyfriend's ex, my son is upstate on a robbery he say he didn't do, and now this coconut is dissing me on the job. So either he goes or I go."

Realizing Weed's insult is just a gust of wind on Suzie's already shaky house of cards, Zarro tries to talk some sense into her. "No one's going anywhere, Suzie. I need you both and you both need this job. He'll apologize and that will be the end of it. No way I'm asking you to love each other, but you two need to be civil."

"Civil? You want me to be civil? That ugly dreads-wearing Rasta man called me ignorant."

"Yeah, and you called him a coconut, so you're even. Now when I get him down here, you are going to accept his apology with all the graciousness you can find in yourself. And then you're going to work three times as fast to make up for the hour you spent locked in the bathroom where nothing got done."

Suzie Q raises her massive shoulders. "Fine," she hisses, "take his side. You men are all the same, balls always stick with balls."

Robert Zarro knows better than to reply. He knows the apology is really all she's looking for, and when Weeds delivers it in Zarro's presence, a dull thud of a mea culpa, Suzie sticks her nose into the air and pirouettes on her thick heel. Robert Zarro also has the good sense to escort Weeds back up to shipping before the wiry Jamaican would hear Suzanne Quentin's gob of foamy spit landing with full contemptuous force onto the dusty concrete floor.

Happy the week is over Zarro is actually looking forward to donning his new suit and driving into Manhattan that evening. Maggie leaves the apartment at noon and takes the subways to Brooklyn to visit Myrna and the friends that survived the apartment fire. He doesn't like her going back to that neighborhood, but Maggie insists. He reminds her to be back by five o'clock at the latest, so they will have enough time to make their seven o'clock reservation.

But five o'clock has come and gone. And since Maggie does not have a cell phone, there's no way to reach her. He will buy her one on Sunday. He mentally adds it to his to-do list. But meanwhile, he begins to imagine all kinds of things. He calls the restaurant to push back their reservation.

He jumps to his feet when he hears the key at the door.

"Oh 'berto, I am sorry I am late," Maggie says breathlessly.

"What the hell happened to you?"

"I try to find Myrna but she is disappeared."

"Maybe she went away for the weekend."

"No. She is nowhere and I am worry the *mara* do something with her."

"Who the hell are these people?"

"*Mara Salvatrucha*. Very bad people."

"Rafael Guzman is part of this gang?"

"*Si*. Rafael Guzman is how you say? The leader."

"I don't want you going back to that neighborhood, anymore."

"I still owe them moneys and they will find me. And if they don't find me, they'll find my family."

"How much do you owe?"

"Three thousand dollars because they bring me here to work for Jackie's Cleaning Service. And then I leave and some of the girls leave and they get mad. The fire is to scare—."

"They're the ones who started the fire? I thought it was an electrical fire."

Maggie looks down at the floor. "No. They make the fire to scare the girls. And scare the whole neighborhood. To show their power. That's what he say. And now I am thinking they have Myrna."

"That's it. This bullshit has gone on long enough. I'm calling Matty's brother. The cop."

"No. Please no *Policías*."

82

Zarro lets it drop for the time being. It's her birthday and she is entitled to some peace.

He lets Maggie get ready first. He turns the volume up on the TV and tries not to listen to her splashing around in the tub, not to imagine the curve of her back, the way her breasts will meet the warm water. She emerges eventually from the steamy bathroom wearing the blue dress, her chestnut brown hair scooped into a beribboned knot on the top of her head, revealing her slender neck. "Looking good Maggie," he says, forcing his hungry eyes away from her.

They park in a pricey midtown lot, and find the restaurant that had made Rick Schwab's top three. Other than McDonald's and The Corner Luncheonette where Trudy McClellan waitresses, it is Maggie's first experience in a real restaurant. Zarro watches as she runs her fingers over the linen tablecloth and taps her spoon gently against the crystal water goblets. Her olive eyes sparkle when the waiter brings over her salad and asks if she'd like fresh pepper. Zarro finds himself completely besotted with her, bewitched by her entire being as he simultaneously suffers from the anguish of not being able to trust himself.

"Is very nice, Roberto," Maggie proclaims as she watches the waiter twist his wrist, sending a rainfall of black pepper dots onto her plate of greens. "Today I am somebody in this very nice restaurant."

And Zarro is pleased that he could make Rafael Guzman and the gang disappear at least for a little while.

"*You* are very nice," Zarro says softly, taking a good, long sip from his glass of Chianti. "And I wish you a very happy birthday."

"Thank you for buying for me the sewing machine. I pay you when it's my turn for the Bullshit Club again."

83

"It's a present, Maggie. Enjoy it."

"I have some jobs sewing already. Louise give me some things to fix, but for her I do for free because she give me all the clothes. But she say she will tell her friends. She has a friend who has the very big chests. Always needs to fix the blouses."

"You did a great job on the curtains. The denim matches the pullout exactly."

"This is because I take the pillow to the fabric store and we match it."

"Well, I appreciate it. The place is really starting to shape up. It's gone from a hellhole to a heckhole."

"I can sew for you something else 'berto. Tell me what more I can sew."

"Maybe you can sew me a goddamn miracle to keep a paying job around seventy-five people," he says under his breath.

"I do not understand."

"Never mind," he says, not wanting to spoil her time. "Eat up, Maggie girl." A vision of the entire warehouse floor comes to Zarro as he sips his wine. He wonders if any one of Schwab's warehouse employees had ever dined in a fine restaurant. Some of them have never been inside a bank. Zarro sees the long lines every Friday at the check-cashing place on Queens Boulevard. They'd cash their checks and have the clerk make out money orders to pay their bills. Suzie Q always brought a stack of bills in with her on Friday. During lunch, she'd close her eyes and throw them high up in the air. Then she'd pay the bills that landed on the table. The rest had a shot at being paid next week. When it was her turn to collect from the Bullshit Club, she caught up on the bills that were past due. He does not want to think what would happen if Rick Schwab decides to pull the rug out from under all of them. He tries to pinpoint the exact moment when he started to give a shit.

The waiter arrives with their entrees and sets them down with an exaggerated flourish. Maggie had Zarro describe every item on the menu before she decided on the shrimp primavera. She moves her chair closer to his and they sample each other's food. Maybe it is the three glasses of wine, or the fine meal they are sharing, or the fact that they are so far removed from their everyday environment, but for once Zarro allows his guard to slip. He takes Maggie's hand in his and squeezes it slightly and she leans toward him and kisses him softly on his just-shaven face.

"Hey, what's all this about?" he asks, pretending to be shocked, a crooked smile working around the corner of his lips.

"It's about I like you very much."

"I like you very much too," he says softly. And then in an attempt to shift the subject to safer ground, he adds, "You know I don't invite any old worker here. I only take the extra special ones. So Maggie, what would you say to espresso and cake? You have some room for dessert?"

"Yes Roberto, I think there is room a little bit."

"Good. Suzie Q loved the cannolis. In fact, the last time I was here, she must have downed three of them. She said they were rich and creamy, the filling as light a feather. On the other hand, Lygia thought the cheesecake was a-okay. I remember her mentioning that the ricotta batter had just a hint of lemon, reminded her of how her grandmother made it back in the old country."

Maggie looks up at him, relieved to see the merriment dancing in his dark eyes. "I will have what Suzie has."

Chapter Nine

By early April the new and improved interactive web site is out there for the world to see. Schwab's Uniform can be liked on Facebook and followed on Twitter. Most of their hits come from individuals rather than companies, and Rick is quick to give Zarro a smug I-told-you-so. "Start packing," he says. "I knew this would be meaningless penny-ante bullshit."

"The jury's still out," Zarro counters. "Rome wasn't built in a day, you know." They're doomed. And he'll be the one to lower the hatchet. Him and his big ideas.

Desperate, Zarro persuades the son-in-law who is unofficially in charge of the sales force, to have the reps visit privately owned Army/Navy stores, costume companies, airlines, and cruise lines. He gets Rick to kick in some advertising money and they run a couple of half-page ads in scouting and flight magazines, both in print and online. Toward the end of April, corporate business starts trickling in. Still, Zarro wonders just how much will be enough to keep Rick Schwab planted in Sunnyside.

* * * * *

One particularly hot morning early in the month of May, Zarro is working with Suzie Q and Maggie pulling stock for a huge order that is to be sent overnight to the San Diego Navy Exchange. Over the din of the sewing machines, the ever-present salsa rhythms, and the incessant thwack of the belt-tipping machine, he hears the son-in-law shout to the head embroiderer to throw the switch on the overhead fans. The office, naturally, is air-conditioned; a king wouldn't work in anything less than a temperate environment. The warehouse, however, is not.

Zarro taps Suzie Q and called Maggie over from the steel shelves. "Get a load of what's about to happen over by embroidery."

They pick up their heads. "See, the son-in-law is turning on the fans."

"That's one fine idea, Zarro," Suzie Q says. "It's hot as the devil's own kitchen in here. Why didn't *you* think of that?"

"I *did* think of it. I was going to switch them on as soon as that order was packed. Take a look over by Narinda and Bupinda. Back behind Despina and Shirley Wong. See those basketfuls of feathers? They're attaching them onto the gowns. It's for some university production."

"You had better go over there and stop him," Suzie Q advises.

"Tell me something. Aren't we as hard working Americans entitled to have a little fun now and then?" Zarro asks. "What good is waking up in the morning if you can't have a good laugh every so often. Am I right Suzie?"

"Well, when you put it that way I have to agree. And all those experts on TV say that laughter is the best medicine. It's listed right up there in the medical books with Alka-Seltzer and Robitussin."

"Roberto, stop him. *Por favor*. Please, I ask you. We will get into trouble. I cannot go back to Nicaragua. Never."

Zarro wonders why she is so jumpy. "Relax. The only one in trouble will be the son-in-law." He smiles when he feels a breeze from the fan. "Look out maties, thar she blows!"

Pink and yellow feathers flutter over the entire sewing department, floating onto faces, hair and clothing. Suzie Q and Zarro laugh until tears run down their cheeks.

Maggie shakes her head. "Is not nice," she chides. "You will get all of us in trouble."

Zarro ignores her. Fuck it. Why shouldn't they have a little fun on the boss's clock? What the hell good is loyalty when it isn't traveling down a two way street?

And for the weeks that follow, all he has to say is, "Gee, it's hot in here. Why don't I switch the fans on?" and he and Suzie Q would convulse with laughter.

Chapter Ten

One Thursday night, not too long after the feather incident, Zarro stays up to do some research. Long past the hour of the *novela*, long past Maggie's practice session with a CD of "You Can Learn English," long after her nightly soak in the claw-footed tub, and long after Maggie falls asleep on the new pullout sofa, Zarro finds something online that piques his interest. He takes a couple of notes, and makes a mental note to call the union rep on Friday. They would be the undocumented workers' natural allies in the workplace. He contemplates waking Maggie up, telling her there might be a way she and her friends could earn an almost living wage, but when he gazes across at her sleeping peacefully under the quilt, he decides it could wait until morning. And after emerging from his cold shower, he towels off, steps into a pair of old flannel boxers, finds his bed and tries to fall asleep.

He tosses and turns for half an hour, a hundred thoughts bumping around his head. He thinks about Immigration. Maybe he could design some training program as a ruse to keep the workers here. Not the H-1B visa—that was for college-educated professionals. An H3 visa? They'd need a detailed description of a training program. They'd need a good immigration lawyer.

Maybe the union could point him in the right direction. Numbers and letters attack him. Eventually, exhaustion overtakes Zarro and he nods off.

But Robert Zarro doesn't find any peace in sleep that night. Instead, he finds himself back within the walls of Dawes Block at Old Bay Correctional. He begins to do battle in his bed, pounding his pillow, and shouting obscenities into the rumpled sheets. He sees the two red rivers of blood running down the back of his legs and he moans. "Get the fuck off me!"

"No, you tagged now, Snowflake. You tagged."

Maggie wakes and stares at the dark. She thinks how nice the new sofa-bed is—fresh and firm and maybe the best sleep she can remember. And yet, she's awake. Why? Then she hears Zarro moaning and moving around in his bedroom.

Startled, Maggie wakes and walks to Zarro's door. Not wanting to invade his privacy, she hesitates for a minute on the outside, debating with herself whether or not to cross the threshold that in her mind is forbidden. She'd been in Zarro's bedroom only when he was out of the apartment. Like a phantom maid, she polished his furniture, and vacuumed the carpet. Occasionally, she darted in to place a pile of his clean, folded laundry on his bed. But she never, ever entered the room when he was home. It is the sound of his pain that forces her hand on the doorknob. She tiptoes over to him and lowers herself onto the edge of his bed. "Roberto," she says softly, stroking the back of his head, "you are dreaming a bad dream."

* * * * *

92

Zarro twists in his sleep. He wants to turn and kill someone, even if it means he will never leave Old Bay.

Then he awakes suddenly, and hears Maggie's voice and feels her touch, gentle, against the violence of his dream. Tears spring to his eyes.

"Go back to sleep," he says. "I'm all right."

Her two hands reach for his damp face. "Did somebody hurt you?"

"Yeah Maggie, they hurt me so bad." He wants to tell someone, has to tell someone.

She put her arms around his neck. "It's okay. They hurt me too."

And where so many times he shunned any touch, tonight he welcomes it. "Hold me, Maggie. Please. Just hold me for a second. I...I can't do this alone anymore. I'm so tired of alone." She is soft and pretty and she is there beside him. Her hair smells of lemons. And he wants her. Oh God, he wants her. He physically aches for her. It would be okay if she just held him for a minute, one minute, so he wouldn't be by himself at Old Bay. "Make it go away Maggie. They keep following me, tracking me down wherever I go."

Maggie peels back the covers and climbs in next to him. She kisses his cheekbone and then his jaw, her lips seeming to taste the salt of his tears. She continues to touch him. Her hands graze lightly over his chest and down to his stomach.

And when Zarro can't bear the torment of that exquisite physical sensation, he whispers hoarsely, "That's enough, Maggie. Go on back to sleep. All you're going to get is hurt. I'm such bad news."

"No, you would never hurt me, Roberto."

With a raging hunger that has lain dormant for three years, his mouth finds hers and she climbs on top of him then, lifting her nightgown over her head, and casting it into the velvety moss of darkness. Back and forth she rocks him and he hears the din of the factory and the pulse of a salsa beat. Then he feels something pulling at him, taking him away from the horrors of himself, and he is floe adrift in a vast rolling sea. It succors him, soothes his febrile machinations. And it feels good and sweet and peaceful. There is no hurt any more, just pleasure's icy salve on a hot, scorching pain. And somewhere far away through the gauze of darkness he hears Maggie softly calling his name. *Ay 'berto, 'berto, 'berto.* He closes his eyes and turns to liquid after that, a thousand dripping stars in an inky sky. Zarro sleeps well for the remainder of that night, his two arms wound around Magaly Ocampo.

An anemic dawn trickles through the half closed Venetian blinds and wakes Zarro. And when he looks over and finds Maggie curled up under the covers, he curses under his breath. Although he had held her all night, he is still taken aback to find her asleep in his bed that morning. After all, it was a dream, wasn't it? She came to him in a dream, some crazy ephemeral hallucination due to overwork. Zarro can't fully understand why she is here, now, in his bed. Quietly, so as not to wake her, he slips on a pair of jeans and a T-shirt and tries to find some answers out his bedroom window. With a quick tug to the right, the frayed cord lifts the blinds, exposing the street below.

And in the somber tones of that misty last Friday in May, a harsh beauty in his adopted neighborhood appears before his eyes. He doesn't find the natural loveliness of the Bentley campus, the clear air, the sunlight playing tag with the leaves of ancient oaks. There are no sloping hills of tended green on the Sunnyside-Long Island City border. In stark contrast, his neighborhood exudes the beauty of human sweat and toil. Gritty brick apartment buildings and pockmarked sidewalks, extant businesses housed in sturdy rectangular warehouses, a line of cars parked with a half inch to spare, a cubist collage signed by an artist formerly known as Hard Work. Zarro realizing that morning for the very first time, his street is so damned ugly it is beautiful. Hard Work greets him outside his window, and he is proud to be a small part of the picture, pleased to be a cog in the wheel of a dying industrial base. It will only die if people let it. He believes it can be saved. Globalization is a bell, a tocsin warning the nation to wake the hell up. Industry can be saved through technology, rather than be replaced by it. Jobs can be made secure through innovation, through smarts. People will have to be willing to invest in the long term, though. It always came down to people, doesn't it? People like Rick Schwab. People—the goddamn weak link in the chain.

And while he is lost in thought, two figures intrude on his personal landscape, two men entering the backdoor of Schwab's. Zarro is surprised that the alarm doesn't sound as he waits for the pair to re-emerge. He gets a better look as the two exit Schwab's garage, a computer in each man's arms. "Son of a bitch," he says out loud as he sees Matty McClellan and an unidentified accomplice. Zarro picks up his wallet from the dresser and rummages through it for Detective McClellan's card. From the kitchen he calls the cell where it goes straight to voicemail. Then he tries the detective's home number and nearly hangs up when an older man's voice comes through the receiver.

"Sorry for disturbing you at this hour. I'm looking for Tommy McClellan. Do I have the right number?"

"You're not disturbing me," the older man answers slowly. "I'm his father-in-law, Sol Barron."

"Can I speak to Tommy, Mr. Barron?"

"What Mr. Barron? The whole world calls me Sol."

"Okay Sal."

"Sol like Solomon. Not Sal like Salvatore. You must be Italian. Italians always say Sal. Anyway at this hour, are you really sure you want me to wake up my son-in-law? Do you *know* what kind of temper he has?"

"Well, if you don't mind. It's an emergency."

Through the phone, Zarro can hear the old man's heavy footsteps as he goes to wake his son-in-law.

"Yeah?" the detective mumbles in a voice honey-thick with sleep.

"It's Rob Zarro. I'm sorry to wake you, but—"

"Sorry to wake me? It's my day off you dumb guinea. I told the Job if a mass murderer was doing his thing on 39th Street not to call. You read me?"

He hears some rustling, a woman's voice, and then McClellan answering her, "Go back to sleep, Sunshine. It's nobody's third cousin, once removed."

"Look, I just saw your brother and some other guy boost two computers out of Schwab's."

"You got trouble sleeping, Zarro?"

"No, not usually."

"Then why in hell are you looking out your fuckin' window at this unholy hour?"

"Forget about it. Sorry I called."

"No, no. Don't pay me no mind. I'm not a morning person, especially not a 'five o'clock in the morning' person. You can't tell by my generally pissed off tone here, but I'm actually *happy* you dropped a dime. You done good, pally. So listen up.

Here's what I want you to do. Play dumb when you get to Schwab's. Let that old bat bookkeeper call the uniforms and let 'em handle it from there. That will give me some time to play with. I'll dig around for those computers…just what I wanted to do on my day off. I'll be back at you later today."

"And what do I say to your brother?"

"Nothing for now. Let me get busy. The other guy, did you get a glance?"

"White guy. Five foot six. Black hair desperate for a comb. Know him?"

"Yeah, the good news is he's not my shit-for-brains stepfather. The bad news is he's Matty's friend, Raymond the Hungarian gypsy thief prick."

By now Maggie is awake and Zarro fills with remorse, realizing just how badly this ended up.

"Maggie," he says, his hands pressed against the doorjamb of his bedroom. "I want you to listen to me. What happened between us last night was a mistake. I took advantage of your good nature and I hope in time you forgive me, but me and you like this together is just plain wrong."

Maggie sits up and draws the quilt around her neck. "You no like, Roberto?"

Zarro moves closer into the room. He lowers himself onto the edge of his bed, his eyes on Maggie. "Oh, I like all right. I…I like very much, but Maggie, we work together and this just can't be." She made her way into his nightmares. She crawled on her belly into Old Bay with me. She saw him lying there weak and helpless. She touched him. She goddamn touched him.

"Who hurt you?" she asks. "Tell me please. You are very sad last night."

"I don't want to talk about this. God, I can't believe I let this happen. Of all the stupid fucked up things I've done, this one has to rank right up there."

"Who would hurt such a fine man?" she asks, sitting up and stroking his cheek.

"Look, don't touch me. I'm not a fine man. I'm nowhere near a fine man. You look at the world with such wide-eyed innocence. But then what can I expect from a girl who marvels at seatbelt technology and thinks chowing down on a can of Franco American is good eating?"

She can't understand what provoked such anger. "Why are you mad on me?"

"I'm not mad at you, Maggie. I'm wicked, wicked pissed at myself for allowing this happen. I got hurt in prison, okay? Your fine man was in prison, locked up for three years because I sold drugs. You know drugs, Maggie. Drugs are not all that different than the glue that those little kids stay high out of their minds on in Guatemala City. And your fine man sold these drugs to make enough money to impress his college fraternity. Fraternity, a group of spoiled assholes out to have a good time on Mommy and Daddy's credit card. This fine man got locked away. And when he first was locked away he got hurt bad. And then he learned how to play the game, figured out who was who. He learned to defend himself so he wouldn't need to hide behind those bullshit affiliations. And when he was out on his own he got thrown in the hole for nearly putting someone's eye out. And your fine man liked hurting this someone. In fact he'd do it again if he had the chance."

She is listening intently, her face expressionless.

98

He continues. He cannot stop the words from rushing out of him. "Then your fine man here got released last summer, left his family in Revere so he wouldn't bring more shame down on them or him, and moved to Sunnyside, Queens. Why here? 'Cause here was far from there. Face it, you just rolled around in the sack with a sick, twisted, drug dealing ex-con. A mistake. You understand now Maggie, or should we make tracks to the UN and hire a translator?"

She understands about half of what he said but all the venom in what he meant. Using the quilt as a makeshift cloak, she stands up and gathers her clothing in order to get dressed for work. Zarro doesn't wait around. He flies down the stairs two at a time, slams the front door behind him, crosses the street, and waits for his day at Schwab's to unwind.

He busies himself between the front office and shipping, avoiding Maggie altogether. He is surprised to see Matty McClellan at work, but there he stands, as if nothing had happened. The police come and go. Marilyn Friedman places a call to the insurance company about the computers. In fact, the day is no more unusual than any other day. At ten thirty, the Roach Coach pulls into the garage and leaves after twenty minutes. Stock is replenished. New orders come into the office by fax and phone, making their way to Zarro's front desk where he marks them up to be picked, blister packed, and shipped.

At lunchtime, one of the embroiderers pulls fifteen faux Fendi purses from plastic bags and displays them on her table. Within twenty minutes, she has sold twelve out of the fifteen to the women who descend upon her three-deep, each of them hungry for a bargain. Not to outdo her, but in the true spirit of a fellow entrepreneur Manuel from shipping, seemingly completely recovered from his bullet wound, empties his deep pockets of the fake ten-dollar Rolex watches he is ready to hawk. At one o'clock when Rick Schwab walks through the warehouse to take his usual afternoon spin in his silver Porsche, all evidence of the lunchtime bizarre has vanished. At three fifteen, Weeds carries a Titan saber and scabbard from the shelf and expertly etches a man's name and rank into the sharp chrome blade.

The UPS truck comes and departs on or close to schedule. And at four o'clock when the workers start punching the time clock and wishing each other a good weekend, Zarro picks up the phone in the back office and leaves a message on the union rep's voicemail. He's just about ready to pack it in, when a sullen-looking Tommy McClellan appears from out of nowhere and parks himself in the spare chair.

"You're somewhat underdressed today, Detective," Zarro says, eyeing the detective's faded jeans and T-shirt. "Where's the suit and tie? You have an image to maintain, no?"

"It's my day off. I think I mentioned that to you about quarter after five this morning, if my memory serves me right. And it fuckin' always serves me right."

Zarro watches grimly as Tommy McClellan stands up and removes a small gun from under his pants leg, removes his wire frames, his keys, his cell phone, his lighter, and his wristwatch, and dumps the entire collection unceremoniously into the bottom drawer of Zarro's desk. Out of two ice-cold navy blue eyes, the cop looks squarely at Zarro and says in a voice of tempered steel, "Now you tell me where he is."

With instincts honed in prison, Zarro knows just what was about to happen, just as well as he knows how powerless he is to prevent it. "Calm down," he says, just as the van barreled into the garage with Matty at the wheel. The detective kicks the desk drawer closed, leaves the back office and pulls his brother out of the van by the neck. In a matter of seconds, the two brothers are rolling on the concrete floor, barreling into stacks of pre-made boxes. A few lingering workers hear the commotion and shout, "Call the cops!" but Zarro tells them to get home and get home fast. One of them *is* the cops.

He tries his best to separate the two brothers. Physically speaking, he thinks Matty, broader and stockier would have it over the tall, lean detective, but the detective has one thing his younger brother didn't have, and that is pure rage.

"Where'd you fence them?" the detective demands as he attempts to smash his brother's face into the floor. "I spent my day off crawling through pawn shops and back alleys trying to save you your job. You know what I was supposed to be doing today, you little shit? I was going to take your niece to the park and then the two of us were supposed to go to White Castle. And if her uncle wasn't such a time suck, that's where we'd be right now, downing belly busters. I've been carrying you for twenty years. And it's no fuckin' way to live."

The two of them roll around for a while and then Matty picks himself up and with his full weight pounces on his brother. Zarro wedges himself between them and tries to separate them, but the two McClellans keep coming together, intent on pummeling each other to the finish. Skin bruises, and becomes pulp. "The best part of you dripped down Daddy's leg," Tommy snarls, punctuating each hostile word with a hard crack to his brother's face.

"Stay the hell out of my life." Matty hammers back, locking his older brother in a chokehold.

The sheathed box cutter that had been in Matty's pocket comes tumbling out onto the cement floor. Zarro and the detective spot it simultaneously. The detective tries unsuccessfully to break free of Matty, his hands groping around the floor for the box cutter. Zarro picks it up and hurls it toward the back of the garage.

"Fuck you too, Zarro. This ain't your business."

Zarro forces himself between them again and works at pulling Matty's hands off his brother's neck only to give Tommy the upper hand.

Seizing the advantage, the detective takes his brother's arm and twists it around his back. "Who took them? You gave them to Raymond to fence? That Hungarian gypsy shrimp. I told you a thousand times to stay away from him. Tell me, Matty. Tell me where he took them."

"I ain't telling you nothing," Matty hisses, freeing his arm and hurling Tommy headfirst against the steel leg of the shipping table.

Zarro is squarely between them now, but it makes no difference. They fight around him, under and over him. It doesn't faze him in the least. It heightens his senses, sharpens his instincts. Civility is overestimated, he thinks. Once in a while people need to get down and dirty. "Break it up already. You're going to kill each other."

"Stay out of this, Zarro. This got nothing to do with you," Tommy tells him, shoving him aside then pouncing on his brother. "You don't know this, but you are becoming our old man. Maybe I look like him but you *are* him. You're a drunk. You piss every dollar away on gambling. What next Matty? You're gonna hit Ma? You're gonna lay hands on her? Then I'll first fuckin' kill you."

"What the hell are you talking about?" Matty yells. "I never laid a hand on her. Get off me. Ow! Shit, I think you broke

102

my nose again, you stupid fuck. I can taste it." Matty leans over his brother and spits a huge gob of dark blood onto the floor.

At that point, Zarro wedged between the two of them, gets punched directly above his eye, receiving the granitic blow that was intended for Tommy. For just a few seconds, he feels the large room reel and then slip out of sight. It comes back slowly, first in ashen pixels, followed by soft pastels, reassembling through a fractured lens. It eventually emerges into harsh full color when his brain is capable of rejoining the wayward images. With a pounding heart, a searing head, blood dripping down his forehead, Zarro is somehow able to locate a pocket of hidden strength and he uses it to pin the detective's chest down with his knee. "Go Matty. Book. I got him. Just get the hell out of here."

Zarro keeps the detective pinned under his weight until Matty's silhouette vaporizes. Slowly, Zarro releases Tommy McClellan, the two of them out of breath, adrenaline still racing through their veins.

Stunned, the cop gets to his feet and with the peak of his remaining wrath, picks up Elmo-the cleaning-guy's push broom and smashes a jagged hole through the windshield of the Schwab's Uniform van, sending a shower of broken glass into and around the vehicle. Then the detective hurls the broom to the floor, finds the back door, and staggers onto 39th Street.

Drained and somewhat dizzy, Zarro goes into the men's room and relieves himself, thinking of Mel Lieb all the while. "Kid, you're lucky. You don't know how I envy you. You're blessed with excellent flow," Mel had remarked when they happened to be in the men's room at the same time. "It's on my resume," Zarro had retorted. "That's what landed me the job." There was the slightest tincture of pink in his flow today that Zarro realizes is blood.

103

Not one to get too excited over a medical situation, he splashes some cold water on his face and then dabs the dark red ooze from his cut brow with a stiff, brown paper towel, the same stiff, brown paper towels used in the Revere public school system. While his breath catches up with him, he wonders how Mel would have handled the situation. Maybe he could have prevented it. Mel had a way with people, a calming influence about him that Zarro is well aware he lacks. He ruminates on this for a while, but comes up with no clear way to rectify his character deficiency. No matter how hard he tries, he will never be Mel Lieb. Never.

He sweeps up the glass, sluices the blood off the cement floor with water from Elmo's bucket and mops the surface clean. He stacks the empty cardboard boxes into neat piles. He removes the detective's gun out of his desk drawer and sticks it in the waistband of his own jeans. He scoops up the keys, the cell phone, the lighter, and the eyeglasses, and shoves them into his pockets. He puts on his Red Sox cap backwards, the long brim throwing shadow onto his neck. Then he sets the alarm and lets himself out, the daylight assaulting his already battered senses.

Zarro walks across 43rd Avenue to Matty's apartment building. The security door is held ajar by a rusted bridge chair and he lets himself in. When his eyes adjust to the 40-watt dinginess of the hallway, he glances at row upon row of smudged gold mailboxes one step up from the sitting area of the shabby lobby. Two mailboxes have the name McClellan on them. One for Barron-McClellan and the other reads McClellan-Emmet. Just my lucky day. They *both* live here.

104

An unkempt woman in a stained terrycloth bathrobe and a lopsided platinum blonde Afro wig approaches him at the bank of mailboxes. "Hey handsome, you looking for someone in particular?" she asks out of eyes that are trying to focus.

"Tommy McClellan for starters."

"My husband is the super in this building," she says, scratching vigorously under the wig's elastic band.

Zarro nods and backs up two steps. An odor emanates from the woman, a stale moldy fragrance that brings his time in solitary front and center.

"Tommy McClellan never has a nice word to say to me. Can I help it if my husband can't get up there the minute something goes wrong? We don't keep spare oven parts in our apartment, you know. But you be sure to tell Tommy McClellan when you see him that the only reason I let him keep that cat of his, is because of his wife."

"I can't tell him anything until you give me a clue on the apartment number. It's rubbed off the mailbox."

"Four-G. His mother's one floor up from him. Nice lady, Trudy. My name's Mrs. Gurtz, by the way. I'm the one to see if you're looking for an apartment. This is a rent-stabilized building you know, very convenient into Manhattan, if you happen to like Manhattan. And cash helps in that situation, whatever you can spare. My husband is the super here."

"So you said."

He rides up on an oily elevator that deposits him with a bone-wrenching jolt on the 4th floor and he finds Tommy's apartment at the end of a long narrow hallway. The little girl Zarro had met on New Year's cracks the door and Zarro spots a

105

red lollipop in her hand. Then a sleek gray and white cat comes bounding out of the small space. "You just lost your cat," Zarro says, as he watches the tip of its high tail disappear around a turnoff in the corridor.

"No, that's Minnew," Aggie says, opening the door wider. "She walks around the whole building. Daddy says she's a mouser. He says Santini our landlord should cut us a break on the rent because of Minnew."

"Who is it?" a female voice wafts into the hallway where Zarro is standing.

"Mrs. McClellan, I'm Rob Zarro from Schwab's."

Aggie stands back, letting her mother come to the door. The detective's wife has large brown eyes, long curly dark hair and a heart-shaped face. Her hands support the small of her back for she is visibly pregnant.

"Hi. I'm Joanna. You called this morning, right?"

"Yeah. Sorry about calling so early."

"Come in. We'll talk inside."

Zarro walks past a foyer where three bicycles are parked against a wall, Aggie's small pink model with two training wheels sprouting on either side, a large red 10-speed, and an even larger black 10-speed, the vehicular version of The Three Little Bears. Joanna sees him looking at the bikes and said, "My husband is quite the rider and Aggie's on her way, too."

"Daddy doesn't wear a helmet," Aggie says. "He has a very big scar right *here* from where he fell." The child lifts her shirt and points to her ribcage, "but Daddy says his head is as hard as a rock."

Zarro nods, knowing full well that her father's scar was not caused by any spill from a bicycle. "Well, he's got that right. They don't make heads harder than his." And then to Joanna, he says, "Would you happen to know where he is?"

"No, I haven't seen Tommy all day. He said he had some stuff to take care of. I'm guessing the stuff he has to take care of has something to do with your call."

"Yeah, sort of."

"You know I've heard so much about you, I feel I know you already. Matty's mentions your name more than once. My mother-in-law talks about you too. And of course you know my friend Louise and her mother Rose."

Zarro can't help but stare at Joanna McClellan. Try as he might, he cannot picture the McClellans as a couple. She is as smooth as silk and he as rough as they come. They walk toward the living room, enabling Zarro to look around. It is a gem of an apartment, Zarro thinks. Joanna McClellan has actually created an oasis, four floors up from the world outside her living room window. Hardwood floors, an area rug, pictures on the wall, furniture that matched. Yes, the McClellans have a real home, unlike his own hodgepodge hole in the wall. An end table full of framed photos catches his eye. There are the usual expected pictures, the McClellans as bride and groom, as well as the progressive stages in Aggie's life that have been captured for posterity. He notices a lone photo of a tired looking woman that Zarro realizes is Joanna's mother, the embroiderer who had permanently abandoned her needles and thread. He stares at the face in the photo, a face that so clearly bore the Schwab stamp of daily drudgery.

"That's my mother," Joanna says, "May Barron. She used to work at Schwab's."

"I'm sorry. I mean I heard what happened."

"My mother missed so much, like our wedding, and Aggie, and this new baby. There are these times I just want to scream at her. And why I'm telling this to a complete stranger, I really don't know."

107

"Any person who wakes you up at five a.m. isn't a complete stranger."

Joanna manages a weak smile. "Well, maybe you have something, there."

Zarro moves away from the end table. To the right of him, is a desk piled high with books. Above the desk three wooden shelves bulge with even more books, spines crammed together, authors indecently forced up against one another. Joyce, Thackeray, Dickens, Wolf, James, and Hemmingway compete for six inches of shelf space. Most of the books look shopworn and have yellow stickers marked "used" plastered on their paper covers, reminding Zarro of the books he bought back when he was in college. And suddenly and unbeknownst to their authors, they convey him back to the prison library.

"Who's the student?" he asks when he is able to wrench himself free of Old Bay.

"Both of us are, actually. Aggie's in kindergarten and I go to Queens College two nights a week after work. Go ahead. Take one if you want."

"You have quite a collection here," he says, eyeing the shelves suspiciously.

"Well, we like to read."

"You and Aggie?" he asks, deftly pulling "Return of the Native" down without disturbing its neighbors. It's a small paperback and with Joanna McClellan observing him with her two large doe eyes, he feels somewhat obligated to borrow something.

"And Tommy."

"Tommy, as in your husband Tommy?"

"Does that surprise you?" she asks with a smile.

"I'd be lying big time if I said no."

"Oh, my husband is *full* of surprises."

"Wonders never cease."

Aggie walks in front of him and twirls the lollipop in her mouth so that it resembles a toothpick and said, "My Uncle Matty calls you that son-of-a-bitch Zarro. He says that all the time to my Daddy. 'You know what that son-of-a-bitch Zarro done to me this time?' "

Zarro bites down on his tongue to keep himself from laughing.

"Aggie," Joanna glares at her daughter.

Ignoring her mother, Aggie continues with her impressions, this time puffing on her lollipop as if it were a cigarette. "Then my Daddy always says, 'Matty, how many times do I gotta tell you to watch your goddamn mouth in front of Aggie?' "

"That's it. Go sit in your room, Agnes May. You and I are going to have one of our little talks later."

Nonplussed, the little girl flounces out of the living room, blond curls bouncing. She sings loudly and off key on the brief journey to her bedroom, "Ma-ry had a lit-tle lamb, a side of peas, a piece of ham…"

Zarro releases his smile when he hears the door close behind her. "A McClellan through and through."

"Thank you for not laughing. Her father can't contain himself. I don't know what goes on at his work, but at home he's definitely the good cop. Anyway, would you like to wait here for Tommy? There's plenty of room on the couch."

Zarro hears belabored breathing from another room.

"That's my dad," Joanna interjects, reading Zarro's thoughts.

"We met on the phone this morning. Sol as in Solomon Barron."

Joanna grins. "You called him Sal."

109

"Hey, it's an altogether honest mistake given my ethnic background. Look, you're going to find out sooner or later, and I don't want to worry you, but your husband and Matty got into a knockdown over at Schwab's. Both of them are pretty banged up."

"You have a deep cut over your eye," she says softly. "It's still runny and the skin is turning black and blue. Here," she says, reaching over to a box of tissues on an end table and handing him one.

"I played referee," he tells her while dabbing the excess fluid out of the cut.

"Where's Tommy now? Is he all right?"

"A couple of scratches, but I'm afraid he'll live. I thought maybe you'd know where I can find either of them."

Joanna folds her arms above the mound of her belly. "Those two," she sighs. "It just keeps on going on and on. Well, you might want to try Buckley's. One or both of them might be there."

"The bar on Queens Boulevard?"

"Yes, but not the topless one. Buckley's is a couple of blocks past the Corner Luncheonette, on the same side of the street, next door to the funeral parlor."

Zarro heads toward the door. "I know the place. Don't get up. I'll see myself out. And if I find him, I'll send him home."

"No matter what you saw, my husband truly loves his brother. It's just the stress. He's working on a homicide that involves a child. It's the way I see him looking at Aggie, trying to piece together how anyone could do whatever it was they did to that kid."

"He must see all types of things in his line of work." He too, had seen things.

"If you do happen to find him, please tell him I said it's okay. He'll understand."

"I will. And congratulations, by the way. When's the newest McClellan making the scene?"

"The doctor says the very last week in July."

"Aggie will be one tough act to follow."

Head still aching, he exits the building and walks up a gloomy 43rd Avenue, hanging a left on Queens Boulevard, searching under the awnings for the bar. It is a narrow, dimly lit place and it takes some time for his eyes to adjust to the darkness. The detective is seated on a barstool. A glass of Scotch is in his left hand and his right hand is submerged in a small bucket of ice. An unlit Newport dangles precariously from his gashed mouth. He is talking to the bartender and he doesn't so much as look up when Zarro sits down beside him, but the detective senses his presence nonetheless. "What will it be, Zarro?" he asks.

"Well, after going three rounds with the brothers McClellan, a cold beer always sounds dandy," he says putting his borrowed book down on the bar.

"He'll have a Dewars," he says to the bartender, a pink skinned bald-headed man with a bushy brown handlebar moustache and two bushy brows to match. The bartender seems to fade into the background as soon as Zarro is served, aware that good bartenders are unobtrusive when they need to be. "Don't you know anything, you Boston bean? Beer you drink when you're thirsty. Scotch you drink when you're empty."

111

Zarro nods. "Thanks, I make it my business to learn something new every day. Jeez, doesn't the alcohol kill your lip?"

"Only hurts the first time. So tell me Zarro, where in the world did you get the idea I was holed up in this here bar?"

"Well, I knew where your brother lived. And then I noticed you lived there, too. God almighty, it's a building chock full of McClellans."

"Yeah, a real Kennedy compound," he sneers. "We got ourselves none of their money and all of their bad luck."

"I got your apartment number from a skanky looking pig in a fright wig who claims she's the super's wife. Not a member of your fan club, I'm afraid. And then I met your lovely wife. She's the one who had a hunch you'd be in here. Congratulations Detective, Rose's daughter Louise is ready to pop any minute and now I see your wife is expecting, too. Must be something in this Queens tap water."

"Either that or some kid's been poking holes in the condoms over at Philly's drugstore."

Zarro smiles. "You mean you're not looking forward to the arrival of yet another McClellan? You have to admit, your daughter is a Class A pisser."

"Yeah, Aggie can definitely stay. But I don't have a clue where we're going to put this baby. That book you're carting around looks awfully familiar. *The Return of the Native*," McClellan says slowly. "Not a happy tale."

"Your wife loaned it to me. Don't tell me you actually read it."

"Yeah I read it," he says with some offense. "Why, did you think I was fuckin' illiterate?"

"Jesus, don't get your horns twisted. I know you can read, I just didn't see you getting into the heavy hitters." Zarro sucks on his Scotch. He doesn't like the taste but he is starting to enjoy the warmth. "Tell me something because I'm really dying to know. How in holy hell did the Southy Irish likes of you end up married to *that* classy lady?"

"As my late Nana Agnes used to say, 'Boyo, don't go questioning God's mysterious ways.' She intervened on behalf of Jo and me. Me visiting her at Elmhurst Hospital when she busted her hip and she making me promise to stop chasing skirt and settle down. Her last words to me were, 'Quit feckin' around Tommy and try to live yourself a day-cent life.' "

"Feckin'?"

"Feckin'. It's an old Irish word, right Pete?" the detective addresses the bartender who was now seated near the cash register, working the Daily News crossword.

"You better feckin' believe it."

"So you're saying your grandmother fixed you up with your wife?" Zarro asks.

"From heaven above."

"What the hell does that mean?"

"What I'm saying is Jo and I got reacquainted at my grandmother's wake. Divine intervention, Zarro. My grandmother pushing us two together straight from the gates of Saint Peter."

"Ah come on, you can't really believe that shit," he retorts. Not for a minute does Thomas McClellan fit into Zarro's image of a religious person.

"This ain't shit, Zarro. This is honest-to-God gospel. You're not doubting the word of a highly decorated New York City detective now, are you?'

Zarro rolls his eyes. "Wouldn't dream of it."

Then Tommy pulls his hand out of the ice bucket, examines it, frowns, and plunges it back in. "You must think I'm

113

some lowdown prick busting into my brother's work and breaking the place up."

Zarro takes another gulp. "I'm not one to be thinking anything. Besides, I haven't been involved in that kind of a beat down since—"

"Oh, say it already, Zarro. Since you were locked up on that drug charge."

Zarro puts down his glass. "Well, well, just how long have you been sitting on *that* one?"

"Actually, I ran you through BCI the minute I laid eyes on that lousy prison tattoo of yours. You having a sheet didn't surprise me none. Besides, a real honest to God college boy wouldn't have lasted two minutes at Schwab's. My brother and his gang of weed-toking mopes would've eaten one of 'em for lunch back there."

"I bet you and Matty must have had a few good laughs about his ex-con supervisor, huh Detective?"

"I never said shit to my brother, or no one else for that matter. Besides, you can see for yourself, I don't exactly walk the path of the saints." Tommy removes his hand out of the ice bucket, once again. "This knuckle is definitely busted. That brother of mine has a typical mick skull, hard as a fuckin' rock."

"A hard head *and* he can pack one hell of a punch."

"Oh, our Matty boy was Golden Gloves once upon a time. But hey, I'm done with him. I'll pay for the two computers he boosted and then I'm done. I got nothing left. I'll sell my sailboat to pay for them, the one thing I own outright other than an old Toyota with a bum defroster. I love that boat Zarro, but Matty's ass needs covering yet again." The detective is morose. Alcohol has melted the topcoat of coolness off him, exposing a layer of underlying woe in its wake. "Hey, how's about we break the no-smoking law. You got a light for a one-armed man,

Peter?" he asks the bartender. Johnny on the spot, the bartender springs to his feet, leans over, and flicks his Bic. Tommy sucking the smoke down like mother's milk.

Zarro feels the drink's warmth expanding into him. He could still feel the pain in his head, but it is dull, bearable. "Come on, a well-paid, dressed-to-the-nines detective crying the money shorts? Give me a break."

Tommy McClellan rubs his knuckle and winces. "You don't get it Zarro, not even a little bit. My stepfather's limo was being hidden in the back of Schwab's for three weeks in order so it wouldn't be repossessed by his ex-boss. My father-in-law's heart medication is running fifteen dollars a pill and he downs four of them a day, and he's already maxed out of his Medicare supplemental. And to top matters off, I got to make sure Matty sends child support for his bastard kid in Turkey—not to mention what gets scooped up by the shys. His vig happens to be more than my rent. Zarro, no salary in the free world will cover my load."

"So who was it that died and left you king?" Zarro sings out loudly, causing the bartender to momentarily glance up from his puzzle.

"Are you drunk already? Jesus, tell me you get shitfaced on half a glass of Dewars," the detective says, sliding over an ashtray.

"Guess I'm a cheap date."

"Guess you ain't much of a drinker, pally. Who left me king? Open your eyes there, Zarro. I'm what's standing between my brother and two busted kneecaps, my stepfather and unemployment, and my father-in-law and not having meds. Anyways, I don't know how and I don't know why but God put me down here to be the patriarch of the family, the whole sorry lot of us including Billy's lousy kids from his ex-wife. But just for the record, I would have cut him, you know. If you didn't toss that box cutter, I would have engraved my initials on my brother's throat, as sure as I'm sitting here."

"From where I was standing that could have gone either way."

"Matty knocking me around was self-defense, nothing more. He don't have real violence in him. He's nothing more than a stupid oversized kid, as loyal as they come. Back when I moved out and got my own place, he lifted the furniture in the lobby and him and that crazy Hungarian gypsy drove it over to my apartment in the Schwab van, 'cause it bothered Matty no end that I didn't have nothing. That's a housewarming gift, Matty style. You should've seen the look on Mrs. Gurtz's face when I returned it after I married Jo and moved back to the building. Zarro, my brother would do anything for me, anything at all, even steal for chrissakes. So I can't make no sense of him setting me off the way he did."

"Shit happens."

"This shit shouldn't happen. Eight hours a day I'm civil to thieves, murderers, rapists, and child abusers. I'm their friend, their priest, their shrink—I'm whatever I need to be. But my brother, my own flesh and blood, him I could have sliced over a couple of lousy computers."

"Well, family always brings out the best in everyone."

"I know that if a bullet don't find me, they're going to carry me out of that shitty apartment building in a box. And I can live with that. But while I'm tossing his usual places for them computers I saw my sailboat disappear on me, and that boat is the one thing me and Jo got to escape. And I need to escape every now and then, need it bad. See you probably don't know this, but this cluster-fuck of a job is ripping pieces out of me. Day after day more and more of me slips away. My wife

116

looks at me sometimes…" His voice trails off for a minute and he is alone with his thoughts. "But the boat brings a little of it back. A couple hours on the water and I can go on another day, ready for whatever hairy ball of phlegm the city of New York can cough up. What am I going to do? Tell me Zarro, what the fuck am I supposed to do?"

"Cheer the hell up for one thing. Your boat is safe. As far as I know, the cops don't have a clue who swiped those computers because Mel Lieb gave everyone and his grandmother a key to the place. There's insurance on them and besides, they grabbed the old ones. We were getting ready to scrap them anyway. So don't give it another thought. I'll handle Matty. Between eight and four he's my headache. And believe it or not, your brother is the *least* of my problems right about now."

"What problems do *you* have?"

"Well, unless I can pull a furry white rabbit out of my ass, Rick Schwab is looking to re-locate to Charleston, South Carolina."

"Shit, don't you *dare* let that sleazy bastard pull out of here. For Christ's sakes, this city *needs* places like Schwab's, places where people can still work up a sweat for a day's pay."

"I'll think of something if it goddamn kills me. And just for the record, I did go to college. It was my *advanced* degree I got at Old Bay Correctional."

"My mistake. Tell me, you got yourself any brothers or sisters out there in Sox country?"

"A seventeen year old brother, Nee."

"Nee?"

"Short for Anthony."

"Get a load of this Pete. An Italian kid named Anthony. Who would ever believe it?" The detective raises his glass and

117

takes a great gulp, draining it in the process. The minute the detective's empty glass touches down on the bar, Pete glances over and raises one bushy brow. The detective declines the silent offer of a refill with a subtle head-shake. "You must be thinking I'm a crazy shit for taking this all on but you tell me Zarro, would you sit back and let *your* little brother get done in?"

"I can't see my brother getting into any kind of trouble. He's the good one. See, in my family, I'm the Matty." He has not been home since last September. He moved out and never looked back. Since his time at Old Bay, Zarro has developed the uncanny ability to compartmentalize the various components that made up his life. He can remove people from his conscious mind for weeks at a time. Now he feels twinges about not seeing Nee, or his parents for that matter. He drains his glass and motions the bartender for another one.

"There's only one Matty in this conversation, and he's my cross to bear." The detective catches a glimpse of the broken blood vessels on his good hand. He looks like his entire body aches and that every breath he draws launches a pickax into his lungs. "Robert my friend, you cannot begin to imagine what kind of hell I'm going to take from my wife when I get home and she takes a good look at me."

"Jo tried her best to convince me you were some kind of nice guy, a literary scholar and a regular prince among men," Zarro replies, making yet another effort to put the images of his own family out into dead space. "Anyway, I told her I'd get you home. And she really wants you to come home. She said to tell you it would be okay."

"See me and Jo got a lot in common. She's the best thing that ever happened to me and I'm the worst thing that ever happened to her. Don't think she didn't have chances, though. She really could have done much better for herself if I didn't get in the way." He mashes his cigarette into the ashtray and looks at Zarro, and the true feelings beneath Tommy McClellan's bruised face are momentarily revealed. Ugly splotches of disappointment and despair emerge through the normally opaque veneer, a broad canvas of his troubled life suddenly exposed for Zarro to see.

Zarro turns away, uncomfortable with the brief glimpse into the detective's soul. "Well God knows why, but it's you she loves."

The detective shakes his head, pulling any visible traces of vulnerability below the surface. "Now I *know* you're drunk. Shame on you Zarro, talking mush in a neighborhood bar. You Beantown gindaloon, didn't nobody teach you nothin' out there in Sox country? The lovey dovey stuff you save for Starbucks when you're knocking back four-dollar-a-pop lattes."

"I can't see you within five miles of Starbucks."

"Jo dragged me there once, and once was one time too many. Give me a cup of real coffee at the Corner Luncheonette any day of the week. A dollar a cup, free refills, and it don't taste like some bitter cockroach-infested Brazilian rainforest."

"Your expert take on coffees around the world is fascinating. And I'm sure you're not aware of this, given your current state, but you have a situation here where a convicted felon has been walking the streets of Queens with your gun. You left it in my drawer along with the rest of your belongings."

"Hand over the gun, Zarro. Forthwith. We sure as shit don't need *you* packing."

Zarro piles the detective's property onto the bar.

"I'm batting a thousand today. See if I couldn't bat cleanup for the Mets today. And I'm near blind without them glasses. Now I understand why them people looked at me all cross-eyed when I strolled into the Edward X. Healy Funeral

Parlor, pulled a chair up to the coffin and ordered a Dewars on the rocks."

"You ever actually shoot anyone?"

"Not with this off duty peashooter. So what's the going rate on windshields these days?"

"Zippo. Didn't you hear? Some homeless guy threw a rock right at Matty when Matty refused to let him clean the windows. Jeez, did you see the cuts on his face, Rick? We are more than lucky Matty's not holding us up for workman's comp."

"You did me more than a solid here. I owe you big time, Zarro. Big time." The detective glances at his vibrating cell phone and sighs. He has a brief, cryptic conversation and hangs up. "More good news," he says under his breath. "It's a race to see what's gonna kill me first, my fucked up dysfunctional family situation or my fucked up dysfunctional job."

Then Tommy McClellan, using his one good hand, reaches for his wallet. Zarro also goes for his wallet, but Tommy won't hear of it. "Forget about it. This one here is on the arm," he says. "You can go digging for your cash when we're doing some *serious* drinking."

"Hey Pete, aside from what I owe you, add on what my brother is into you for, and what the hell, I'm in a generous mood. Include my stepfather in on the deal, too. We're on the family plan."

"Billy's paid in full when his horse came in and Matty settled up in his own way. Your brother, generous soul that he is, gave me a gift of a brand new Foreman grill."

"You mean a newly *stolen* Foreman grill," the detective clarifies.

*   *   *   *   *

120

They exit Buckley's and head toward 43rd Avenue. Tommy, who can hardly hold himself up straight, draws a number of stares from passersby. But the detective stares right back until the pair of inquisitive eyes retreat into their sockets. "Hey pally, you ain't pissing blood are you? I mean other than that dinger on the eye, you took a couple to the kidneys if I ain't mistaken."

"So far so good," Zarro lies. "How about you? Jesus, look at you, you can't even walk right."

"Me? Nah, not a drop. My piss is as clear as Campbell's chicken noodle," the detective answers. And the way Tommy responds with such buddy-buddy exuberance, Zarro knows for certain his friend is lying as well. "You need a hand cleaning up Schwab's?"

"Been there, done that, but thanks just the same. Besides, we filled our 'hire the handicapped' quota the day we hired your idiot brother. So Thomas, why don't we show your wife you're still in one piece, and then I'll drive you down to the emergency room."

"Over my fuckin' dead body you will. The odds suck in the emergency room. Them doctors can kill you easy there and then pin it all on the big man upstairs. You really do know nothing, Zarro." Then the detective stops mid-sidewalk and tries to straighten his battered body out. "As bad as it hurts now, I know that tomorrow's gonna be five times worse."

"Lean on me."

"Screw it. We only got one more block." But he leans on Zarro just the same, and Zarro wonders just how many of his ribs are cracked. "I look bad, huh?"

"Like shit warmed over."

121

"That's how I feel, minus the warmed over part. Tell me something, why in hell do you keep Matty on? Why don't you just can him already?"

"Well for one thing, your brother is as strong as an ox. Shows up every day rain or shine and does the work of three men. He can count to fifty and even blind drunk he knows the stock better than most. Besides, he provides me with comic relief. For instance, I love the way Matty handles the UPS guy. Like most of them, this UPS guy is a brown-shirted Nazi who cares about one thing, keeping to his precious schedule. One day last week our shipment wasn't ready exactly on time, nothing unusual here at Schwab's. Our Mr. UPS was not a happy camper—and he had to let everyone know it, loud and clear. So your brother jumped up on the shipping table, dropped his drawers, and mooned the brown shirt with that hairy ass of his."

The detective manages a partial smile out of his cut lip.

"Wait, there's more. Picture this. Marilyn Friedman, on her way to her car, sees Matty's broad butt on display, and shouts out, 'Hey Matty, you really ought to take a washcloth to that thing.' I'm telling you Thomas, where I sit, you just can't pay for this kind of entertainment."

"It's scary. Mel Lieb used to feed me stories like that once upon a time."

"Maybe I'm the ghost of Mel Lieb."

"Do yourself a big favor, Zarro. As soon as you hit your doorstep, wash down a couple of aspirins. Trust me, you're going to have a head out to *here* in a couple of hours."

"I have a head out to here right now."

* * * * *

122

Zarro leaves Tommy McClellan at his building with a wish of good luck, and contnues on to his own place. He sees Rose's son-in-law Hector out front on a ladder and Zarro asks him what he is doing up there.

"Measuring for new windows, eyeing the damage around the old frames. Hey Zarro, what do you say we rent one of those sprayers and we power wash the bricks next weekend?"

"You tell Rose we'll do it for a plate of homemade gnocchi. Homemade, now. She has to make the well with the flour and the beaten eggs."

"What in the world is gnocchi?" Hector asks. "I'm *Cubano*, remember?"

"Dough, potatoes. Rose will know and be sure to tell her I like mine swimming in marinara, and I like my sauce without sugar, a little grated Parmesan on top, fresh parsley if she happens to have any laying around in the house." And gathering inspiration from his visit to the McClellan's tastefully appointed apartment, he adds, "Then the weekend after that, let's pull up the old carpets and sand the floors. When that's done we can polyurethane them, shine 'em up nice like a bowling alley."

"I know. Don't tell me now, you'll do that for a plate of lo mein?"

"No way Hector, lo mein I can get on Roosevelt Avenue. I want homemade sausage and peppers, half the plate hot and half the plate sweet. And I want toothpicks sticking out of the hot ones, because when it comes to food, I'm not into surprises. I'm telling you, after the two of us get through, this will be a regular luxury building. Rose will have to hire a doorman."

"I don't know Zarro, why don't you just walk around Sunnyside with a sign hanging around your neck? 'Will Work For Italian Food.' But before you take all this on, think about it.

123

We'll start whipping this old house into shape and you can count on my mother-in-law raising your rent. I'm telling you straight, *Primo*. No matter how you slice it, the rent is going up."

"No, she'll raise *your* rent, Hector. I'm *paysan*, remember?" Then, almost as an afterthought he asks, "Did you see Maggie?"

"No, but I just got out here five minutes ago."

Maggie has her own set of keys at this point and Zarro wonders what he will say to her after his caustic words of this morning. He enters his apartment with an anchor for a heart and is met with only the steady hum of a refrigerator motor. He finds a note on the kitchen table, held in place with Maggie's key ring.

Dear Roberto,

I go to live on Lygia's sofa. I borrow the suitcase in the closet and I give to you on Monday. I leave you the blue dress because you spend much moneys and maybe you can sell, yes? Please do not sell the sewing machine. Maybe yes you can drive it to me some day so I can never be hungry. Roberto, I'm sorry I make the mistake with you last night and I'm sorry you go to jail. I don't know this other Roberto from the jail. The Roberto I know is a fine man, very nice. I see you Monday at work.

Maggie Ocampo

Chapter Eleven

He reads the letter four times before he brushes her printed words across his lips, folds the paper and places it into his night table drawer. He notices that Maggie had cleaned before she left. He can smell a combination of furniture polish and Ajax cleanser. A fresh set of linen is on the bed, but it doesn't stop him from touching the pillow where Maggie's head had rested. When he sees her rebuilt Singer sewing machine in the corner, a pale shadow of lonesomeness creeps up on Zarro. It sneaks up slowly, from behind. He *has* to get out of the apartment. Zarro finds a gym bag in the closet. And for the first time since he moved to New York, he feels an overpowering urge to see his family in Revere. After swallowing two much-needed aspirins, he packs a couple of things, locks the door and, drives half a block to the Sunoco station to top off his tank. He won't arrive in Revere until one in the morning, but that doesn't seem to matter. He *has* to go home.

Zarro plies himself with high-octane roadside coffee in order to remain awake behind the wheel. But he is determined to get there. He turns onto his street at ten to one, glances up at the old Dutch colonial, unlocks the front door and inhales the scent of home, an exquisite bouquet of tomato sauce, parmesan cheese, Revere Beach, and Murphy's oil soap. He climbs the stairs, and gently wakes his mother. Marie, thinking she is seeing an apparition at her bedside, screams at full voice, waking up her bewildered husband.

"Are you crazy, Robbie? You could have given the both of us a heart attack. What's the matter with you?" Marie yells at her son. But once she catches her breath, she relents. "Look Dom, he's home." And Zarro can't stop hugging them, realizing how he has missed them. He lets his brother sleep, saving the surprise of his return for the morning. When he finally lets exhaustion overtake him, he crawls into his old bed and sleeps for a good solid ten hours.

When he wakes, he looks around for Maggie, and then realizing where he is, sits up and comes down to the kitchen to get something to eat. He answers a barrage of questions about his life in New York while his mother shovels food into him.

"Other than the cut over your eye, you look better than the *menza morte* your father brought home in June."

"Gee thanks."

"So what happened to your eye?" his mother asks.

"I cut it on the top drawer of a file cabinet."

"It's really deep and I don't like the looks of it. The edges are turning black and blue. I've seen plenty of cuts in my day, but I've never seen anything like this. I'm getting the Bactine."

"Forget about it. That's going to sting like holy hell."

"Never mind. Hold still." She dabs the solution on the cut with a saturated cotton ball. "The last thing you need is an infection."

"Ow. Jesus Christ, Ma. It's dripping." Zarro makes his way to the kitchen sink and flushed his eye with cold water. "Great. Now I'm cut up *and* blind."

"The optometrist where I work can see you. He's a very good doctor. He gave your father his eye exam. I get an employee discount at Pearle."

"No Ma, I don't need a doctor. I'm telling you it's nothing. It's *above* the eye that got cut."

"Those file cabinets are dangerous Rob," his father says, with just a scintilla of sarcasm. "Did you put in for workman's compensation?"

Zarro shoots his father a look. "First thing Monday morning."

"So tell me about that girl Maggie who answered your phone," his mother says.

Zarro tries his best to block Maggie's image from reappearing in his head. Whenever his mind zeroed in on her, he'd think of the night they had shared and he'd get tight in the groin and weak at the knees. "I told you. She's someone I work with who lost her apartment in a fire. Anyway, she's found herself a new place by now," he says impatiently.

"She sounded so cute on the phone. She called you Roberto. Where is she from?"

"I don't remember."

Anthony is intrigued. "She *lived* with you like on a full time basis, day *and* night?"

Marie Zarro hushes him. "That's enough Anthony. The kitchen table is no place to discuss this. Unless it's in the presence of my two best friends over a hot cup of espresso and a box of fresh *suiadel*."

Zarro smiles and lets Nee's fertile teenage mind wander.

*   *   *   *   *

Saturday evening he sees his paternal grandparents, his aunts, and uncles. If he could, he would scoop them up and taken the whole bunch of them home to Queens. Home to Rose's house. Home to the Sunnyside-Long Island City border, on 39th Street, a half block past 43rd Avenue. Home, where he is just beginning to feel comfortable.

He lets his mother's arms linger when the company leaves and it just the two of them, and he tells her about Trudy McClellan, the overworked waitress who reminds him so much of her.

"See Robbie? God puts me where I can watch over you," she says, her words a much needed poultice on Zarro's overworked conscience.

"I haven't been much of a son to you."

His mother strokes his dark blond hair. He wears it short now, not much to hold onto. "I'm so glad you came home to see us. That's all I care about now."

"You know I missed you and-and everybody. But I had things I needed to work out, that's all."

His father corners him later on that night, asking him once again if he's ready to work at his construction firm, but again Zarro politely declines with a, "Maybe one day, Dad."

"I don't understand you. You would rather work for strangers than your own family?"

"I would rather stand on my own two feet than get handed a paycheck just for being Dominick Zarro's son."

"I wouldn't just hand you a paycheck. Believe me, your two uncles wouldn't go for that, not even a little bit. You'd learn the business, just like you learned that military business. There's

128

a lot to learn in the construction business. Look Robbie, I'd never force you to work with me if you wanted to be a doctor or a lawyer…but to do the same thing for strangers? It gets me right here," his father says, tapping at his chest.

"Dad, I'm not saying never. I'm just saying not right now. People are counting on me, whether they know it or not."

"Maybe I'm counting on you, too," his father says after a long pause.

When Zarro gets Anthony alone, he feels him out about what is really going on at home in his absence. He senses the tension between his parents, a tension he thinks would have dissipated as soon as he had left the house.

"You behaving yourself, Nee?'

"I'm working fifteen hours a week at Shaw's market. I'm taking two honors classes at school, math and science, and that burns a lot of time. And this summer I'm increasing my hours at the supermarket to thirty-five so I can save up for a used car. Got my eye on Steven Ianello's Altima, which according to his brother will be on the market next November. I'll be driving in the fall. I got my permit now."

"So you're telling me all you do is study, work, save, and go to school?"

"Not exactly. I hang out too."

"You don't go down to the beach at night and get tweaked on vodka and smoke, do you?"

"No, Robbie. No offense, but I'm not you."

"Good, 'cause that's one of my biggest fears." Nee should learn something from his mistakes. "Now maybe you can tell me what's up with our parents?"

129

"What are you talking about?"

"They seem…I don't know, on each other's nerves."

"You got me."

Zarro presses on. "Is it the business? The two of them are so over the top. Jesus, can't you see it?"

"You don't let go, do you? You want to know when they were over the top? Try the year of your trial when you sat for hours in your room staring into space while Daddy had to shake the uncles down for money. Better yet, try the three years you shut them out completely and wouldn't let them see you. Three years. Mommy cried every night for three years. You know what that was like hearing that when you're trying to get to sleep? It wasn't bad enough when Nanny and Grandpa Scioffo died in that crash. Oh no, you had to put her through worse. So if they're both crazy now, you can thank yourself for that, Robbie. You made yourself dead to them and then you came back for ten minutes only to pick up and leave all over again, and just now you stroll in wearing a smile on your face and looking for a TV Land rerun"

"Well Nee," Zarro says, "don't you even *think* about sparing my feelings."

"You asked. Do you want me to lie to you? Lies are *your* thing, right? 'I'll be home for Christmas. I'll try to make the ride down for President's Day weekend. Definitely for Easter. I'll swing down for Mother's Day.' All you do is feed us your bullshit."

"Hey, I sent flowers for Mother's Day." Maggie had reminded him to do that. Apparently, they had Mother's Day in Nicaragua, too. *La Dia de la Madre*, she called it. He recalls Maggie being very quiet on Mother's Day, very subdued.

"If you think this is about flowers, you have your head up your ass."

130

Zarro presses his lips together. Where is the little kid that used to idolize him, season after season? When hockey was nearly finished, they'd squeeze in a season of basketball. And after mud season, March in Massachusetts, baseball. Where is that Nee who sat in the stands when he was pitching for Revere? 'Work the batter Robbie!' he'd shout in that high-pitched voice he used to have—a bag of Big League Chew beside him on the dented metal bleachers. 'Careful, there's a force at second.' 'Good eye,' he'd yell if Zarro checked his swing when he was at the plate. 'Come on Blue, are you blind?' if the call didn't go in his brother's favor. Zarro would have given anything to put that Nee in front of him, the eight-year old gap toothed Nee, with a mouth like a seven-ten split. "You have no right sitting in judgement of me. You don't have a *clue* what I've been through."

"Back at you."

"You know what Anthony? You wouldn't have lasted all of ten minutes at Old Bay," Zarro lashes out.

"You can't last more than fifteen minutes in this house," he snaps back.

Zarro turns to walk away, but Anthony stops him. "Hey, you want to ride over to Kelly's?"

"Roast beef, Nee? You shovel a load of shit in my face, and now you're hunting down a roast beef sandwich on Revere Beach?"

"Yeah, I guess I am."

"Fine. You say you got your permit? You drive, my treat," he says, tossing his brother the keys to the Camaro.

"Rob?"

"What now?"

"I never drove a stick."

"Today must be your lucky day. Roast beef, the keys to my Camaro, and as if that's not enough, you also got in a couple of good shots without getting the ever-loving shit kicked out of you. You pulled a regular hat trick, Nee. I'm telling you, your life won't get much better than this."

"So, are you a Yankee's fan now?" Nee asks on the way to Kelly's.

"Never happen."

"You root for the Rangers?"

"Give me a break, Anthony. It could be a hell of a lot worse, you know. I could have moved to Montreal, or T'ron'o as they say up in Canuck country."

"Not funny."

"I'd like to sing you a song, before you completely screw up the clutch. "O Ca-na-da!" Zarro belts out in his best lilting tenor, as with any true hockey fan, the words of the Canadian national anthem are as familiar to him as his own. "Our home and na-tive la-nd!

"Sometimes I hate you," Nee says, trying in vain to hide his smile.

"True pa-triot love in all thy sons com-mand. With glowing hearts we see thee rise, the true north strong and free! Come on, Nee. You can carry a tune. Just the virgins now."

"From far and wide, O Ca-na-da we stand on guard for thee…" Nee sang out alone.

"All right, enough is enough. Sox, Pats, Celtics, Bruins, and that's all I have to say on this matter."

"And that's forever, right?"

"Forever or until you lose your virginity, whichever comes first." Zarro answers.

*   *   *   *   *

Right after Sunday dinner, after a promise to visit more often, the Camaro heads west and South. Behind the wheel, Zarro wonders if Revere will ever again be called home. He senses a new skin is forming around his bones, and that skin is beginning to fit comfortably in the borough of Queens. Silently, he even congratulates himself on the distance he has put between himself and Old Bay. Not bad for an ex-con, he says to himself now and then on the ride down to New York. *Going, going, gone*, he thinks, willing away any of the uneasiness his visit produced.

Chapter Twelve

At ten-thirty Monday morning, Zarro corners a very apologetic Matty McClellan whose broken nose is taped securely into place. Earlier, he'd told Matty what to say about the van so his brother wouldn't have to pay for it, and Matty was grateful. He is still grateful.

"Quit thanking me. You're not going to like what I have to say, but I'm going to say it anyway. Matty, before you get the windshield fixed, I want you to march your sorry ass into Marilyn Friedman's office and tell her you're naming your brother as co-signer on your paycheck."

"What have *you* been smoking this weekend?"

"Your brother has enough on his plate. He's got himself a kid and one on the way. He has a sick father-in-law to take care of, and what you're doing to him doesn't help matters. You really think it's fair that every time you can't cover the spread, your brother has to make it right?"

Matty looks down at the floor. "Don't put Tommy and fair into the same conversation. You know what he done to me, Zarro? He had two of his cop friends pick me up at Buckley's Friday night on some bullshit back tax charge. Them two cops took me out of the bar in bracelets, in front of everyone, and threw me in the pokey for the night. So forget about involving my brother in my pay. I ain't some kid you put on an allowance."

"That's exactly how you've been acting, like some oversized brat looking for big brother to pick up the broken pieces. Matty, if you could run your own life, the Schwab garage wouldn't have looked like Boston Garden after a night at the fights. So this is the way it has to be."

"Let me get this straight. My brother comes in here, busts the place up and now I have to hand him my paycheck? I don't like it at all."

"After what you've pulled, I don't give a flying fuck what you like. So let me put this to you real simple. The way I see it, you got yourself two choices. Either you name Tommy as co-signer, or I stroll into Rick's office and tell him just who it was who lifted those computers, because I *saw* you out my bedroom window. I saw you with my own two eyes, *capisce?*"

"Maybe you saw wrong."

"Maybe you'd better get moving before I change my mind and give you up."

Matty curses Zarro under his breath as he walks down from the warehouse and into Marilyn Friedman's office.

And when he comes back, Zarro approaches him again, pulling Matty into the corner of the garage. "Now hand over your keys to the place," he says quietly so there is not even the slightest possibility of anyone overhearing the conversation.

Scowling, Matty pulls the keys off a ring he kept dangling from the belt loop of his jeans. "I can't believe you're doing this to me. I swear to Christ, Mel Lieb is rolling in his grave."

"When you boosted those two computers, that's when Mel rolled."

"Here, take 'em off me. And why don't you give my keys to that toothless Pollack retard, Spacious, the idiot you hired out of that sheltered workshop for morons in Greenpoint? Give *him* my keys that I had on me since Mel gave me the set when I was seventeen years old."

"You refer to Roman by his name between the hours of eight and four, none of this Spacious shit. You know something, maybe I *will* give Roman your keys," Zarro says. "He comes in. You show him what to do, and he does it. I'll take a hundred guys like him over you any day of the week, and you know why? 'Cause I can count on him, and I plain old can't count on you."

Matty turns his back and starts to walk away.

"Yo, get your ass back here. I didn't say you could leave."

"I thought we were done."

"I'll fuckin' tell you when we're done. After you run the van over to get fixed, I want a physical count on those Navy rating badges downstairs. See if it matches with what comes up on the inventory system."

"There's over seventy bins of rates, four types in a bin," Matty says. "You got your poly, your gab, your sateen, your—"

"I don't need the Southy likes of you telling me what's in those bins. Should take you all day if you do it right. And I *know* you're going to do it right because I'm going to spot check the bins myself."

"Who's gonna pack stock upstairs?"

"Anyone but you today."

"You're giving me *women's* work to do, Zarro? Is that it? You're punishing me with *women's* work?"

"Call it whatever you want, but that's your job today."

"This is out and out bullshit. You actually want me to stand downstairs in the middle of a bunch of women and count rates? Do you know how embarrassing that is? Do you know how the guys upstairs are going to break my balls about this? The Spanish boys will call me a *maricon,* which is some kind of Spic faggot. And Weeds will put that shit-eating Jamaican grin on his mug and call me Moms."

"Live with it and count yourself extremely lucky you still *have* a job. And consider yourself even luckier that I don't talk Rick into installing a GPS in the van. Wouldn't that be sweet? I'd know when and how long you stop for a beer and when and how long you pull off the road for some on the job lap action. Right away quick that Matty McClellan bullshit would fly out the window. No more 'Sorry I'm late Zarro, the line at the goddamn post office was unbelievable.' With this system in the van, I'd be able to tell if you you've even *been* to the goddamn post office. On some of the newer models, a manager would know for certain exactly how long it takes his driver to have a cold one *and* get his rocks off."

"I don't need nothing like that, Zarro."

Zarro shrugs. "The jury's still out on that one. Oh, before I forget, one more thing, Matty."

Matty gives Zarro a good, long stare. "What?"

"We're through now, just so there's no doubt in your mind. You have yourself a nice day."

It is after the Roach Coach comes and goes, that Zarro realizes he hasn't seen Maggie all morning. Not that he'd know what to say to her. He asks her friend Lygia who tells him that she left on Sunday night with two *Policías,* a tall, dark handsome man and a short Puerto Rican lady.

Zarro closes the door to his back office and calls the detective's cell. "What did you do with her?"

"Easy boyo. The day after me and Matty had our little squabble, Maggie saw me in Philly's drug store where I was able to persuade Philly to hand over a few pain pills for his favorite detective. She told me what happened to her friend Myrna who she suspects is at the mercy of a gang of inked up Salvadorian street thugs into drugs, human trafficking, murder, prostitution, and any other evil you can dream up. So, I put Maggie in touch with an old friend, Milagros Santiago who heads up a gang unit in Brooklyn. A Puerto Rican dyke who happens to be one of the best cops in the city."

"And?"

"And your *seniorita* will be helping us out for a little while. As an informant. Nothing more. She volunteered. Seems to me she was tired of the world taking advantage of her."

"Any harm comes to her and I'm holding nothing back. I don't care if they lock me up for life."

"Gee pally. It sounds like the two of youse have more than a casual boss-worker relationship."

"We have *no* relationship. But that doesn't mean you have the right to get her involved in all this." He had kicked her out of his house and into harm's way.

"She came to me with information on the arson and the possible kidnapping of her friend. Nobody forced her. This is all her doing. So relax, she's in good hands. And that's all I'm saying."

"Well fuck you. That's all *I'm* saying."

Chapter Thirteen

Maggie went back to Sunnyside on the Saturday morning after she left Roberto's apartment, but she did not go there to see Roberto. Roberto was angry at her. He had his secrets and his sadness. His past. But she had her secrets and her sadness, too. Her past. The country she couldn't go back to. The family that abandoned her. And Sergio. Even thinking his name brought tears to Maggie's eyes. *El Terremoto*. The Earthquake, the day the earth shifted beneath her feet. The day everything changed. No, Roberto didn't know about any of that.

She had returned to Sunnyside to pick up a prescription at Philly's drug store for Lygia from Schwab's because Lygia was kind enough to let her stay on the sofa after Roberto got so angry. She spotted the nice *Policía* there, talking to Mr. Philly the druggist. The detective had bruises on his face, but he smiled at Maggie and they struck up a conversation. Maggie hadn't woken up that day determined to change her life. She started her day like every other day in America. Looking over her shoulder. Afraid. But her friend Myrna's plight, that day, emboldened her rather than intimidated her. Maggie was tired of being yelled at, tired of being taken advantage of, and tired of being nobody in this country. And she wanted the *Policía* to help find her friend Myrna. If she didn't help Myrna, who would?

"Can I talk to you outside?" she asked the detective.

The detective followed her out the door. "What can I do for you?"

"I wish to tell you about bad mens," Maggie began. And she didn't stop talking. About Myrna who was missing. About the gang. About Rafael Guzman. And that is how she started to become someone who wasn't nobody.

Chapter Fourteen

When the union rep gets back to Zarro, the two of them arrange to meet at Schwab's after business hours. Zarro's mind is on other things when he finally meets Steven Sarian, a youngish guy dressed in Dockers, the UNITE union rep. He expected the man to be bald, paunchy and chomping on a stump of a cigar. But Sarian has a prominent Adam's apple, chews cinnamon gum, and has a full head of wavy brown hair. Zarro informs him about the fifteen non-union undocumented workers out back, and Sarian springs into action. He removes a tablet out of a case and rests it on Zarro's desk.

"This needs to be documented. Give me names. Dates of employment. Wages."

"Why?"

"What do you mean, *why*? These workers are being exploited."

"Calm down. I'm the one who called you, remember?" Zarro reminds him.

Sarian chews furiously on his gum. "And now you're afraid to rock the boat."

Upon hearing the word afraid, Zarro counts silently to ten. "I'm not afraid of shit. But I want to know what you have in mind."

"Did you happen to hear about our walkout at the meat processing plant in Texas?"

"Can't say that I did."

"Two hundred meat packers, most of them undocumented, shut the place down for the day. We sent a strong message. Workers are not disposable."

"You're not talking about a strike here at Schwab's?"

"Why not?"

"It's a little hotheaded, no? You got people who are afraid to lose what little they have. Besides, fifty people marching around 43rd Avenue isn't exactly going to generate any kind of attention."

"The days of the small, individual strikes are over. We coordinate this strike with others. Hotel workers. Food service employees. We gather our membership from every business that can't outsource to China."

Zarro cannot concentrate for the life of him. He wonders where Maggie is. The detective told him not to worry. But he is damned worried. He can't help it. "A strike is the last thing we need, right about now."

Sarian looks up from the tablet. "Why did you call me down here, Zarro? You're obviously not into this."

"You're right. My mind is on about a hundred things right about now. But I sure as hell didn't sign up for the Norma Rae thing," Zarro says, remembering the movie he watched in his AP government class back in high school. "I thought you'd have some suggestions on getting worker visas."

144

"You must be aware that there's no blanket visa that's going to magically grant legal worker status on undocumented workers. It's strictly case-by-case."

"But the union has a legal department."

"Naturally. We live in a litigious society."

"Then get me the names of some decent immigration lawyers. When people aren't afraid to get their asses kicked out of the country, they might be more willing to stand up for themselves."

Steven Sarian fishes a few cards out of his wallet and fans them out on Zarro's desk. "You can tell your boss that UNITE demands that those workers be a part of our union."

"Wake the hell up. You can't demand shit. Piss Schwab off and trust me, he will yank the whole operation."

Sarian gathers his belongings and rises from his chair. "We will follow him to wherever he sets up shop."

"That won't do the people here any good."

"Don't underestimate the power of UNITE."

Zarro also stands up. "Don't underestimate the power of greed." He unlocks the front door to let Sarian out. "Look, I'm on your side. Give me some time on this. I'll get back to you."

Sarian reaches into his pocket and pulls out a fresh pack of cinnamon gum. "Interested?"

"No thanks, I'm trying to quit."

Zarro wants very much to share with Maggie the conversation he had with Sarian, get her take on the whole thing. But Maggie no longer lives with him. Maggie is gone. Each night he returns to an empty apartment. The prospect of a lonely evening spent in front of the TV depresses him. Desperate

145

for company, he falls into *The Return of the Native.* He reads for escape, just like he did at Old Bay.

Chapter Fifteen

A month passes and Zarro has some hope on the business front. Orders are starting to come in now. What started as a trickle is growing into a cascade. He hires three more people for the warehouse. Still, he wonders just how much will be enough to keep Rick Schwab in place. And he has some doubts about the fifteen undocumented workers earning a living wage or holding a green card.

But on a personal basis, Zarro makes an attempt to live his life as a normal, single guy in his mid-twenties. He begins to hit the clubs on the weekends and he is well on his way to developing a social life. After his night with Maggie, he sees it is possible to separate sex from violence *if* he's careful. As long as they don't get too close I'm in, he reassures himself every weekend.

And Maggie is gone. So, as he does with other people and events, he sweeps their encounter into the back pocket of his mind. He meets lots of women on his time off and he beds most of them. He decides it is the very best of both worlds. They afford all of the needed physical release without any of the emotional pull. For never does he feel so dangerously exposed with his bevy of back-to-back one-night stands, as he had with Maggie.

But there are those times when he wakes up in strange apartments and has to study the sleeping face on the neighboring pillow and try to come up with a name. On a lazy Sunday morning in June, after spending a particularly pleasurable Saturday night romping between the sheets, the girl he has spent the night with suddenly bolts upright in bed and asks, "So tell me, who's this Maggie?"

Zarro yawns and stretches, thinking he could sleep another two hours easy. He pries his eyes open, taking in the face of his companion, a well-built redhead named Dawn Costello who spends most of her evenings in Sunnyside topless, long legs wrapped around a metal pole at Gallagher's on Queen's Boulevard, good-naturedly tolerating the customer's jokes about the crack of Dawn. It was Matty McClellan of all people who had introduced the two of them the night before, for much to Zarro's surprise Matty occasionally works as a fill-in bouncer in the club and had buttonholed him as he was walking up Queens Boulevard. "Let me know if anyone in particular rings your chimes," Matty said. "I know 'em all."

Zarro nodded, taking a seat at the bar, adjusting cautiously to his unfamiliar surroundings. Teasing. It's all about teasing. All about power. Control. Maybe he couldn't do this. No, he would do this. He was going to enjoy himself, goddamn it. He deserved to enjoy himself. He'd keep it light. That a boy, Kicker. Keep it light. And as he sat there, silently conversing with himself, a voluptuous redhead began to yell at a customer. Embarrassed by the stares, the man got up to leave and the redheaded dancer, naked to the waist, followed him out of the club and onto the busy boulevard, loudly calling him every name in the book. Matty, who had been standing guard at the

148

door, ran after her with a coat. "Jesus Dawn, cover yourself up. You're giving all of Queens a free show."

Within a couple of minutes, the dancer returned to Gallagher's visibly upset. Zarro had noticed that despite her lack of composure, she did manage to finish her set and make a lot of money in the process.

"Wow. What the hell was that about?" Zarro had asked Matty, intrigued by the new world in which he found himself.

"Oh, that's just Dawn Costello getting pissed off at a customer. She got that typical redhead temper on her. But you say the word, my man, and yours truly can arrange for a private dance in the backroom. And she's a genuine redhead, too. Collar definitely matches the cuff. The only downside about a place like this is you gotta keep your hands at your sides at all times, boss. Rules is rules."

Zarro looked Dawn over. She had beautiful smooth skin that seemed to shimmer under the club lights. And her waist-length hair wasn't really red, not in that avoidable Old Bay orange sense. It was more of a copper shade, the color of a just-burnished penny. He could handle that kind of orange. She had some hell of a rack on her, too. It might be nice to get lost in there, he thought. "Matty, do me a favor and ask her to join me at her break. I'll make my own arrangements, thank you very much."

"Suit yourself," Matty said. And Zarro did. He didn't take his eyes off her all throughout her set. The athlete in him admired the gymnast in her. Effortlessly, she could shimmy up the pole and support her weight upside down by just a crossed pair of ankles, all to the beat of the music. Once upside down, Dawn could do other gravity defying feats, feats that involved a tongue and her own two half-dollar sized nipples. Quite impressive, Zarro thought. He wondered where in the world a dancer such as Dawn could have picked up such skills? Certainly not at Miss Annette's School of Tap and Ballet (unless Miss Annette was leading a double life after she tossed her tutu into the wash.)

At three o' clock that morning Dawn drove the two of them to a chrome-faced diner where they sat down to an early breakfast. She explained to him why she had to run into the street after that cheap bastard who didn't leave her two cents after she spent a solid half hour "dancing" in his lap. And then not to leave a tip? What a set on that man!

By four o'clock Zarro was inside Dawn's spacious co-op in Forest Hills. Dawn kicked off her four-inch stacked-heeled brown leather cowboy boots, the ones that replaced her working shoes, (six-inch, platform based, stiletto-heeled black patent leather pumps) He sprawled out on her sofa and rubbed her aching calf muscles through the denim of her stretch jeans. Slowly and methodically he worked his way up and by the time he reached her thighs, Dawn motioned him toward her bedroom. Without wasting much time, he picked her up and carried her there in his two strong arms. Then he lowered her and himself onto the pink and purple swirl of a bedspread, all the while chanting to himself his weekend rosary: Be gentle. Be gentle. Be gentle.

Zarro was pleased to discover she was still wearing her black G-string. He wondered if G-strings were all she wore. She probably had a drawer full of them, one for each day of the week. And while those pleasant musings meandered through his head, she began teasing him, playing with those beautiful shimmering breasts, turning around and lowering and raising her very firm but ample bottom onto and off of his lap. "You don't have to do that," he said. "You're not working now, are you?"

150

"Sorry. Force of habit."

"I don't need much in the way of teasing," Zarro said, kissing her face. "You've had my interest for hours already." Be gentle, Kicker. You're not in Old Bay and this isn't about power. The girl doesn't want to hurt you. She just wants to fuck you.

"I've been looking at you all night," she murmured in his ear. "So far, I like what I see."

Throughout the remainder of the night, they made love feverishly. Physically drained, both had fallen dead asleep at first light, and now at nine a.m., a mere five hours since his estimated time of arrival, Zarro does not know it, but he is about to be royally hassled.

"Good morning, Dawn. Now tell me what you are talking about."

"Do not play dumb with me. Do not *ever* play dumb with me. You called her name last night. Maggie. Over and over. I heard you loud and clear."

"Oh, *that* Maggie! Don't give it a second thought, Dawn. She's my little sister," Zarro says, silently cursing his big mouth.

"I think you should leave now. Get yourself dressed and get the hell out of here."

"Come on Sweetheart, it's not even nine fifteen."

"I don't care what time it is and I don't care how good a lay you are. Any guy who shouts out his sister's name when he's coming quarts is one sick puppy. 'Don't stop Maggie. Oh Jesus, I'm almost there Maggie. Thank you, Maggie.' That's really twisted in my book."

"You don't understand," Zarro says with some chagrin, locating his black dress jeans on Dawn's purple carpet. "We happen to be a very close family."

"Don't you get it? *I'm* supposed to be the fantasy here. Men call out *my* name when they're doing their wives and girlfriends. They're not supposed to call out *their* names when they're doing me."

Zarro realizes he is car-less right about the time the elevator deposits him in Dawn's lobby. It is Sunday morning, but the neighborhood is already bustling. And it is *his* kind of neighborhood, one brimming with restaurants and grocery stores. The sweet doughy smell of freshly-baked bagels beckons him and he is never one to decline the call. Zarro tastes his first ever bialy, the dusty onion taste reminding him of the outer texture of an onion-filled stromboli his mother baked and then brushed cornmeal across the top.

After three attempts, he finds someone on the streets who is fluent in English. And the way the foreigners look at him with such contempt, with such a sense of superiority, it takes everything he — the grandson of immigrants — has to quash the urge to flatten them. Finally, a native New Yorker directs him to the bus that would take him via Queens Boulevard all the way west to 39th Street and beyond if necessary. Maybe it is Zarro's imagination, but *that* person looks at him strangely too. Ah, it's probably my Boston accent, he thinks. In ten minutes, Zarro boards the bus and heads home. He vaguely remembers something about Hector and Louise's baby son being baptized today about two minutes before he vaguely remembers making the commitment to attend.

152

Both Rose Petruzzi and her son-in-law Hector are outside when Zarro makes the scene. Rose, broom in hand, is attacking the litter on her two front steps with gusto. Hector has his truck jacked up in front of the house and is about to change the front passenger tire.

"All set for your grandson's big day?" Zarro asks his landlady who squints at him rather intensely from her large black eyeglasses.

"What a wise guy you are. Do I *look* like I'm ready? Does the house look ready for the thirty people we're inviting back from the church for macaroni and porcupine balls?"

"Porcupine balls? Gee Rose, how did you ever get past their sharp quills to castrate the little critters?"

"Are you trying to be funny, Robert Zarro? Because I'm telling you, I'm in no mood."

"Not in the least. I never heard of such a delicacy, that's all."

"Are you trying to tell me your mother never rolled her meatballs in rice, fried them in oil, cooked them in sauce and served them over macaroni?"

"No, I would have definitely remembered that. But I get it now. It's the rice that turns an ordinary meatball into a porcupine ball."

"Ab-so-lute-ly, Robert Zarro. Now, the christening is at three o'clock sharp, right Hector?"

"Right. Three o'clock," he says.

"God, I hope these front steps look clean enough for my sister. And forget about the inside steps. Youse two put so much of that polyurethane on the staircase that every single speck of dust shows when it's sunny outside. The two of youse should have left well enough alone. That's the trouble with your

153

generation, nothing is good enough for you. Are you listening to me, Hector?"

"Hanging on every word."

Rose clutches her broom and shuts the door behind her.

"Can you use a hand?"

"Yeah *Primo*, give me the lug nuts," he says to Zarro. "I'm almost done here."

Zarro stoops down next to Hector and hands him the lug nuts to be tightened.

"Look at you man," Hector says. "You're glowing."

"Chalk that up to me getting laid last night."

"No, not that kind of glowing. Look at yourself. You must be into some kinky shit because you got this glittery stuff all over your face."

Zarro gets up and moves to the truck's side view mirror to take a look at his face. It is true. Won-der-ful, Coun-sel-lor, the light of a thousand stars dance upon his countenance. He is a living, breathing human firmament. Then it suddenly dawns on Robert Zarro that it is Dawn, or more accurately Dawn's shimmering breast makeup that has somehow made its way onto his face. So *that's* what those people were staring at, he thinks. It wasn't the goddamn Boston accent. It was his sparkly face. "I think a shower is in order," he announces to Hector, as Hector is about to tighten his last lug nut.

"Give me a fifteen minute jumpstart because this grease on my hands is way worse than that glitter on your face. Grease is some nasty shit. And if we both take a shower at the same time, Rose won't have enough hot water to mop the hallway floor so it will be nice enough for her sister. Then Rose will be one miserable mother-in-law for the entire day."

"Ab-so-lute-ly," Zarro agrees.

154

Zarro waits for the McClellans to arrive at the church and after he greets Jo and pulls on one of Aggie's pigtails, he requests a word in private with Tommy. "Go on in. I'll be there in a minute," Tommy tells his wife.

Zarro raises one eyebrow and waits for the detective to talk. "I called you last night. You didn't answer your cell."

"I was busy."

"From what I hear, you were gettin' busy with Dawn Costello."

"So?"

"So, I wanted to give you the heads up before you seen it on the News."

Zarro feels the blood rush out of him. "Seen *what* on the News?"

"Myrna's been killed. They slit her throat and Maggie saw it."

"Jesus Christ. You promised me she'd be safe."

"Gangs are now a homeland security issue. They rank right up there with Johnny Jihad. So the F.B.I. got involved where they had no business being and those humps fucked it up because they don't know shit about anything local. So that poor girl paid the price. And unfortunately, your *señorita* saw it go down and she went from being an informant to a Federal witness."

Instinctively, Zarro grabs the detective by the collar. "You bastard."

"Easy boyo," the detective says, and Zarro releases his grip.

"This ain't my doing. The good news is she's out of harm's way. She's squirreled away in a secure location. So be patient, Zarro."

"Patience is overrated."

"And don't think I didn't see you on the surveillance tape, two nights ago. At least you're not as dumb a guinea as I thought. You knew enough not to wear your Sox cap and park your Camaro within a five block radius. That much I'll give you."

"Did you really think I was going to sit by and do nothing? It's been six weeks. Six goddamn weeks. I feel responsible for her. We work together."

"Maybe you can bullshit yourself, but you can't bullshit me. You *work* together, my ass. Would you be pacing up and down the streets of Bushwick if it was Marilyn Friedman?"

"Yes, I'd like to think so."

The detective grins. "Keep your ass out of that neighborhood if you want to live to see your next birthday."

Three church bells sound the time. "Come on, Detective. Let's not keep Jesus waiting," Zarro mutters. He would go back, though. He'd just have to play it smarter. Zarro is confident. He is, after all, a graduate of Old Bay Correctional College. And Maggie is not going to testify against Rafael Guzman if he has to kill the bastard, himself. While the priest drones on, Zarro sits quietly in the church and begins to plan. Out of the blue, the words of Machiavelli pop into his mind. "The prince must be sly like a fox and intimidating and frightening like a lion...." Once in a while, Zarro's education ambushes him.

156

Chapter Sixteen

At noon, a couple of hours before the start of the Fourth of July weekend, Zarro is sitting in his back office with a ham and cheese from the Roach Coach. It is so busy lately that most days he doesn't have time to walk to the luncheonette. But eating at his desk is fine by him. Busy means business. Busy means they had half a prayer of remaining in Queens. He has a can of grape soda at his lips when a smiling and very casually dressed Tommy McClellan comes strolling in, shoves aside a stack of paperwork and slides himself onto the top of Zarro's desk.

"Not again," Zarro says, putting down the can. "I just finished cleaning up from your last visit."

"Not to worry. I come in peace, my son."

"You're lucky Schwab left early for the day. I don't need grief about him seeing you here."

"It don't take a genius to figure out he'd be long gone with a three day weekend coming up."

"Actually, I'm glad you're here. I've been meaning to stop by and give you back the book your wife loaned me. Many happy returns," Zarro says breezily as he returns *The Return of the Native,* placing Joanna McClellan's paperback on the top of the desk.

"So, Maggie's back, as promised," Tommy says, picking up the book. "Have you talked to her?"

"Only about military insignia and accessories." Once, their eyes locked but he couldn't summon the words to describe just how furious he was with her for putting her life at risk. Just what the hell was she thinking?

"Did you catch today's Daily News?"

"Yeah. Sox beat the Yanks 5-3. I saw the game on TV, anyhow."

"No shithead, the front of the paper."

Zarro pokes around his office for the paper he had bought earlier that morning, along with a cup of coffee. Eventually, he locates it under a tray filled with trouser blousers.

"*'F.B.I Nabs Gang Terrorizing Brooklyn.'*"

"A bunch of glory seeking humps. Turn to page three."

"Well, well," Zarro says, spreading the paper out onto his desk. "They even provide a chain of command. Looks like the corporate structure over at Proctor and Gamble."

"The Bureau is into diagrams," the detective says. "They picked up a few low level nobodies. But there's one important name missing."

Zarro looks up from the paper. "Rafael Guzman. Don't even think of telling me she has to testify."

"Easy, boyo. Alls I'm saying is the F.B.I. blew it big time."

"You gave me your word that you and your carpet munching P.R. cop friend would look out for her."

The detective raises an eyebrow. "A little respect, Zarro."

"My cousin Angela likes women, so that makes it A-okay," Zarro says, his voice tinged with sarcasm. "A highly

158

decorated detective once told me you're allowed to make fun of your own."

"You got every right to be pissed. But neither me or Millie has much juice with the Feds, on account of we're just NYPD. But, no need to panic. We got her out, safe and sound. The Feds think she's in the wind. From the get go, we made sure she didn't use her real name. They're looking for someone named Nancy. Sometimes being under the radar has its benefits. So just keep Maggie out of Brooklyn until you hear different," Tommy warns.

"For all I know, she's *living* in Brooklyn. So, I'm going to take care of this myself." It is time to put his plan in action. Counting on other people is a complete waste of time.

"You really don't know what you're dealing with, Zarro. I'm warning you. Leave it to the professionals before you end up on a slab."

Suzie Q knocks on the Plexiglas and pokes her head around the closed door before Zarro could answer the detective. "I wanted you to see my Fourth of July costume, Zarro."

"Stay there just a second, Suzie." Zarro turns his attention back to the detective and says in a very low voice, "You don't happen to have any Black relatives do you?"

"Had me a Black partner once upon a time."

"Well I don't give a fuck, McClellan. You're *still* going to be politically correct. Do not let that 'n' word fall out of that sewer trap of yours, *capisce?*"

The detective crosses his heart and Zarro opens the door for Suzie. She has draped her torso in the colors of the American Flag. Her size ten feet are crammed into size nine sparkling, silver pumps. On top of a silver wig, she wears a green crown, a felt replica of Lady Liberty's headpiece. "Stunning," Zarro says. "You really outdid yourself this time. Believe it or not Suzie, this

159

gentleman, and I'm using that term very loosely, is Matty's brother Tommy."

"Mmm mmm mmm," Suzie Q says. "Baby, there is *so* much good looking in this here room, I'm getting douche chills just thinking about it."

The detective laughs heartily. And Zarro says, "Douche chills? I'm eating my lunch, Suzie. And I think I just might lose my grape Coke all over your patriotic American costume if you even think of bringing that up again."

"What in hell is a grape Coke? Coke don't come in grape, last time I checked. This is soda, Zarro, grape soda," the detective informs him. "Nowhere on this here can does it say Coke."

"Where I come from, everything is Coke. Grape Coke. Orange Coke."

"Tell me something Lady Liberty, how in the world do you work for this guy?" the detective asks.

Suzie Q shrugs her massive shoulders. "Oh, me and Zarro are soul mates. Us two is *always* speaking the same language," she says with an exaggerated wink. Then she hobbles out of Zarro's office atop her high heels, closing the door behind her.

"Anyways, it's our annual 4th of July barbecue I'm inviting you to," the detective says. "Hector and Louise put it together at your place every year."

"If it's at *my* place, why do you need to invite me?"

"Hey, don't expect me to explain McClellan logic at work. Seriously pally, it's a good party and we'd like you to be there. Rose has a pool out back, one of them above ground numbers. And I have a couple of cartons of confiscated fireworks fresh out of Chinatown. Trust me, we'll have a blast, one way or another."

160

"Well, thanks for the invite. Count me in. So Thomas, how's your extremely better half holding up in this heat?"

"Jo's almost ready to hatch so like the old song, I ain't got no loving since I don't know when. Anyways, I already got you penciled in for the two o'clock feedings."

"What are friends for?"

Then Tommy McClellan jumps to his feet and slams a fist onto Zarro's desk. "You know something, Zarro? My hunches are fourteen-karat gold, no, *eighteen*-karat gold. You couldn't keep yourself off her, could you?" You bad, bad boy. I knew that platonic thing was a crock of shit the minute I heard it."

"What are you talking about?"

"Stand up a second and take a good long look at your seniorita, Zarro. She's pale as a ghost and munching fast and furious on a bunch of Saltines."

Zarro gets out of his chair and looks over at Maggie. "It's ninety five degrees back here so it's kind of hard to retain that just fresh feeling. And we manual laborers get hungry, you know. Especially at lunchtime."

The detective shakes his head. "No, no. I got experience in these matters. Trust me. That one has that Saltine-crazed 'I'm two months pregnant' look. So tell me Ro-ber-to, just exactly when was it you slipped her that real hard Italian pepperoni?"

Zarro's knees buckle under him and Tommy is quick with a chair. Then Zarro puts his head down on his desk and as he sat there, the words, "What am I going to do?" come tumbling out onto the hard, gray metal.

"Oh relax there, pally. You ain't the first person in the world to knock a girl up. My little brother Matty has it down to an art form. But then again, he uses the 'don't worry babe, I'll pull out' method of birth control. Ah come on. Pick your chin up. You got choices, you know. Now why don't you sit back and

161

tell me how it happened?" Grinning from ear to ear, the detective pulls a pad and pen off Zarro's desk and pretends to take notes.

Zarro picks his head up and says. "Put that down, will you? You're enjoying this just a little too much. Anyway, you know goddamn well how it happened. Should I draw you a picture?"

"Shame on you Zarro, I ain't talking angle of the dangle here. I'm talking motive. For instance," the detective begins, sporting a mock-serious police department demeanor, "did the seniorita in question set a trap for you so she could score the almighty green card?"

"No, no. It was nothing like that. It…well, hell, it just sort of happened one night and…and I couldn't stop."

"'It just sort of happened one night and I couldn't stop' is the worst case scenario of all, because friend of mine, now you got yourself one big decision to make. So let your all time favorite cop lay out your three choices."

Zarro remains silent and lets the detective have his say.

"You got yourself Choice A, which is to take care of the mother and child like the decent hardworking bastard we've all come to know and love. Then there's Choice B, do the college boy thing where you get to hold her hand and pay for the baby's murder while it's floating around safe and warm in her belly, sucking on its cute little thumb. Or last of all, Choice C. Ignore the situation and let her raise the kid all by herself. C is not a real choice for you, Zarro, because that saintly but perpetually horny Jewish ghost of Mel Lieb wouldn't let you do that. B is not a choice, neither, 'cause dollars to doughnuts, you served ten o'clock mass with Father Guido at Saint Vinny's in Boston. And like they say boyo, once a good Cat-lick always a good Cat-lick."

162

"It was nine o'clock mass with Father Sebastian at St. John Vianney in Revere."

The detective smiles. As sympathetic as he is to Zarro's plight, there are times he really enjoys being right. And this time happens to be one of them. "Did Mel ever tell you the one about this girl who offered her honor and the guy who honored her offer? And all night long he was on her and off her."

"Get the fuck out of here, McClellan. I swear, every single time you cross this threshold, it's a goddamn head-on collision."

"*Adios* Papi. See ya on the Fourth."

Zarro peers onto the warehouse floor from his back office. He watches Maggie enter the ladies room and he leaves his office and follows her in. She is bent over the sink, splashing cold water onto her face. She jumps when she spots him and he takes a minute to adjust to his unfamiliar surroundings. On one of the stall doors, is a hand-written a sign in Spanish and Zarro asks for a quick translation.

"It says in Spanish but it rhymes in English. Wait. I remember. Suzie Q say it all the time. It's a famous American poem. If you sprinkles when you tinkles, please be so neat and wipe up the seat."

"Yeah, and I once knew a man from Nantucket."

She looks up at him quizzically and he says, "Never mind. Are you just about through in here?"

"Yes, Roberto. I am through," she says, pulling out a rough, fibrous brown paper towel from the dispenser on the wall. "I know it's time to get back to work. I'm sorry I'm late."

163

"Come into my office and close the door. We need to talk."

She follows him into the warehouse office. "Sit down," he says.

Maggie can see Roberto doesn't look very happy. "I hope you don't fire me because I take too long at lunch."

"This has nothing to do with lunch or breakfast or a goddamn midnight snack. Tell me Maggie, just how long were you going to keep it a secret? When the hell were you going to tell me about the baby you're carrying?"

Maggie sighs, her olive green eyes plummeting to her lap. "It's a mistake you say. Everything we do is a mistake. We are workers together and it just can't be, you say. So there is jnothing to tell you. *Nada.*"

"Have you been to the doctor's? Or were you too busy fighting crime?"

"There is a clinic in Lutheran Hospital."

Zarro leans against his desk. "I don't want you in a goddamn clinic. I want you in a regular doctor's office where they have a fish tank and a big pile of Good Housekeeping magazines."

"I have no insurance to pay."

"Well that's about to change. That one I'm working on. I just need a little time." Time is always circling too damned fast at Schwab's. Time, the dirtiest word of all.

Maggie shrugs. "Okay. I see you Tuesday."

"Come home with me later."

"You don't want me, Roberto. I am a mistake and the baby is a mistake. One time I tried to wash your toaster in the sink when it was plugged on, remember? And I don't know what a seatbelt is for. And I talk funny."

164

"Big deal. They tell me fifteen times a day I talk funny, too. Listen, from now on, you can sew for most of the day. Get off your feet. You like?"

"Yes, I like."

"Tell Lygia I'll be by with the car later to get your things."

"I'm too weak and too hot to fight with you, Roberto."

They are out of Schwab's and in Zarro's apartment by four thirty. "You have new windows," Maggie says, spotting the white vinyl frames. "Hector does a very good job."

"Replaced the fat screen with a flat screen and I bought an air-conditioner too," he says, reaching for the switch. "Sit down. I'll get you a glass of ice water."

"You're not angry on me, Roberto?"

"Shocked beyond belief is more like it. Look, I want to do my part. I'm a fine man, remember?"

Maggie glances around the apartment. The frayed carpet is gone, replaced by diagonal slats of honey oak which catches the rays of late afternoon sunshine. Still, the apartment doesn't look half as clean as it did when she had lived there. Dirty dishes are piled in the sink. The kitchen table is dotted with multicolored stains and a handful of bumpy crumbs. The curtains she had sewn for the living room need laundering. "When the baby is born, you give me some money for the baby and I clean for you, Roberto."

"I'll give you money for the baby and you *don't* have to clean for me. In fact, I think we should get ourselves down to City Hall and get a marriage license. You'll be on my insurance then and in three, four years you're almost guaranteed a green

165

card. At least let me do the right thing, here. You know, for the baby."

"This is how you say, a make-believe marriage, yes?"

Zarro looks at her. "So? Believe me, we won't be the first ones to do that in the City of New York. Plenty of people make mistakes and plenty of people cover them up with a marriage license."

"I am just making sure. After the baby is born I will leave."

"Let's just take it one day at a time. Next week we'll work on getting the marriage license." She came to him in a dream. And they got good and caught. And this is the price he has to pay.

"Myrna is dead," she says softly. "Rafael Guzman cut her throat because she run away from where the gang keep her and make her sleep with mens. I see it. And he laughs with his gold teeth. And my friend was screaming. And everyone run inside. And say nothing to the *Policía*"

"I know. I'm sorry. Tommy McClellan told me what happened. But jeez, Maggie. That could have been you. What the hell were you thinking, getting involved in this?"

"Every day I wake up afraid. I don't want to be afraid anymore. And in this country, I should not have to be afraid."

"Where have you been living all this time?"

"In a hotel. In Queens. It's very nice. They have these little soaps and shampoo in a little bottle. And sometimes Tommy McClellan, the good *Policía* come to visit."

"And what were you doing?"

"I was wearing a wire. And I help the *Policías* to arrest the *maras* who burn my house and kill my friends and kill Myrna." Maggie looks into his eyes. "Did you miss me?"

166

Zarro looks away. He walks over to the refrigerator and finds a beer. "Of course I missed you. We were one person short when it came to pulling stock."

"Don't you want to call your mother? She will be a grandmother. Your father will be a grandfather. And your brother will be the uncle, yes?"

"Yeah, yeah. That language software has worked miracles on you. I'll give them a call later, announce our engagement. God, I can't wait for this one to hit the fan. You know what? I'm going down to the pizzeria. Bring us back some good Sicilian rice balls." He puts the beer down. He never could take *agita* on an empty stomach. But this, this baby thing is beyond *agita*. How could this have happened? Once. They were together all of once. His mother whispered to her friends all the time about couples who have to try for years on end. There was no trying here. This was easy, effortless, a goddamn mistake all around.

Chapter Seventeen

When the door to their apartment closes, Maggie goes to the sink and washes out her empty glass. She finds a bottle of Windex on the countertop and a bottle of Murphy's Oil under the sink where she had left it, and she begins to clean Zarro's apartment. She thinks about one of the women she used to clean for, back when she was at Jackie's Cleaning Service. The woman had reprimanded her for using Windex on the mirrors. Chemicals weren't natural, she said. It was not good for the children to be exposed to chemicals. Scrub that peanut butter and jelly off the mirror with plain water. Do you understand plain water? If you don't know, ask, the woman said. Maggie tried to explain as best as she could, in her new language that plain water wasn't going to be enough to remove that dirt. The woman had let her naughty American children eat in every room of that sticky, messy house. But the woman did not want to hear Maggie's explanations. She lost her patience and called Maggie an ignorant girl. And when Jackie drove Maggie to the next job, she yelled at her, told Maggie that the client was always right. Who are you to tell a client the correct way to clean a house? Don't ever forget you are nobody in this country. Yes, Jackie, was right. Except now when she helped the F.B.I. and the department of *Policías*, she is somebody. Somebody they need.

Maggie doesn't say a word to Roberto about the glossy purple lipstick she finds in the bathroom that she knows isn't hers, or the unfamiliar pair of tiger striped panties she discovers when making Zarro's bed. She just leaves the items out in the center of the newly cleaned and polished kitchen table, and when he saunters in with the hot rice balls, he gives Maggie a very dark look, and tosses the items unceremoniously into the trash. After they eat, Zarro drives to Lygia's by himself and brings her things back to his apartment, heeding the detective's advice to keep Maggie out of Brooklyn.

"Well, well, what do you know? It's almost time for Rosa Salmaje," he says flatly, the rice balls sticking him right where he breathes.

"That story is finished. I watch Monica Rodriguez now."

"Nothing ever stays the same, huh Maggie?"

"Roberto, I want to tell you something. And then maybe you don't want to go to City Hall next week. I am not so true with you."

"I'm listening."

"My baby with you is not my first baby. I have a baby boy before I come to this country. The night I come to your bed, you say you were hurt. Me, I was hurt too. In my country there were the American soldiers. They come in the helicopters to help with the floods. And I was walking in Leon, my town, to get to my school and two of the soldiers follow me. And I run, but they run faster. They drag me where nobody is. And then one of them climb on top of me and the other hold my mouth closed. I smell their sweat and hear them laughing and feel a ripping in my skin and then I don't remember any more. I wake up and there was grass and mud in my hair. My clothes were ripped into

170

pieces and I am hurt and I have blood. I look up and I see the red leaves of the *malinche* tree and a *tecolote,* you say in English an owl. The *tecolote* looks at me with the bad luck and the whole world turns red like the blood. I tell you I come here alone, but this is not true. I come here with my baby, Sergio."

Weakness washes over him and he leans against the wall for support. "Where is this baby?"

Maggie looks down at the floor. She knows she is supposed to open her mouth to get the words to come out, but it is such an effort. It is less difficult to be quiet, much easier not to say the words.

"Where's the baby?"

She tries again to locate her voice and at the third attempt it rises to the surface. "After this happen, I want to leave my home. Because everywhere I look, I think I still see the soldiers, waiting for me, hiding in the corners. And every time I breathe the air, I still smell them. And when I lay in my bed, I still feel them and they are all over me. *Bastante, por favor.* Enough, please I tell my dreams because there is nothing left to me. And my father is not talking to me because he see me get fat when we go to the beach. So I take a long, long walk to my aunt's house and I stay with her until the baby come out."

"And after the baby was born?"

"I come back home because I think my father will love the baby when he see him and be so happy that I name him his name, Sergio. But he take one look at my little boy and call him a *yanqui hijo de la gran puta.* They are ugly words and I do not want to hear them. I want a new life in this country. So again I say good-bye to my mother. She give me some money she save from when she work the looms to make the cloth and then I take the baby and we ride the vans and the busses to this country."

"And then?"

171

"Then my baby get so sick from the bus. It's hot and I don't have fresh water and I don't have enough milk. And the baby cry and cry on the last van, the van to Brownsville. So crowded with us. And the *mara* scream shut up to me. Shut up your baby you stupid whore. And by the time we stop, the baby is very quiet because he is no more breathing. Me and this girl from Honduras we bury him where the van rests. My baby is under the ground in Mexico, *descansa en paz*. He rest in peace. I wrap him in my shawl, because all the time his little hands like to touch it. I save a little piece of his hair. He was blond, just like you Roberto. I write a poem for him. *Mi Nino Chele*. My little blond boy, asleep in the earth. I walk above you, but I am with you. My heart beats for you. *Mi Nino Chele*."

By the end of her story, Maggie is crying softly into her hands, but Zarro sits mute. Paralyzed, bolted within the iron gates of his own tongue-tied prison, he cannot tell her how much he understands. And just like the aftermath of the solitary night they had shared, when she touched a place in him he thought was long dead, Zarro immediately begins to construct another wall to separate them. Powerless, the tender, bruised Robert Zarro keeps a safe distance from Maggie.

"I *still* want to go down to City Hall," is all he can manage to get out of his mouth. "Go put your show on. I'm going to lift a little bit." She went through worse than he did. *She* lost a child. She had to bury her baby. Goddamn it, say something to her. Tell her you'll be there for her. But his words strangle in the back of his throat. He sits down at the weight bench.

*   *   *   *   *

172

That night they fall back into their old routine. Maggie takes her bath in the claw-footed tub. Zarro tops his workout off with a cold shower. She reacquaints herself with the blue denim pullout sofa, and Zarro tosses and turns in his bed, unable to wrench his mind free from the clutches of his personal morass. Dear God, he thinks. Give me the strength to get me through my poor excuse for a life.

Chapter Eighteen

Zarro never makes it to Louise's annual Fourth of July party. Instead, he takes Maggie up to Revere to meet his family. It is an awkward ride up, Maggie chewing on what she referred to as Teek-Tocks, doing her best not to get carsick, Zarro preoccupied with his parents' reaction, wondering just how he will break it to them. And although Maggie doesn't show yet, Marie Zarro takes one look at her future daughter-in-law emerging from the car pale and shaky on her feet, and asks her when she is due.

"The middle of February," Maggie answers honestly while Zarro, hiding behind his shades, busies himself with their solitary suitcase.

"You know I was two months along with Robert when his father and I got married."

Zarro pulls his head out of the hot trunk. "And here I thought I was premature."

"Only in Revere is there such a thing as a nine pound premature baby, Robbie."

"I'm shocked, Ma. *Shocked.*"

"Your father can be a very persuasive man. I guess you can say he swept me off my feet. Anyway, there's so much to do.

I'll call Father Sebastian. Maybe he can dispense with the Pre-Cana but I'm sure he'll still want to hear your confession. And another thing, did it ever occur to you Robbie, that your very own mother could have gotten you a discount on those sunglasses? Why am I the last person you come to, for anything?"

"I'm sorry. I didn't think." He honestly can't tell if his mother is more unsettled that he didn't purchase his sunglasses at Pearle Vision or that a bombshell just got flung into her lap. "And about my confession, that would tie Father Sebastian up through September so Maggie and I have decided to go to City Hall in New York." He doesn't dare look at Maggie when he says it because he knows Maggie had nothing to do with that decision. She'd still be living with Lygia if he hadn't confronted her.

"Why are we all standing on the curb?" his father asks. "It's hot as hell out here."

"One second, Dom. No big church wedding? Why not?"

"Marie, leave them alone. Not everyone wants the *agita* of a big church wedding. You have to order flowers and figure out where to seat the two cousins that have bad blood between them. Who needs it?"

"How about a small church wedding? Just the family."

"City Hall will do just fine, Ma." A trip to City Hall would be enough to get her on his health plan. They could petition Immigration for a green card. He'd put her name on the checking account and on his credit cards. They'd hook up a landline, and get a home phone number to show stability. The marriage would have to look real enough to fool the nitpickers down at Immigration.

They follow Dominick Zarro from the street into the house, Maggie admiring something every step of the way. Zarro

176

introduces her to his brother Anthony and Maggie smiles up at him and says, "You are the brother who will be the uncle."

"What do you say there, Anthony? How does the name Uncle Nee grab you?" Zarro teases.

"Whatever floats your boat, brother. Wait a minute. Are...are you saying? You mean? You mean you—"

"Very well put, Uncle Nee. The model UN would be proud of those extra smooth oratory skills."

Maggie and Zarro pretend to be the happy couple for the remainder of the day. That night when the family goes down to the beach to see the town's fireworks display, Maggie begs off, because she is exhausted. Zarro stays back at the house with her. "You have such a very nice family, Roberto. Everyone talk like you in this house."

"Everyone in the goddamn state talks like me, Maggie."

"Maybe I go to sleep now. It is a long ride in your car. And the baby make me so much tired."

"Come upstairs. You'll sleep in my old room. I'll take the couch down here."

She nods. "Your family, they don't know we will have a make-believe marriage next week."

"And they don't *have* to know," he says curtly, walking her up the stairs. "Listen, after we get the license you're coming with me to Citibank. It's important for your name to be on the account so Immigration doesn't have any suspicions that our marriage isn't legit."

"The bank? Oh no, 'berto. They will send me back to my country."

"The only place Citibank sends anyone is on a long line." He places the suitcase on the bed. "So let's make this happen."

She takes a few items out of the bag, in a feeble attempt to avoid further conversation.

"Goddamn it Maggie. You're signature *has* to be on that account. Do you understand?"

"Yes."

"Then stop busting 'em. No one at Citibank has the authority to send you back to Nicaragua."

"Oh 'berto, I am afraid of the banks."

"You're afraid of the bank, but you're not afraid to wear a wire to put a killer behind bars. That makes perfect sense." He takes her chin in his hand and looks into her olive eyes. "Come on Maggie, do you really think I'd let anyone take you?"

She picks up her shoulders and pulls away from him. "That will make the mistake go away, yes?"

"I don't want to get rid of you. You happen to be one of the best workers I have," he says, his attempt at levity free falling, the journey ending with a resounding splat.

She looks up at him, still unconvinced. "I see the bank on the Eyewitness News. There are soldiers with the guns."

"They're not soldiers. They're security guards. The guns are to make people think twice about taking off with the bank's money."

"You will be standing next to me?"

"Darlin', they'll have to separate us with a crowbar."

"A crow-bar?"

"Never mind. I'll be right next to you, I swear."

"I will think about it."

"Good. Now get some sleep, Maggie girl."

"Not yet. First I want to look at your things in the room." She walks over to the shelves that line the walls. "How you say this?"

"Trophies. Hockey, baseball. I was into sports." She is completely out of context in his old room, Zarro very much aware of his past and present colliding right before him within a ten by twelve space.

"Tro-phies," she says slowly, trying the new word out on her tongue. Then her eyes move around to his desk. She picks up the picture from the high school prom. "This is your girlfriend, yes?"

"That was taken a long time ago. Anyway, my girlfriend days are over and out. *Finito-Benito* Magaly Ocampo. The word on the street is I'm getting married next week."

"Yes, you will be my *esposo*."

"I suppose so," he replies, once again failing to coax a smile out of her.

"Goodnight, Roberto."

Once Maggie is settled, Zarro goes back downstairs, sits back on the sofa and sifts through a couple of sections of The Boston Globe. He becomes a little nostalgic as his eyes wander over the familiar names of local politicians, and ballplayers. As an M-80 explodes nearby, a vision of his golden retriever appears, Zarro remembering how Clem hated the Fourth of July, how the dog hid under a bed, whimpering at every loud noise.

In a week's time he'll be married to Magaly Ocampo, illegal alien. Married in name only. Married so she can obtain health insurance. Married so she could remain in the United States. He thinks back to the one night they had together, and he

179

momentarily lets his protective guard slip away. He is hiding, hiding under the bed, no better than old Clemmy. Then he refutes the logic of his own conscience. Yeah? Says who I'm hiding? I'm marrying the girl, aren't I? I'm doing the goddamn right thing.

His parents are back by eleven-thirty. Anthony, they tell him, went out with some friends. "It's hard to keep them in the nest once they learn how to drive," his mother says wistfully.

"Nee's a good kid Ma," Zarro reassures her. "And being you're a regular with the envelopes at church, I don't think God would punish you with two like me."

"Maybe you were a challenge, but you are certainly not a punishment. Why do you talk like that?"

"We like Maggie very much," his father says, changing the subject. "She seems like a very sweet girl. I hope you two will be very happy."

"Thanks. I really wasn't sure how you were going to take all this in." They must be shockproof by now. They must ask themselves what next, every time they see him. Just what will our Robbie pull this time?

"Is Maggie's family living in New York, too?" his father asks.

"No, her family is back in Nicaragua. She came up by herself. She's here illegally, if you hadn't guessed."

"Oh, the poor thing," his mother says. "All alone in a big city. Strange language. Different customs. I just don't know how people do that."

"Don't ask me." Zarro replies. "You get taken advantage of. Even by your own people. It's a tough go all around. And Maggie has these crazy fears that anyone in a uniform can grab her off the street and send her away. She thinks the security guards at Citibank are working hand in hand with Immigration."

"You know Rob, in some countries the bank *is* run by the government."

"Yeah, I guess. I never thought much about it."

"But what does all this mean for the baby? Will my grandchild be an American citizen?" his mother asks.

"Are you aware of what you're saying, Marie?" his father asks. "Of course the baby will be an American. It will be born in the States, no?"

"Dom, I'm just checking. I'm new to all this," she says with an edge in her voice. "Robbie brings home a pregnant girl out of the clear blue, and I'm supposed to think clearly? And now Anthony out all night. *Marrone a mia.* Who can take this? My nerves are shot to hell. No wonder I can't stay off the Tylenol PM."

Suddenly it hits Zarro that he's going to be a father. The baby would grow. It would be a real, live person. It would take up space and have a voice. It wouldn't always be a blob of cells safely hidden behind Maggie's shirt. He has to be strong now. Strong. He'll have to take care of this baby. He'll have to feed it and clothe it and take it on educational vacations. His mind is on the old North church, the reenactment of the Tea Party on the Beaver II, and the entire length of the Freedom Trail. Yes, he'll have to suffer through that another time, but it would be for the baby. He will do it willingly for the good of the baby. He will lift when they got back to New York. He has to keep strong for the baby.

"Rob?"

"Yeah Dad?"

"Where did you go? You looked a little out to lunch, there."

181

"I'm tired, that's all. Maggie went upstairs about an hour ago."

"Are you saying you want to join her?" his mother asks.

"No. I'll sleep on the sofa, Ma. We're not married *yet*, you know."

Dominick Zarro chuckles. "Only you, Robbie. Only you. In fact this whole situation reminds me of the time my brother Benny dated this girl from Maine."

"Uncle Benny was seeing a girl from Maine?"

"Oh we're talking years ago, way before he met your Aunt Carmella. The girl was real provincial, from a real old-fashioned religious home, real devout people. Her parents kept their daughter on a short leash, never let her out of the neighborhood. I'll even go out on a limb here Robbie and say your uncle never got to Bangor."

"What are you *scoccing* him about now, Dom? He's doing the right thing and you're giving him the business. Like he said, they're not married yet. So he knows that they should sleep in separate places. And I really don't see how your brother Benny has anything at all to do with Robbie sleeping downstairs."

"Listen to yourself, Marie. The girl is two months along. What difference will it make *now* where he sleeps?"

"To me there's a difference."

"Well Rob, you heard the boss. Downstairs for you. And if you have any intentions of sneaking upstairs tonight, the third step is loose, *capisce?*"

"I have no such intentions," Zarro says matter-of-factly.

"Well, I'm going to bed," his mother announces. "This has been some day. You think my friends have days like this? A crazy day for them is a mother-in-law coming to visit, a pipe breaking, maybe a car that doesn't start in the Star Market parking lot."

182

"I'll be up soon," Dominick says to his wife as he gently eases himself into the club chair that faces the sofa.

"So, how's it going with the business?" Zarro asks his father.

"Can't complain. The thought of being a Grandpa is making me feel my age. Oh, did your mother tell you, the VA wants to operate on my ear, after all these years? I told them as nice as I could they could go to hell. I don't want Uncle Sam anywhere near me with a knife. Besides, I got no time for an operation. I got myself a business to run while I can still hobble around."

"Cut it out. You're not old. Dad, I know you would like nothing better than for me to quit my job and take one in your company, but I don't see myself doing that yet. This conversation hangs between us every time I see you."

"Robbie, it was wrong of me to pressure you last time. You seem happy. The people in New York are treating you good. I got no right telling you how to live your life. You're a grown man, soon to have a family of your own."

"You got every right in the world to tell me anything. You're my father. You stood by me when that whole thing went down at school. You borrowed money from the uncles to pay the lawyer. You sat next to me in the courtroom and listened how your eldest son thought he was smarter than the law. You watched his scholarship go down the drain. In a million years I could never repay you what you and Mommy did for me. And I just want you to know that if things ever go sour at Zarro Construction, you just say the word. I'll drop everything for you. Everything, *capisce?* I'll be there in a heartbeat."

Dominick Zarro nods his head slowly. "That means a lot to me." Then he rises from his chair. "A grandfather," he says wistfully, running his hand over the top of his favorite club chair. "I can't believe it. I'm as old as goddamn dirt."

"So Uncle Benny never got to Bangor?" Zarro asks with a grin.

"That joke definitely sailed right over your mother's head."

"And thank Christ for that."

Chapter Nineteen

Despite Detective McClellan's warning, Zarro spends much of his free time in Bushwick, Brooklyn observing comings and goings, patterns of behavior. For as long as Guzman walks the streets, Maggie would be in danger. He learns the rhythm of the neighborhood and how to avoid the street cameras. And although it does not come naturally to him, he is patient. He learns what time of day Rafael Guzman and his clique collect their "taxes," where the drug sales are going down, and what streets the Feds use to park their vehicles. One night in June he witnesses another gang move into MS territory. That ends in gunfire, and is tailed by the caterwaul of sirens.

At 2:00 on a Sunday afternoon, Zarro finally makes his move. And he is prepared. A box cutter is sheathed in his pocket, just in case. He follows Rafael Guzman and a small boy into the Burger King on Myrtle Avenue. It is a bonus having the kid there, Zarro thinks. Even a gold-toothed, power-hungry inked psychopath like Guzman won't want to make a scene in front of his own son. But even a glimpse of Guzman causes the blood to rush to Zarro's gums, leaving his mouth tasting of metal. Zarro is on high alert, prison alert, but he manages to slow his breathing. Don't wring his neck. Be sly like the fox.

185

Zarro buys a Coke and parks himself at an adjacent table. He spots the cameras on the wall facing the cash registers. He looks closely at the other patrons in the restaurant. None appears to be part of the gang. Guzman tears the paper off the boy's hamburger and hands it to him.

"Your son?" Zarro asks.

Guzman stares ice at Zarro, but doesn't acknowledge his existence.

"Allow me to introduce myself," Zarro says. "I'm a detective from Waltham, Massachusetts."

Guzman flashes his devil horn sign and his little boy does the same. "So?"

"So I need someone with your particular talents to sling base for me. Has a street value of thirty thousand."

"And why you gotta come all the way to Brooklyn to do that?"

"Can't do business in my own backyard. Too many eyes."

"I don't make deals with no law enforcements. Do you know who I am?" Guzman asks. "Sure. Everyone knows you. You're on You-Tube. You're Hollywood."

Guzman nods, pleased that his reputation is spreading. "Then you know I hate cops."

The little boy offers Zarro a French fry and Zarro declines. "Well," Zarro says. "If it's not MS, it will be the Kings. Makes no difference to me."

"The Kings are pussies. They're Boy Scouts. All about community service. You don't want nothing to do with them. You need businessmen."

"So, you want in?"

"My crew is up for it."

186

Zarro forces himself not to think of Maggie whose clothes got splattered with Myrna's blood. Or of the girls who died in the Christmas Eve fire. "Look for a white van. New York tag. Make it the last Friday of the month. Wait 'til midnight. Hernandez Park on the Knickerbocker side. Twenty Gs."

"Ten"

"Fifteen and no bullshit. A simple business transaction."

Guzman considers the proposition. "How do I know this isn't some half-assed five-oh set up?"

"'Cause I'm the one with the merchandise." He gives Guzman his number from the burner phone he bought just for this purpose. "Any problems, hit the cell."

Guzman nods. Zarro picks up his drink and heads for the exit. The little boy waves good-bye but Zarro does not wave back because if it all went down as he envisioned it, the little boy would be minus a father.

Chapter Twenty

In mid-July not too long after Zarro's sit down with Rafael Guzman, a huge order arrives via fax from Evelyn's Costumes in the city. Zarro requests a meeting with Rick Schwab.

"We don't do meetings here," Rick says. "This is a family owned business, not Johnson and Johnson. So park it and we'll talk."

Zarro closes the door to Rick's office. Normally he is oblivious to the cut and color of Rick's wardrobe, but he cannot help but noticing today. Rather than the usual navy blue or grey, Rick is in some muted shade of orange, and the tie that hangs from his neck is a bright orange plaid. Orange, the color of pain and humiliation. "We'll talk, but as soon as you pick up that phone, I'm out of here."

For the first time in a long time, Rick Schwab holds his calls. "This better be worth my time," he snaps.

"I take it you saw the fax," Zarro begins.

"Of course I saw it. Now get busy and take care of it."

"That's it?"

"Zarro, if you're hungry for pats on the back, you're working for the wrong company. I find that every time you

189

throw a worker a compliment, it comes to haunt you when he holds a rifle at your head for a raise."

"An interesting theory. Look, in case you haven't guessed, I'm not sitting here looking for money and I'm smart enough not to ask you for the right time of day."

"So why *are* you here?"

"I met with the rep from the local and they're all going in the union. It's a done deal. All that's left is the paperwork."

"Please tell me why in hell did you rock the boat now, Zarro? Marilyn told me you married the one with the eyes. Maggie. She's in the local now and on her way to getting her green card, isn't she? So what's this altogether crazy obsession of yours with that godforsaken union?"

"Well, I can't marry them all, can I? Even the Mormons don't do that anymore."

Rick Schwab picks up his gold nail file and begins giving himself a halfhearted manicure. "I can't pretend I like it. It's costly and more importantly, it's unnecessary. And don't kid yourself Zarro, one call from yours truly can undo the whole deal."

"Do that and I'm gone."

"Tell me you're threatening to walk over the fate of fourteen unskilled illegal aliens. Do you know how asinine a move that is?"

"Since I turned up at your doorstep business has increased at least twenty per cent. And single-handedly I dragged your anemic, over-the-hill Mom and Pop ribbon and patch company first into the twentieth and then into the twenty-first century. You owe me something here."

"You got a raise and a generous bonus."

"It's not always about money, you know."

"That union throws enough weight around. I was on the phone with them ten minutes ago. Seems that gum-chewing yahoo who replaced that old soup-stained Yid from the local wants me to let Shirley Wong and that entire inscrutable gang from Flushing, take off Chinese New Year next year, with pay. Can you believe the unmitigated gall of those people?"

"Jesus Rick, you act like you're dealing with the Teamsters. All it buys your workers is a halfway decent wage, a paid vacation, and something to retire on."

"The way I see it Zarro, nothing could be finer than to be in Carolina. Shall I hum you a few bars as you're exiting?"

"Don't throw that shit in my face now, not after this costume contract came through. There's life in this business. We'll have to jockey cars out of the garage and into the street because I need to make room for stock. I did everything I was supposed to do, and *now* you want to cut out of here?" Control, Kicker. Self control. Don't get out of the chair. Keep your hands at your sides.

"It always remains a possibility. And that possibility will keep you on your toes," Rick says, a hawkish glint emanating from his eyes.

"I'm not married to this job. My father's on my case every time I see him to get out of here and join his construction company."

"The door's always open, Zarro. What's stopping you?"

"*You're* stopping me. Every time I look at you I know that's just how I don't want to end up."

Rick Schwab leans back in his chair and laughs. "You're funny, Zarro. Completely off your rocker, but funny. And it's a good thing I have a thick skin."

"Tell me Rick, just what kind of king do you want to be?"

191

"Now you're losing me."

Marilyn Friedman taps her bony knuckles against the partition. Zarro gets up and rolls the window open. "No calls. Not until my sweet guinea ass is out of this office."

"Well excuse me all to hell," she snipes. "You give someone a little power and right away it goes to his head. Happens all the time."

"Hey, why don't you up the dosage on your estrogen, Marilyn?" Zarro shouts at the old bookkeeper. Then he rolls the window shut. "I asked you what kind of king? Do you want to be the well-loved dictator that people pledge their undying loyalty, or do you want to be the evil power hungry king everyone is looking to dethrone?"

"They can't dethrone me, Zarro. I own the joint. I'm the major in this majordomo, in case you've forgotten."

"You know, I never met your father, but I've only heard good about him. Mel Lieb must have mentioned to me about a hundred times how your father took care of his workers. Get it? He took *care* of them. He didn't purposely go out of his way to shaft them."

"Mel Lieb was a sucker for any sob story that reached his ears and my father was not much better."

"A king has an obligation to his subjects."

"This king has an obligation to the bottom line. And rumor has it I'm running a business, not the Robert Zarro Community Center."

Zarro considers Rick Schwab's point for a moment. His boss is not entirely wrong. Schwab's Uniform is a business and businesses need to make a profit. He takes a breath and switches gears. "From what I learned in college, the best way to get more out of employees is to give them a small raise."

"How does that work?"

192

"Psych 101. The raise will motivate the workers because they will want to live up to your expectations. Believe me. They'll work twice as hard."

Rick Schwab replaces the nail file on his desk. "I don't want to *believe* anything. You will show me, with actual numbers."

Zarro nods. "You'll have an Excel spreadsheet in your Inbox next month." He remembers what his accounting professor once said in class. *Figures can't lie, but liars can figure.* So, he'll just have to finagle a set of numbers to show his boss. Piece of cake. "Okay fair Marilyn. Our majesty will now be receiving his calls. And I'm sorry about that estrogen crack."

"What are you sorry about? I'm flattered that you think I'm still young enough to be getting hot flashes."

At noon, Zarro places three twenties into Suzie Q's hands and asks her to do him a favor and go down to the 99Cents store on Queens Boulevard. "Bring me back every pair of cheapo plastic sunglasses you can lay your hands on."

"It's a cloudy day, Zarro. What you wanting sunglasses for?"

"I'd like to spread a little indoor sunshine."

"You buggin' on me, white boy?"

"Not at all. Tell me, did you happen to catch Schwab's suit and tie today, Suzie?'

"Oh yeah, Rick look just like a Florida tangerine." And then when it gels, she clicks her tongue, and shakes her head. "Zarro, the devil is riding you fast and hard today."

By twelve thirty, fifty-five people have a cheap pair of sunglasses at the ready. And at one p.m. when Rick normally steps through the warehouse to get his car out of the garage for a leisurely lunch, fifty-five smiles and the black plastic shades that hood a hundred and ten eyes are there to meet him.

"Everyone's a Goddamn critic," he shouts onto the floor as he hurries up the hill to make a getaway.

Chapter Twenty-One

At four o'clock Steven Sarian enters the garage with a union lawyer in tow. He sets up a table and schedules time with each department supervisor. But Rick Schwab doesn't get to see the meeting. He has already turned his silver Porsche eastbound onto the Long Island Expressway and calls his wife. "Thanks for the fashion advice on the new suit," he says. "The summer coral was a big hit."

"I hear sarcasm in your voice. Pierce Billings from the club had worn something very similar last Friday night and it looked great."

"Good for Pierce Billings," Rick says. "Pierce Billings is a gynecologist. He doesn't work in a warehouse with seventy-five wannabe comedians. No naked woman with her legs waving in the breeze is going to give *him* grief over his choice of suit."

Rick Schwab fumes as he sits in traffic, ruminating on the events of the day. The entire incident had Zarro's special brand of arrogance written all over it. They're all going in the union, he told him in that obnoxious diphthong laden Bostonian twang. Narth for north, bawx for box, pahk for park, stawk for stock, it was enough to drive anyone to drink. Besides, who does Zarro think he is *telling* him anything? True, business is starting to pick up. That much he had to give him. But that's beside the point, isn't it? It doesn't erase the fact that his warehouse manager has the brass balls of a professional cat burglar to go ahead and mock him like that.

"My brothers and sisters," the rep starts, "we are here to work with you. Mr. Shuldiner, our lawyer, will work with any undocumented worker in order to start the process on obtaining a visa. This is the first step in becoming a permanent citizen. If anyone in your department is undocumented, have them line up before me. We must petition the Immigration on a case-by-case basis. Some of you might be eligible for a labor certification on a Schedule A. Some of you can apply for political asylum. If someone can translate for me..."

"Go wake Elmo-the-cleaning-guy up," Zarro tells Maggie. "He's sleeping behind the supply closet. I'm sure he wants in on this."

Maggie comes back all upset. "He is not sleeping. I shake him and shake him. Elmo is dead. This is so sad, 'berto. What are we to do?"

"Are you sure? The man is one heavy sleeper."

"Yes. I am sure. His hand is cold and all the moneys fall from him and I put it back in his pocket."

"What money? What are you talking about?"

"It was his turn in the Bullshit Club."

"Lucky him. I'll see the money gets to Elmo's wife. Christ, I'm going to be here all night now. Don't say anything yet. I'll hold off on the nine-one-one call until the place is cleared. They'll think I'm calling *la migra* down on them. Jeez, poor Elmo, huh? Timing is everything in this sorry life, right Maggie?"

"Roberto, I have to sit down."

"You all right?"

"I…I just don't know. Something feels funny inside of me. I stand too much today. It is very busy. And Elmo is dead. I can't believe this."

"Listen to me, go into my office and call the doctor's. I'll have Matty run you over to check you out. I have to stay here until the medical examiner arrives for Elmo. I'll have to call Elmo's wife. I swear to Christ I'm not cut out for this, not even a little bit."

Zarro shouts for Matty and he jogs over. "Listen up. I need you to drive Maggie over to her doctor. Doctor Adair. He's the same guy your sister-in-law uses."

"Yeah, I've been there with Jo when my brother couldn't get off work in time. The doc in Rego Park, right?"

"That's the one. And I want you to take it easy on the bumps, *capisce*? That's my baby in there."

"Baby? Oh, I get it now. So that's why youse two got married in a hurry. Maggie's having a baby! Way to go, Zarro. Jeez, why didn't you say something? I gotta get a pool going. Boy or girl, pounds and ounces, day it makes the scene. It takes time to make a chart like that. It don't happen overnight, you know."

"Never mind. I want you to sit in the waiting room while the doctor checks under the hood. No way I want you leaving her off at the curb and taking off somewhere."

"I know I act like a complete asshole sometimes, but I'm not an idiot."

Zarro nods and claps his hand on Matty's shoulder. "I appreciate this. And call me from the doctor's, you hear?"

*   *   *   *   *

The cops arrive quickly, but the medical examiner is another story. As he waits for the phone call from Dr. Adair's office, his mind lights on a hundred things and all he feels is helpless. Not knowing what is up with Maggie causes his thoughts to career like a just shot pinball. He tries to take his mind off her by immersing himself in work. Soberly, Zarro packs up an order for the mortuary at Dover Air Force Base. War has created a steady supply of customers, both in life and in death.

He knows it is bad news as soon as he hears Matty's voice on the phone. "I'm sorry man."

"Can I talk to her?" Zarro stands there, supporting himself against the gray metal desk, waiting to hear her voice through the receiver.

"Roberto," she says weakly.

"I'm sorry, Maggie. I should have been there with you."

"Dr. Adair says I should rest now in the bed so Matty will drive me home."

"Let me talk to him, okay?"

He comes on the line. "Yeah, Zarro?"

"Look, do me a favor and walk her up the stairs. If she can't walk, carry her. And then come on back to Schwab's. I need you to wait here with Elmo-the-cleaning-guy. You'll get paid for your time. I need to get home. I want to be with her."

"Why the hell do I have to wait with Elmo?"

" 'Cause he's dead."

"Boss, are you sure he ain't sleeping?" Matty asks, but Zarro has already hung up.

198

* * * * *

Zarro is pacing the floor when Matty parks the van inside the garage. When Matty opens the door, Zarro hands him a set of keys. "I'm out of here. You lock up."

"I'll give these back to you on Monday."

Zarro looks him up and down. He starts to say something and then he stops. "Whatever," he said when he is halfway able to gather his thoughts.

Maggie's skin is ashen against the navy blue sheets on Zarro's bed and he brings her a glass of lemonade. Her hands shake the glass and he takes it from her, holding the glass at her lips, himself.

"You marry me for nothing, Roberto."

"Please don't say that." He puts her hands in his. "You're hands are like ice. I'll bring you another blanket." He takes her quilt out of the pullout couch and places it around her. He pulls the Venetians closed and the room falls into shadow.

"You marry me because you are very nice and you don't want me to have a baby all alone. You say it is a mistake and you are right."

"I don't want to hear you say that again." His words haunt him. A mistake. Maggie was carrying a mistake. How in God's name could he have said those things? Where the hell was his head?

Maggie looks at him. "I am tired. I try to sleep a little. Matty bring me to your bed. He does not know I sleep on the sofa and I don't know how to say it."

"It doesn't matter. Do you need anything?"

199

"Matty knock on Louise's door and she bring her baby to Miss Rose and Louise drive to the *farmacia* for me. There is much blood and there is laundry."

"I'll take care of the laundry. What did the doctor say?"

"He say it happen sometime when there is something wrong with the baby. It is not from standing too long or working too much. He say it is Mrs. Mother Nature. Dr. Adair doesn't know we have a make-believe marriage in the City of New York, so he say we can try again in the little while after I am healed and after we have mourn-ed. I think that is the word. It means to cry. But I have no tears left in me to cry and I don't want another baby, Roberto. My babies don't ever live." Her voice is resigned, as she lay in the bed as stoic as an early martyr, so accepting of her fate. And it tears Zarro apart.

When his cell sings out, he jumps on it so not to disturb her.

"How's Maggie?" Matty McClellan asks.

"Resting. Look, thanks for helping me out today. I won't forget it any time soon. What's the deal with Elmo?"

"They just rolled him out the door, took 'em long enough. Poor bastard. I guess Schwab will have to get someone else to wash his precious silver Porsche next Friday 'cause Elmo's on a permanent nap now."

"A permanent nap sounds real good to me," Zarro says. "I'll see you Monday." He continues to hold his cell in his hand after Matty hangs up. He takes a deep breath and makes the call to his family. More sorrow for them. All he ever does is bring them sorrow.

Then, he silences his phone and goes back into his darkened bedroom and watches Maggie sleep. It should have been a happy day. After all, he did it. He had everyone in the union now. He should have felt proud for orchestrating the move, proud for finally doing something decent in his life, but as he gazes at Maggie's pale face on his pillow, Zarro is well aware that any gains he made that day are overshadowed by loss. He convinces himself that if he had paid a little less attention to work and a little more attention to Maggie, he wouldn't be in this situation. Regret lodges in the back of his throat like a bitter lozenge.

Chapter Twenty-Two

Zarro doesn't know how long he's been in the chair, listening to Maggie's steady breathing. He becomes aware of the stiffness in his joints as the room slowly turns from grey into blackness. He stands up, stretches his limbs and feels his way through the shadows into the kitchen. The light is on and he notices a pot on the stove that does not look at all familiar. He lifts the lid and peers in, pastina in chicken broth, a soup from his childhood, a soup his mother made when he was not well. He turns the knob on the stove and a blue flame jumps to warm the pot, the floating pastina looking like the small seed pearls women in Schwab's fasten to a costume. When he turns away from the stove, there is Maggie, pale and shaky at his table.

"I didn't hear you get up. How are you doing Maggie girl?"

"Okay."

"Rose left this for you. She must have let herself in. She brought you chicken broth and pastina. It will make you feel better." When it begins to boil, he ladles out a bowl and then returns to the table with a spoon and a napkin that shake ever so slightly in his large hands.

"Miss Rose is a very nice lady to make this for me." Maggie dips her spoon into the bowl and takes a sip of the hot soup. "It tastes salty, like the tears I cannot cry," she says, bringing another miniscule amount to her lips.

"It will give you strength. You need that now," he says bringing a bowl for himself to the table.

"And big, strong Roberto, what does *he* need?" she asks, gazing steadfastly into his dark eyes.

But Zarro looks away and does not answer.

Maggie returns to work in a couple of days, gradually regaining her basically sunny nature. Only a few of her close friends at work even knew about the pregnancy, and when they whisper their 'I'm sorrys' and their '*Que lastimas*', Maggie quietly reassures them it is the will of God and Mrs. Mother Nature. Zarro, on the other hand, turns bitter despite the doctor's reassurances that no one was at fault. He blames himself for the loss at every chance he can get. He blames it on the drugs he did in college. He blames himself for making Maggie stand on her feet before he knew she was expecting. He blames himself for his indifference, which prompted her to wear a wire for the Feds. And he blames himself for not taking her to the doctor, himself. His guilt feasts on his profound grief, a determined parasite out to kill the host. He is short-tempered at work and very quickly his staff learns to stay out of his way, if they know what's good for them.

At seven thirty in the morning on the Monday following Maggie's miscarriage, Zarro sits staring into space, positioned on the last stool at the Corner Luncheonette sipping hot coffee from a thick white, red rimmed mug. Trudy McClellan approaches him from behind the counter and tells him how sorry she is. Matty had told her what had happened. Zarro just shrugs and goes back to his coffee. The wound is so deep, so painful he doesn't want to talk about it, doesn't want to think about it.

"It happened to me too, you know," Trudy goes on, unaware of how far the depths of his sadness reach. "Years ago. I had a 'mis.' Between my daughter and Matty. Everyone said it was for the best, but it was still very upsetting."

Zarro nods his head, hoping the conversation has ended, hoping she will change the subject, thinking if he slams his cup down on the counter it will shatter into sharp, jagged slivers. But the waitress doesn't hear his thoughts.

"My mother said I shouldn't cry. She said what never made you laugh must never make you cry. Tough old broad she was, my mother. I really think they're made of stronger cloth, those from the other side. But let me tell you, I cried buckets, Robert. Buckets."

Zarro doesn't say a word. Head bent, eyes hooded, he pushes off the stool, reaches into his pocket and slams a fistful of money onto the scratched Formica counter, over-tipping the waitress as usual.

Chapter Twenty-Three

On the last Friday of the month, shortly before the two of them have to be at work, Zarro watches Maggie neatly pack her belongings into a borrowed suitcase. "I really don't know what your rush is, Maggie. You might as well finish out the summer here. I have air-conditioning."

"You have air-conditioning and new windows and clean bricks and the nice polish floors. You and Hector do a very good job to make the house very pretty. Still, I will go. We don't have to make believe any more, Roberto."

"There's no rush. Joanna and Tommy had their baby and they're having a little party tonight. Matty will be there and Trudy from the luncheonette. Louise and Hector should be there with Frankie. And Rose, ab-so-lute-ly Rose. I'm telling you Maggie, you'll know a lot of people. It will do you some good to get out, socialize a little."

"Okay. I will leave on Saturday morning. Shirley Wong knows someone who has a room in Flushing. Then on Monday I will call the special agent from the F.B.I. I want to testify against Rafael Guzman. I will live in a hotel with little shampoos and soaps. They promise for me a new name and a new life. Finally, I will be someone in this country."

"Goddamn it. I don't want to hear about this again."

"Do you want me to buy the baby a present at lunchtime? Manuel in shipping is selling baby clothes."

"Please, no clothes that fell off of a truck. Buy something legit on Queens Boulevard. They had a girl, Sally Elizabeth McClellan." He peels a couple of bills out of his wallet. "And as long as you're going, I'd appreciate it if you'd get a little something for their older daughter. Aggie must be around six."

"A doll?"

"Yeah that will work. You know I can still remember feeling very ignored after Nee was born. What about you? You don't talk too much about your family. You have any sisters or brothers?"

"Yes. Four sisters and three brothers. I am the oldest one." Once we were a happy family. We went to the beach at Corinto, ate clams and played in the water. One minute happy and the next minute sad. Fighting, arguing when we came home. My father say, 'Why is she so fat? Why is her stomach so big?' Marta from next door, banged her hand on the window, to make sure everything was okay. In eighteen years, she never heard such noise coming from the Ocampos."

"That's some big family, Maggie. I get that you and your father are on the outs, but what about the rest? You must miss them."

"They have a cell phone now. I call to tell them the money is coming."

"When you get your green card you can visit them, you know. Go back and forth *no problema*."

"I will *never* go there again, Roberto," she snaps back. "My country is soldiers and pain and the explaining to my mother about why I am pregnant. My country is where my father do not believe what happens to me, where the owl is

208

watching me under the blood red leaves of the malinche tree. My country is where my father call me a prostitute, and where my mother was too weak to defend me. I am not stepping my foot there."

Zarro quickly changes the subject. "Look, I don't want to force you to go to this party tonight, you know. Maybe it's too soon after our experience to go looking at another baby. It might upset you, Maggie."

"Looking at another baby will not make me sad. Do you think I will not see another baby forever? I see Louise and Hector's little boy in his car seat yesterday."

"I just want to make sure, that's all. They'd understand if we didn't stop by later, being it's so soon after."

"First you invite me to the party 'berto, and then you stand there and give to me all the reasons why I should take the subways to Shirley Wong's friend tonight."

Nothing else is said after that. Maggie continues packing. Zarro leafs through a catalogue that one of Schwab's suppliers sent him. At ten minutes before eight Maggie zippers the borrowed suitcase, pushes it up against the wall, and the two of them leave the apartment.

Without uttering a word, they cross 39th Street and walk into the back entrance of Schwab's Uniform together. It is okay to be seen together now; they are married after all, make believe married in the City of New York. They will be together for one more day, Zarro thinks. One more day and then she would call Detective McClellan and force him to take her back so she can testify. Maggie, he realizes is ready for her new life. Her new life without him.

"You're very quiet this morning," Zarro says to her, breaking their awkward silence, as they enter the open garage and walk toward shipping. "Did I say something to upset you?"

209

Maggie tosses her head, unknowingly sending the fragrance of lemons in his direction. "Sometimes I think it is very good to be quiet. You can think all your thoughts when you are quiet."

"Yeah, well clue me in darlin'. What thoughts are you thinking?"

"I'm thinking that I will punch my card in the clock and you will hand me the orders and I will pick them. And the orders will be good, no mistakes, and you will say 'Thanks Maggie girl,' and then you will hand me some more. And I will make those good too. And then you will say, 'Go sew Maggie. Take a load off.' And I will sit at the machine and sew. And then I will find Suzie Q and Lygia, eat my lunch and then run fast to the store to buy the presents. And then I will pick more orders and do more sewing until four o'clock. Then everyone will say 'It's Friday, *Gracias A Dios*. Have a nice weekend.' And Suzie Q will say, 'Girl, don't you do anything I would not do.' And then I will go to the apartment and get the laundry and take it to the Laundromat on 43rd Avenue. I will come back and cook the macaroni for you not too soft the way your mother shows me and I will clean the apartment. This is only the thoughts of me. A poor girl who comes on the buses from Nicaragua can have no more thoughts."

"Jeez, you really sound like you could use a break in the routine, Maggie. I'm real glad you think you'll be able to come with me tonight."

Maggie waits her turn to punch her timecard. The warehouse begins to fill up with workers and many mill about before the day officially begins. Maggie feels her face get hot. "And you will be even *more* glad tomorrow when I leave. Then you can call the messy whore with the purple lipstick and the underwears with the stripes of a tiger," she says angrily, loud

210

enough for everyone to hear. "You can have a fun party with this messy girl. And she don't have to pick the orders and cook your food and clean your house. I am thinking I would like very much to be this girl, because she is not a mistake, no? You *wanted* this girl in your apartment, Roberto. You invite her and her purple lipstick and her underwears with the stripes of a tiger."

"For the love of God, the whole place doesn't have to know our goddamn business."

"I don't have to talk to you anymore," she shouts even louder than before, her voice filling the factory with an out-of-character crescendo. "Not on the inside. Not on the outside. Not nowhere. Your mistake will be leaving on the subways in the morning. I will live in a nice hotel and have a new name."

Workers scurry from the time clock, pretending not to listen to Maggie's tirade. "I find for me another life," she shouts at him. "I hate what you do to me and I hate you."

With his dark eyes boring holes into every object in the line of sight, a wounded Zarro walks toward shipping.

"Yo, what are you two idiots staring at?" he growls at Matty and Weeds when he turns around. "Got nothing better to do? Just say the word and I'll fuckin' give you something better to do. Nothing but dead weight the two of you are. I swear to Christ, I could replace both of you with a pair of gorillas from the Franklin Park Zoo."

Matty and Weeds go back to their cartons and when Zarro is safely encased within the Plexiglas walls of his back office, Matty turns to the wiry Jamaican and says, "Do you *know* what kind of evil mood Zarro's gonna be in all day?"

211

"Our man Z in a bad way. Today would have been an excellent day to call in dead."

Zarro makes it his business to avoid Maggie. He hides behind his desk in the front office and works on purchasing. He just doesn't get it. He had done the right thing, and it still ended up so wrong. She hates him. She resents him. And for what? Zarro wonders. For taking care of her? For giving her a place to stay? For making sure she had health benefits for their unborn child? Where had he gone wrong? He had been respectful, caring, concerned. What more does she want? He never asked her to clean for him or cook for him. That was *her* idea. And now she is shoving *that* down his throat.

Frustrated, he looks up at the series of numbers on the computer screen, but all he sees is her borrowed suitcase waiting in his living room. To hell with her. She'll be gone by Saturday morning. Going, going, gone.

Zarro remains in the front office until four fifteen in the afternoon. He waits for everyone in the warehouse to punch out so he can avoid any possibility of contact, and then he will lock up for the weekend. Safe and alone, the way he is meant to be. Up the hill, however, he hears raucous laughter, Matty's and Weeds' laughter. He obviously startles them, because they are sitting in the back office, two sets of work boots on his desk. With them, a frightened looking short, skinny, jug-eared kid who couldn't have been more than eighteen years old is in their presence. Matty has Zarro's Sox cap on his head, backwards, the

212

way that Zarro usually wore it. Silently, Zarro stands in the doorway until Weeds motions to Matty and their feet fly to the floor, both of them standing up simultaneously. "Oh Zarro, where've you been hiding? We thought you left for the day," Matty says, trying to look innocent, hoping his eyes do not give anything away.

"Use the brains that God gave you. If I up and left for the day, who would lock up? Who would set the alarm? Not you. Not *ever* you. And we have a new code now, just in case you were wondering."

"I really didn't think about that," Matty replies.

"You don't do too much thinking, do you?"

Matty looks to Weeds for moral support, but his friend's gaze is impregnable.

"Where's your manners? Aren't you going to introduce me to your friend?" Zarro asks as he rips the cap off of Matty's head and puts it on his own.

"Sorry, boss. This here is Jose from Ecuador. From the street he seen the picture of the soldier and now he wants to enlist in the U.S. Army. Right Jose?"

"I look to find recruitment station."

"Jose be as smart a fellow as our Spacious," Weeds says, trying not to giggle. "So we're recruiting him, right Matty?

"Why do you want to enlist?" Zarro asks the boy, who wears an expression of total confusion on his face.

"I need the job. My cousin who I live with say to try recruitment station. He say I no long can live with him with no job. Go join the Army, he say. They take anyones."

"You have papers?"

"I have my cousin's social security number. He say I can use."

Zarro nods. "You like to travel, Jose? The Army moves around all the time."

"I don't so much like to travel. I like in Queens. The bread is very good in the Turkish bakery on Queens Boulevard. Could I sign my name for the Army in Queens?"

Matty and Weeds can no longer contain themselves, the two of them bursting out in a fusillade of laughter. "The Turkish bakery, you believe that?" Matty says. "I knocked up that baker's daughter ten years ago. And you should have seen the buns on that girl." Weeds is listening, his smile a mile wide. Matty says, "Mmm, they were the finest buns this side of Skillman Avenue. What kind of baked goods do you like, Weeds?"

"I like sweet cinnamon buns, hot sticky buns—"

"Shut up you two," Zarro interrupts. Then he addresses the boy. "This is a *pre*-recruitment station. This particular unit stays put to ensure the safety of the neighborhood. No travel is involved."

"Can I sign my name for this Army?"

"We don't take anyone. Are you in shape?"

"I no understand."

Zarro eyes Matty and Weeds. "Corporal Matthew McClellan here, will demonstrate the concept of being in shape. Corporal, let's all move out of the office where there's more room for you to drop and give me fifty."

"Are you crazy?"

Zarro stares ice at him. "Do it."

The group reassembles in shipping. Matty drops to the floor and begins his pushups. Weeds thinks that is the funniest thing he's ever seen. He slaps Zarro's back. "You a snap, Z."

"Corporal Weeds, quit your fraternizing and show Jose here what a crunch is."

The Jamaican finds a spot on the floor next to Matty and begins a series of off-kilter drug-impaired modified sit-ups.

"Can you do this?" Zarro asks the boy.

"Si. You want me to show?"

"At ease gentlemen," Zarro says to Weeds and Matty. "No Jose, I'll take your word on it."

"You're nuts, Zarro. Go the hell home. You need a long rest," Matty says when he catches his breath.

Zarro ignores him and turns to the boy. "The pre-recruitment station is looking for people who do as they're told."

"I do that," the boy assures him.

"Do you have any special skills? Do you know computers? Sew? Drive?"

"No skills. No. I sorry."

"Don't be sorry. You've come to the right place. We specialize in people who can't do a goddamn thing. Both Corporal McClellan and Corporal Weeds are prime examples of the type of soldier we specialize in."

"I can learn something, yes?"

"At this time the pre-recruitment station is looking for someone who can clean. Floors, windows, sinks, toilets. Our last recruit went AWOL, that's 'absent without leave' in Army talk."

"You pay me something in this Army? My cousin is looking for the moneys all the times."

"Yes. The government is offering its special minimum wage package for anyone with a cousin's social security number. You can start on Monday."

"Si. What time is the hours here?"

"Eight to four, Monday through Friday. You'll get a weekend pass where you can go home to rest."

"Do they give to me the uniform?"

215

"Listen to this fuckin' imbecile." Matty elbows Weeds. "He wants a *uniform!*"

Zarro stares at Matty again. "Go downstairs and pull me a pair of Army Sergeant's chevrons, the brass ones. No, eighty-six the brass. Bring me the twenty-two karat anodized ones. Nothing but the top of the line for our newest recruit."

"Have you lost it, boss?"

"Do it."

Matty goes down the hill and into the aisle that housed the metal chevrons.

Then Zarro turns to Weeds. "Get him an apron."

When both men are before him, Zarro slips a blue denim apron around the boy and pins the chevrons on either side of the cotton bib. "We will call you 'Sergeant Custodian' from now on. Sometimes we'll forget and just call you 'Custodian.' How does that grab you, Jose?"

"Sergeant Custard, *si.*"

"And I'll be inspecting your work each day. I'm looking for sparkling sinks, floors that shine, urinals you can eat your lunch out of. See me Monday at eight o'clock and we'll set you up with your weapons."

"Weapons?" the boy asks, his eyes wide with wonder. "You meaning the guns?"

"Nah, no guns. Broom, mop, ammonia, paper towels, a bucket or two. That's about all the artillery we issue in a pre-recruitment station."

"*Si.* That is good. Mister, you my boss, yes? What should I call you?"

"Call him friggin' crazy," Matty says under his breath.

"Insubordination," Zarro glares back at him.

"That too hard to say," the boy says quietly. "My English is no so good."

"Call me Zarro for short," he says shaking the boy's hand and following it up with an exaggerated salute. "Congratulations, Sgt. Custard, you are now a member of Schwab's division of the U.S. Army, first cleaning brigade."

The three men watch the boy leave through the open garage door. It is Matty who breaks the silence. "You don't have to say it, boss. We know we done wrong. We took advantage of some foreign idiot who thought this is some military recruiting station."

"Get out of my face. You make me sick, humiliating that kid 'cause he's new here and he doesn't know which end is up. How smart do you think *you'd* be if I threw you down in the middle of Ecuador? Tell me. You think you'd come off so goddamn clever?"

Matty and Weeds look at each other.

"Look at you, two bleary-eyed bullies, cranked on God knows what, the both of you."

"Lighten up, it's Friday," Matty says.

Zarro lets Matty's words hang in the air for a minute, hoping he'll realize just how stupid they sound. "Lighten up, it's Friday," Zarro echoes. "Why don't you tell it like it really is? Tell the whole story for once in your life. It's Friday and you thought your pain in the balls supervisor was gone for the day. Lucky us, we got the place to ourselves. What better time to take advantage of the situation, right guys?"

"We sorry Z," Weeds adds, remembering what had transpired that morning, he and Maggie having words in front of them. Zarro, in that evil mood and then him disappearing into nowhere for hours.

"Everyone is always sorry, aren't they? So, where are you two hiding your stash these days? Back file cabinets still the place? Jeez, you look surprised. You didn't think I knew about

217

it? Oh, I know all about it. I know every goddamn inch of this place. Wait here, gentlemen."

"Come on, Zarro. We said we're sorry. Just forget about it, huh?"

But Zarro is already up into the garage, pulling open cabinet after cabinet, slamming them shut when nothing but yellowing paperwork is revealed. After ten attempts, he locates a three-quarters empty bottle of Southern Comfort that he places in his left hand as he continues pulling open drawers with his right. He returns to the office with the bottle and a bulging paper bag, placing both items on his desk. "Well, let's party hearty," he says, unscrewing the cap on the Southern Comfort, and taking gulp after gulp, the sweet burning beverage blasting a quick path down into his gut. *"Salute."*

"Boss," Matty says, alarmed by the completely unreadable expression on Zarro's face. His eyes are cold, Matty thinks. His brother Tommy looks like that sometimes. It scares him, those cold eyes, scares him more than anything in the world. And he was Golden Gloves once upon a time.

"Don't 'Boss' me. It's Friday, right? You said so yourself," he says taking another pull from the bottle. Then he peers into the paper bag. "You got weed in there? I'm game," he says expertly rolling a nice fat joint for himself. "Been a long time."

"No Zarro. Take it easy on that smoke. It's lethal island-type shit. Why don't you forget about it?" Matty suggests.

"And why should I?" he says licking the seam, lighting the end and drawing the smoke into the deepest cavern of his lungs where it rolls around until he lets it out.

"Because you're our boss. It ain't right."

"Well Matty, I'm tired of being right," he says already feeling a light buzz, experiencing the happy confluence where

218

smoke meets drink. Zarro takes another swig from the bottle. "Right has gotten me nowhere. Wrong has gotten me nowhere. Both right and wrong have gotten me nowhere. So it's wrong's turn today. You play the odds. That's just the luck of the draw, right Southy?"

"This is about you and Maggie this morning," Weeds says. "You're all jangled from that woman. A woman can do that to a man. Whip you 'til you're beaten down."

"Let's not go there Corporal Weeds," Zarro warns, popping one of the pills and taking two more swigs from the bottle which he quickly follows up with a double hit from the joint. "Maggie is my wife. So don't you ever, ever even think of saying one word against her. She's my wife. Magaly Ocampo Zarro is my wife. We were married in City Hall. Make-believe mar-married in the goddamn City of New York." Two more tokes. "And now she wants to leave me for real. 'Cause she hates me. Hates me in a b-big way." His slurred words bump about the small room. "We were going to have a baby, you know, but the baby's dead before it's born. All the babies are dead now. All the goddamn babies are dead—"

"I'm putting this away. You had enough," Matty says pulling the remainder of the joint out of Zarro's hand. "I told you this is powerful stuff, Zarro. Two tokes and it knocks you right on your ass."

"Are you of all people talking moderation to me, Corporal McClellan? Now that's a real hoot, that is. That's even fun-funnier than that poor South American kid thinking he's going to be all that he can be. Don't you think? Are you deaf? I *said*, don't you think?"

Matty tosses the now empty bottle into the trash and walks the paper bag back into the nether regions of Schwab's

219

garage. "Come on let's get the fuck out of here," he says on his return.

Zarro attempts to get up. "Jesus Christ," he says, falling back into the chair. The second time he is all the wiser, making sure he braces himself against the desk. "Well you weren't shittin' me. That's some wicked fine stuff, there," he says, finally unhooking the keys from his belt loop after two unsuccessful attempts. "Wicked, fine stuff."

"You gonna be okay, Zarro?" Matty asks when they are all outside.

"Oh don't worry none about me," he says, waiting for a break in the traffic to cross the street. "I got all the balls up in the air. I'm a regular madician. Ma-gi-cian."

"Wait up. Don't let Maggie see you like that. Here. I got some Visine in my pocket. Weeds, give him a mint or something."

"Tools of the trade, huh Matty?" Zarro mutters as he squirts the liquid into his dry, reddened eyes, wetting a good portion of his face in the process. Then Zarro tries to peel the paper from a new roll of Lifesavers. "Fuck it," he says. "This is her-her-metically sealed."

"Here Z, let me do this for you," Weeds says, peeling the paper and handing Zarro the first one from the roll, an orange Lifesaver.

"Orange? Never orange. Orange is the color of pain and hu-hu-miliation. I wore orange for three years at Old Bay. Three years of my sorry life. That's more than a thousand days in decimal talk, one, zero, zero, zero. Did Zarro miss a zero somewhere? That's pretty funny, huh?"

"How about the red one then? Red a good color for you?"

Zarro pops the red one in his mouth, his tongue flapping about helplessly, unable to find the hole at the center of the candy.

"I'll see you at my brother's house tonight. How do you like that? I'm an uncle for the third time," Matty says. Zarro has enough sense left to see that he is trying to change the subject, trying hard to blot out what is before him. That he's thinking, *Zarro, of all people. It just ain't right.*

"Third time. That be nothing," Weeds says. "I be an uncle fifteen times. Maybe sixteen now. I lose count. You have a good sleep, Z. Get into bed and let the sleep take care of you. Tell your wife a fierce headache come sneaking up on you. She never know you been feeding your head."

"She'll know something's up," he says softly. "She'll think her fine man's been inhaling Resistol like those poor, wretched kids in Gua-Guatemala City, those raggedy-ass kids who don't have enough to eat. Maybe she'll feel sorry for her fine man, her precious 'berto who fucked everything up."

The two men watch Zarro zigzag across the street. "Look at him," Matty says in disbelief. "The guy can't even walk a straight line. He ain't used to that Jamaican shit. He's really messed up on it."

"Don't go blaming the weed, man. That island medicine cure depression, women's troubles, men's troubles. Helps you concentrate, relax you, make you study hard. It's a best friend when you be needing a best friend. It's the fire he put in his belly that make him sick like that. Southern Comfort. Why don't they call it what it really be? White man's poison."

221

"Did you hear what come out of his mouth about wearing orange for three years?" Matty asks as he watches Zarro enter Rose's building. "Weeds, you thinking what I'm thinking?"

"Well, now that depends what you be thinking man, don't it?"

"I'm thinking that maybe our boss spent some time locked away, like in a jail."

"Locked up in a jail. Listen to you. You crazy, Matty. Z a rich white boy. He know all kinds of business things like supply chain management, whatever that be. I say he spent three years in the private school where they wear an orange uniform. Old Bay, he say. Some strict Catholic school on the water where the nuns like to take the ruler to your hands if you don't do your sums correctly."

"Yeah, you're probably right. Shit, I don't know what's what anymore. Seeing Zarro like that is freakin' me out big time."

"That Maggie have him in a bad way. It's all *her* fault he like that. She bringing their troubles into work for everyone to hear, making him miserable and him taking it out on us."

"You don't like women much, do you Weeds?"

"I like them just fine. I tell you I have myself a woman, a good woman. She cook jerk chicken and curried goat on Eastern Parkway in Brooklyn. She one-third owner of the restaurant. When I had caught that terrible chill this winter, my woman come running to my apartment feed me the jerk and seal me in lemons."

"What did you say? She sucked you like a lemon, jerked you off, and cooked you in the pot with the chicken and the goat?" Matty asks, the question and the accompanying snicker assaulting his co-worker's two ears.

222

"You an ignorant fool, Matty. You don't understand so you go making your stupid jokes. My woman squeezed the lemon juice on my skin to seal out the cold. She *cure* me with lemons. By the next day I was right."

"I never heard of such a thing. How the hell does a lemon juice bath fight a cold?"

"It go deep down into the bottom layer of the skin. All that good vitamin C get itself absorbed and attack the cold."

"Oh whatever. You people gotta have the most bizarre customs on the fuckin' planet." Matty puts a fresh toothpick in his mouth and begins to work on it with his back teeth. "So you serious with this woman?"

"Very serious, Matty. Tonight I'm going to eat that good jerk chicken and ride her 'til she *beg* me to stop."

Matty snorts. "Anyways, have yourself a good one." He extends his hand, the Jamaican grabbing it, their friendship bound by ten years of side-by-side toil, any serration by racial and cultural lines all but hammered smooth by the work they share.

"There be no need to say that now. I always have a good one. Matty, you ever be wondering why Z keep calling you Southy?"

"I swear, Weeds, sometimes it's like you're right off the boat. Southy is like a southpaw, a lefty. I still got me one hell of a left hook you know," Matty says, affecting one of his better stances and jabbing Weeds' right shoulder. "I was the great white hope of Queens once upon a time."

"And now you the great white dope of Queens. Will you be looking at the time, Matty? Wasting the weekend we are," the Jamaican says and hurries himself to the #7 train.

223

Chapter Twenty-Four

Sally Elizabeth McClellan is a little pink-faced bundle with dark hair and grey eyes. Zarro pockets the obligatory cigar, punches the detective in the arm and proceeds to tell him he is running a regular harem. Maggie fusses over Aggie and the baby and then Joanna McClellan introduces her to her father and shows her around the apartment. Trudy and her husband Billy are there as well as Joanna's elderly Aunt Adele—Sol Barron's older sister—and her husband Uncle Jack. Apparently, they also live in the building. Zarro is surprised Hector and Louise aren't there, but he figures they are just late. He hands Aggie the doll that Maggie has picked out for her. "This one's for you kiddo," he says. "Being a big sister will take everything you got, if you do it right, that is."

"Thank you Zarro," Aggie says. "My Uncle Matty was wrong about you. Anyway, Mommy says I can't say son-of-a-bitch any more or I have to sit in my room. By myself."

"Your Uncle Matty's wrong about what?" Matty says opening the door to the apartment, letting Minnew the cat in, in the process.

"That Zarro is one son-of-a-bitch," the little girl tells her uncle.

"Aggie!" Joanna cries out. "I don't believe you. What did I tell you last time?"

The detective smiles. "Come on, Jo. No harm done, huh? Our little angel just said he *isn't* a son-of-a-bitch. Now how can you possibly find anything wrong with that?"

"Yeah Jo, what's wrong with that?" Matty asks his sister-in-law. "My niece is just speaking her mind. And I like that in a girl. You should be happy she won't grow up to be one of those balls breaking babes that make you guess why they're pissed at you."

Joanna shoots both of them a look.

"Agnes May McClellan," Tommy says to his daughter, "please cut me a break before your mother throws me and your Uncle Matty out in the street. Everyone in this here room knows Zarro isn't a son-of-a-bitch, so there's no pressing need to mention it every single time you run into the guy."

"Uncle Matty teached me a song when we were playing cards," the little girl says to Zarro.

"You mean when you were trying to *cheat* him at cards," her father adds.

"That's only because he was trying to cheat me," Aggie counters.

"Anyways, you sure you want to sing that for company?" her father asks, wisely walking his daughter a few yards away from his wife.

"Yes, because it's funny." Aggie begins marching around the living room, her fuzzy pink slippers tapping a beat against the hardwood floors. "Sal-va-tion Ar-r-my. Sal-va-tion Ar-r-my. Put a nic-kel in the drum. Help another stink-in' bum...."

Matty, joins in loudly from the kitchen. He grabs two Heinekens from the refrigerator and tosses one over to Zarro.

"Hey, what about me?" Trudy's husband Billy shouts over the duet.

"Put a nic-kel in the drum. Help another stink-in' bum," Matty echoes his niece.

Zarro watches this, amused, then he happens to catch Joanna's disappointed expression from the kitchen. He figures Matty hates to upset her in any way, because he knows how much he genuinely likes Jo. They both agree there is nothing *not* to like about Jo. And not that it is saying much, but she treats Matty *far* better than his own brother does.

Matty must have seen her expression, too. He says, "Can it Aggie. Your mother's gonna stick you in bed early if you don't put a sock in it." Then he turns his attention to his stepfather as he hands Zarro the beer. "Two hands, one butt. And that guy you're sitting next to is my boss, so go help yourself." He pops the top off the Heineken. "Besides, that tip you gave me on Sapphire's Reward didn't pan out the way you told me it would, did it? Now I gotta scratch 'til Banker Brother throws me a couple of pennies outta my next paycheck, so thanks a lot for nothin'."

Matty turns to Zarro. "You feeling better now?" he asks. "I never seen you like that."

"Just peachy, thanks for asking." And then, not wanting to be part of another family feud nor a Matty McClellan counseling session, he walks over to Trudy and gives her a congratulatory kiss. "Can I bring the grandma some coffee?"

"Sit down, Robert. You don't have to do that," Trudy says. "And when I get up, can I cut you off a piece of that foot-long on the table?"

"You stay where you are. I'd like to serve you for once," he says, thinking it is good to see the waitress off her feet. Thinking it is good to put a little distance between him and

227

Maggie. After he awoke from a two-hour sleep where his dreams spun around his head like a carousel gone haywire, they had an abysmal dinner. It couldn't have been the food, because he didn't recall actually tasting a bite of it, his stomach queasy from his prior indulgences. It was the two of them, uncomfortable, awkward, their conversation of the morning hanging between them like a thick mass of tropical humidity.

"Ain't that sweet, Billy? He wants to *serve* me. I'm telling you, his mother in Boston who looks just like me raised him right. I wonder just where it is you find sons like that. Jesus, get this goddamn cat off of me. Fifteen people in a room, and that slimy thing has to find me. And she leaves me dead mice on the doormat. It's disgusting. You hear that, Tommy? That evil cat of yours is leaving me presents."

"Yeah Ma, I took her around the building and showed her which apartment was yours. Don't mention it."

"Don't get yourself too used to being served, Trudy. Not in your line of work." Billy says, tossing Minnew gently onto the polished hardwood floor, the cat landing on the pink pads of its feet with a dull thump.

Then Trudy's husband turns to Zarro and says, "By the way, thanks for letting me park my limo in the garage a while back. Thank God I won't be needing to do that no more. The repo man can go hunt down someone else." His eyes sweep the room. "Hey Solly, you driving for Rainbow Cars tonight?"

Joanna's father nods. "I gotta leave in an hour. You?"

"Light night, just a quickie at Kennedy. Run some executive broad into the City. Saturday I got a full day. I'm doing a wedding party out on Long Island. And I'm telling you, Solly, sometimes they're worse than proms. So if you happen to see me Sunday morning scrubbing puke out the backseat, you'll know how it went."

228

Sol Barron settles deeper into his recliner. "If I were you, I'd sell the limo and drive car service. You don't have all that glamour but it's way less aggravation."

Zarro hands Trudy her coffee. Then he sits down next to Matty on the sofa, Matty gulping his cold beer, Zarro taking a couple of half—sips just to be social. They are talking about nothing in particular when little Sally Elizabeth starts to fuss. As if none of them had ever heard a new baby cry, all conversation in the room comes to a halt as Tommy parts the starched white netting that comes between him and the infant. He picks up a cloth diaper and throws it over his left shoulder. Then in fascination, they watch as he leans over the cradle, picks up his new daughter, and gently places her on his shoulder. Like the pro that he is, he begins to pat the baby's back, his chin nestling against the dark down of his daughter's little head.

It is Trudy who breaks the silence with, "Ah, look how cute she is." And with that utterance, the company goes back to whatever conversation they had neglected to finish, all the company with the exception of Robert Zarro, that is.

Robert Zarro continues to watch the baby take comfort in her father's capable arms. And as he hears Sally Elizabeth's little kitten cries subside into contented breaths, a peculiar inverse reaction takes place within him. Zarro fills up with immeasurable sadness. As strange as it is, he seems to be absorbing any discomfort or anxiety the detective has dispelled in his little daughter. Zarro cannot understand what is happening to him; he can only feel it. He realizes he has to leave the room. So he places his barely touched beer down on a coaster and makes a hasty excuse to get out of there.

*　*　*　*　*

Twenty minutes later, Tommy hands over his new daughter to a very willing Grandpa Sol, and joins Maggie and chats with her for a while. Then he turns to his wife, whispers something in her ear, and exits the apartment building in search of Zarro.

The detective starts his car, all the while cursing the emperor of Japan and all his subjects when the defroster yet again fails to do its job. He swipes at his windshield with an old towel that he keeps on the floor just for that purpose, and when partial visibility is attained, he drives up Queens Boulevard and double-parks in front of Buckley's. He is known in Buckley's, and in every other business in the neighborhood. People don't hesitate to pull him aside in order to stop and chat with him. But always the cop, his eyes scan up and down the Friday night crowd as he makes idle conversation. His friend, however, is nowhere in sight. Then he stops thinking like Tommy McClellan and starts thinking like Robert Zarro. And based on personal experience, he knows Robert Zarro is not a serious drinker. He drives to Zarro's apartment, but he comes up empty as well.

He is about to get back into his car, when he notices a pale yellow light radiating from the narrow windows above Schwab's garage. He tries the handle on the warehouse entrance and sure enough, it is unlocked. He finds Zarro leaning over the shipping table, placing blister packed stock into large cartons, the radio blasting lively Spanish music onto an empty floor.

"Rackin' up the overtime, pally?" the detective asks.

"There's no overtime for managers. I don't punch a clock."

"Then what the hell are you doing here, Zarro? One minute you're at my place nursing a Heineken and the next minute you're packing stock here at Schwab's."

230

"I came here to be alone, so do me a favor and leave me alone, okay?"

"No, *not* okay." the detective says, lowering the volume on the radio. "I'm *not* going to leave you alone. Just like you tracked me down and stayed with me when my busted up hand was in an ice bucket, I hunted you down and like it or not, I'm gonna stay with you. And fondest regards from Patti, that's P-A-T-T-I the waitress in Buckley's, not P-A-D-D-Y the Friday night bouncer. Hope you're aware she's Pete-the-bartender's eldest daughter, his very pride and joy. My brother Matty sees her now and then, up and down, in and out. You get the picture, right?"

"I get the picture."

" And Matty was sure to tell me all about the gold stud she wears in that very special place. I swear, if that ain't the sweetest thing, the two of youse sharing the same girl. Now, how do you like that? Matty, Patti, and Zarro. You got to admit, it has a real nice ring."

"Excuse me for a second while I go throw up." He would have liked to forget all about P-A-T-T-I the waitress. That gold stud in her special place definitely abraded him in *his* goddamn special place. He didn't notice it right away either, but by the next morning he was not a happy camper.

"Anyways, when I asked if she seen you she said no, but I should be sure to ask you if in your travels you happened to come across her pair of extra lucky tiger striped panties," McClellan says and smirks.

"You can tell her they weren't so goddamned lucky. Maggie found them and I had to make a nice three point shot with them right into the trash."

"You paint a real pretty picture there, Zarro. If things wash out at Schwab's, you could always do the Knicks' play by play."

231

"You must mean the Celtics, don't you?" he says, annoyed and turning his attention to his work.

"All right, Zarro. But if you don't mind, I'm gonna have my last cigarette of the day, Tommy says. "I promised my wife I wouldn't go above half a pack, and you know I take my promises seriously."

Zarro doesn't say anything after that, and neither does the detective. He realizes that if Zarro wanted to talk, he'd talk. But standing and doing nothing doesn't come naturally to Thomas Patrick McClellan. With a lit Newport dangling from his mouth, he begins to lay the finished orders into cartons, much in the same way Zarro is doing.

"Ah, why don't you just go ahead and say it already? I know why you're here and I'm ready for your best shot. So fire away. 'Zarro you great guinea wop, you couldn't even make a baby.' Go ahead. Get your laughs in, McClellan. I couldn't even knock her up right."

"You must be hurting real bad, Zarro," he says, pausing to take a drag. "And I know I'm one sorry excuse for a human being, but normally I don't kick a man when he's down."

Zarro glances up from the carton. "You know what Maggie said to me? She said, 'You married me for nothing, Roberto. You felt sorry for me. We made a mistake and we had to have a make-believe marriage because you didn't want me to be alone. And you wanted me to have health benefits for the baby.' That's where her head is. We have no reason to be married, now."

"Well? Is she wrong?"

"Not really. It *was* a make-believe marriage. I *did* want her to have insurance for the baby. I *did* want her to get her green card."

"Yeah?" The detective pushes a button to cut a pre-measured length of shipping tape. "So what are you saying to me here, Zarro?" he asks, sticking the cigarette back into his mouth so he can smooth the tape over the seams on Zarro's carton with two free hands.

"You don't know what she's been through. American soldiers raped her when she was no more than a kid. And then her father threw her out of the house when he found out she was pregnant. She gave birth to the baby but she wanted to get away. Wanted to start over. Just like me. So she takes this baby, and boards buses, cars, overstuffed vans and makes this grueling trip to Honduras, then Mexico, and then over the border to Texas. Only the baby didn't survive the trip. It dehydrated. She buried him at a rest stop. At a fuckin' rest stop."

"That sucks. I'm sorry to hear that."

"But wait. Then she comes to New York and has the good fortune to meet me. A drug dealing ex-con who at least knew enough not to touch her. Until one night, one night when his prison nightmares came to life, the brutality playing over and over. And this girl came into his bed and comforted him and brought him back to life. She chased those horrible dreams away. And after she spent the night holding him in her arms, what does he do the following morning? He tells her it was all a mistake and throws her out of his house and into the arms of the gang."

Tommy says quietly, "On account he was scared. He was scared because he bared his soul to her. And he felt real exposed. Because when you're exposed you can't be in control. And where you spent the last three years, you needed to be in control. So you backed away. Oh, I know just what you're about, Zarro. The Job puts me there, too. And I fight *there* every fuckin' day of my life."

233

"You know what I was doing when she left me?" Zarro asks. "When she was risking her life to be part of a botched Federal investigation? I was out there doing my very best to forget her, humping every girl in sight."

The detective shakes his head. "Don't go beating yourself up about that. You didn't know what her situation was then. Besides, a guy acting like a jerk is a rite of passage, like pissing your name in the snow."

"Me acting like a jerk doesn't quite describe how I treated her." Zarro slams his hand down on the packing table. "I turned my back on her after she had given herself to me. But you know something? I actually *wanted* that baby. Maybe not at first, but then when I got used to the idea, I was looking forward to it. Because having a baby means having a future. Having a baby means you don't just have a stinking lousy past that you have to lie about, and cover up with bullshit. But God must have looked down and said, 'Not so fast, Zarro.' Well, I can understand it. I did some pretty fucked up things in my life. I brought shame onto my family. I know *I* should be punished. But why her? What did she ever do but totally give herself to me? And yet she keeps going on. Day after day, she picks herself up, dusts herself off and starts fresh every day. I wish I had an ounce of her strength, I really do."

"Did you tell her any of this? Did you ever sit her down and tell her what she means to you?"

Zarro grabs another box and begins filling it with officers' Marine Corp garrison cap devices. "Oh, it's too late now. Her bags are packed. She's leaving first thing tomorrow morning. *Adios* Roberto. Our make-believe marriage in the City of New York is history, as far as she's concerned. She can't wait to testify against Rafael Guzman. Wants the F.B.I. to give her a

234

new name and a new identity. Wants to be someone in this great country of ours."

The detective throws the remainder of his cigarette on the floor, crushing it under the heel of his sneaker. "Tell her what you said to me. Give her a reason to stay. I'm telling you Zarro, you need to keep an eye on her for now. You don't want her nowhere near this cluster fuck of an investigation."

Zarro shakes his head, fast. "It's too late. She had it out with me this morning, in front of the whole place. She's disgusted with me, fed up with her life. We're history."

The telephone rings, its sound piercing the night quiet of the warehouse. "Who the hell could *that* be?" Zarro wonders out loud.

"Sit tight," Tommy says, walking down the hill into Zarro's back office.

"Schwab's," he answers cheerfully. Then he pauses. "Sure, this is Lowery Bakery. You want *what*?" He pauses again, a big grin spreading around his face. "For you, not a problem." Then, "Anything else?" And finally, "Thank you for your order. Have a good night, now."

"What's that all about?" Zarro asks when the detective emerges wearing a wicked smile.

"Some space cadet from a catering hall thinking this is Lowery Bakery. You know, I could really get to love working here. I just took down an order for six dozen Kaiser rolls, so get right on it, pally. They need 'em by five a.m."

"Seeded or unseeded?" Zarro asks glumly.

"Come on Zarro, let's book before Schwab has to put me on the payroll."

"Give me a second. Just throw over that box of Purple Heart ribbons. Yeah, that's right Sherlock, they're the purple

235

ones. Look, I'm sorry for ruining your night. I took you away from your family, Jo's family."

"Our whole family rents in that building. I see them every day whether I want to or not. Anyways, I got people up my ass all week. We got Jo's know-it-all sister Arlene and her two spoiled brats heading in from Jersey tomorrow in their minivan. Then I'm hosting twenty thirsty cops on Sunday, and half of them guys are serious Emerald Society drinkers. Rumor has it I might actually see my sister, too. And that's a real honor, Zarro, 'cause Princess Teresa Ann don't leave Manhattan too often, unless it's to fly to London or Barcelona."

"Your baby is beautiful. You-you and Jo make such pretty kids." Zarro says softly, trembling, wiping a tear on his sleeve, and turning his head to conceal his sorrow. "I'm sorry. I—"

"Easy there, boyo. I got a hunch you and Maggie will have pretty kids, too. And you know my hunches are always on the money."

"No way it's ever going to happen for me. Inside I'm rotten, ugly, and dead. Of course my kid dies before it's even born."

"Listen to me now. Get yourself home," the detective says to Zarro. "Hang the guilt you're walking around with in the closet, pour yourself a stiff drink and pull yourself together. I'll walk your *seniorita* home in a little while. My car's parked in front of your house so why don't I leave it there for now and drive it back after I drop her off?"

"Thanks. I…I don't have too many friends, not since—" Zarro grips the sides of the shipping table. He tries as hard as he can to stifle his sobs, again pivoting his entire body to conceal week's worth of emotion that is finally overpowering him. "I'm sorry…I'm losing it…"

236

The detective puts his hand on Zarro's back. "Shh. Rob, everything is going to be alright."

"I'm just trying to h-hold it together at the job, at home. I'm trying to keep everyone employed. All around I'm so goddamn over my head." Zarro pulls away from his friend and wipes his eyes with the bottom of his T-shirt. "And now I have to worry that my soon to be ex-wife is going to be snatched off the street by the F.B.I, and tossed in Witness Protections where either I'll never get to see her or she'll be killed because she knows too much. I can't lose her. You might as well drain the blood from my veins."

The detective produces a pressed white handkerchief from the pocket of his jeans and hands it to Zarro.

"And today I fucked up," Zarro says, wiping his eyes. "Mel, God rest his soul, would have been disappointed in me big time."

"Hey, even a saint like Mel took a good belt of his schnapps now and then on Schwab's clock."

"I'm not talking a sip here. I got good and wasted on the job. I raided your brother's stash and smoked it down, right in front of him. Topped it off with Southern Comfort. And Matty of all people trying to stop me, begging me actually, and me getting high scaring the crap out of him. I rocked his predictable little world where he gets to screw up and I get to bust him."

"Yeah, Matty told me. He was real worried about you."

"I'm real worried 'about me too. Look at me. I'm a friggin' basket case." Zarro tries to steady his breathing. He brings the handkerchief to his face again and cleans away any remnants of his remaining tears.

* * * * *

237

Tommy leaves him alone for awhile, and Zarro continues to wipe his eyes, clean his face. He smells menthol in the clean white cloth, menthol from Tommy's pack of Newports. The scent sweeps him home to his childhood, a long ago ride on the Blue Line with his Grandpa Scioffo, a menthol-tinged white handkerchief having been extracted from the depths of a trouser pocket jingling with change, ready to dab a trail of chocolate ice cream from Zarro's six year old face. 'You say nothing to your *nonna*, eh? She no like you eat ice cream before supper.' Unwanted tears form in the corners of his eyes again, the memory becoming a conduit for years of underlying sorrow, guilt, and regret. Grandpa Scioffo is dead. Nanny Scioffo is dead. And he didn't shed one tear at their funeral, not one. His folks called him at college, broke the news. Bus crash they kept saying. Bus crash. The drive to Revere, the wake with two closed coffins. Oh, he dosed himself real good for the funeral. Shock, his family must have thought. Poor Robbie, he's taking it so bad, it's like he's not even here.

Zarro looks around for Tommy, and sees him nearby, in the shadows. "I don't know what's happening inside," Zarro says, and chokes a bit. "It just sort of hit me, my grandparents are dead, the grandparents on my mother's side. They were killed in a bus crash."

"Jeez, when did that go down?" Tommy says, coming back to Zarro's side.

"Years ago. And...and it's hitting me, all of a sudden, right smack in my face," he says bringing the handkerchief to his eyes again.

"It's reaching you now because you can deal with it now. It's them giving you a sign from heaven above that you're up for it."

238

"I'm not up for much of anything," Zarro says, trying his best to blink back his tears.

The detective's hand lands on Zarro's trembling shoulder. As if instinctively, he begins patting Zarro gently on the back, much in the way he did with his baby daughter earlier that evening. "Come on, let it all out, boyo. You let it out."

And after Zarro had a good let-go and the detective is assured that Zarro is somewhat composed, the detective seems to snap back into his ordinary everyday demeanor. "Jesus Christ, quit sniffing already and give that leaky faucet of yours a good blow," Tommy commands. "No need to be shy. Believe me, the twenty-year old Maytag in my building sure ain't smart enough to know the difference between your snot and mine. And Zarro, as long as us two are close enough to be mixing up our body fluids, let's get one thing straight. I have heard all I ever want to hear about this make-believe wedding bullshit. Get yourself home and make this right with Maggie, forthwith. I want to dance with my Jo at a real wedding. And I'll tell you what. I'll even make that boring as shit drive up the Pike for an open bar and a plate of fried guinea rubber bands."

"Calamari," Zarro says quietly into the handkerchief. "And it's a good thing I like you." Zarro suddenly straightens and looks directly at Tommy. "Holy shit, what time is it?"

"Eleven twenty. Why? You got a bus to catch?"

"You might want to alert your good friends at the F.B.I. that in forty minutes their white van that's staked out near that park on Knickerbocker will be visited by Rafael Guzman and company."

"What the fuck are you talking about?"

"Guzman might be under the impression there are some drugs for the taking."

239

"Drugs? Zarro, go on home, before I murder you. Didn't I expressly tell you *not* to get involved?"

After Zarro locks up, Detective McClellan calls Detective Milagros Santiago. "Bad news, Millie. Just heard the NYPD reinstated the height requirement."

"What do you want, McClellan?"

"The proverbial shit has hit the proverbial fan. And if you want to look like a hero, get your taskforce to that park over on Knickerbocker forthwith because the Salvadorians are about to hold up the F.B.I. van"

"Why would they do that?"

"Millie, no time for explanations. Get on it. We'll talk later."

Chapter Twenty-Five

When Zarro enters the hallway of Rose Petruzzi's house, there are raised voices coming out of Louise's apartment, and a deep gurgling sound as well.

"Ma, I'm telling you he didn't mean it," Louise shouts at her mother. "It was an accident."

"What kind of a kid is he, Lou-Lou?" Rose yells back. "Eleven years old and he does something stupid like that?"

Zarro knocks on Louise's door. "You ladies okay? I thought for sure you'd be over at Tommy and Jo's tonight."

"I definitely would've been there," Louise explains, "except for our little water problem."

"Little water problem? Does this look like a *little* water problem? Four inches on the bathroom floor. My grandson Frankie flushed his brother's diaper down the toilet. We're flooding, Robert Zarro. Flooding!" Rose yells at him.

"Did you shut the water?" Zarro asks.

"Of course. Do you think I'm helpless, Robert Zarro?" Rose squints at him through her black glasses. "I know the plumbing in this house better than I knew my late husband's hairy coulie."

Hector arrives from the basement carrying a plunger. "Here, I found it."

"No, you idiot, I want the snake," Rose shouts at him. "S-N-A-K-E, she spells. "Don't Cubans know what snakes are?"

"Ma," Louise fires back. "Don't talk to Hector like that."

"It's okay," Hector says to Louise. "She's an old lady. A crazy old lady." He starts talking to himself in Spanish, Zarro listening in fascination to the live and in color version of "I Love Lucy" that is being played out right before his eyes.

Rose grabs the plunger out of his hands. "I'm a crazy old lady? Is that what you said? I'll show you what a crazy old lady can do." She takes a good swing and hits Hector on the shoulder with the business end of the plunger. "That kid of yours is an ab-so-lute devil. Imagine flushing a diaper? And not just any cheap supermarket diaper. Oh no, my fancy daughter Louise has to buy top-of-the-line Pampers. That's worse on the pipes than a sanitary napkin and two-ply toilet paper glued together."

"You need help?" Zarro asks.

"Are you kidding? Floods are the ab-so-lute highlight of my mother's life," Louise says.

"Enjoy then," Zarro says, closing Louise's door behind him.

By twelve-thirty, Maggie returns to the house, escorted by Tommy McClellan. "You're married to a good man," he says to her as she fumbles around for her keys. "The salt of the Earth."

"Yes. I always say Roberto is a fine man."

"And that big blond *goombah* is head over heels crazy about you."

242

"I don't understand."

"Crazy. *Loco. Loco* in the *coco* for you."

"No," Maggie says. "Now *you* don't understand."

"I do *so* understand," the detective insists. "He just spent an hour making me understand. He loves you a lot, Maggie. And I hope you give him a chance to work up the courage to tell you."

"Courage? Big, strong Roberto is not afraid of nothing. He take my lawyer by the neck and he almost choke Mr. Quinones to his death. He yell at the boss Rick Schwabs. All the time they fight so very loud. No, he is not afraid of nothing and nobody."

"Except for one thing, Maggie. He's afraid to lose the one person he loves. You."

Maggie ignores his words and changes the subject. "Please tell me why is Rafael Guzman still a free man."

"That's not your worry."

"It *is* my worry. He killed my friends. I had Myrna's blood on my blouse. And he was laughing with his gold teeth. Laughing because he thinks I am scared to say something. So, I am ready to go to the F.B.I. and be a witness. I am ready to get a new identity. And live far away in Florida with a new name for me."

"I like Maggie O. Zarro. Has a nice Irish ring to it." The detective does not have the heart to tell Maggie that the Department of Justice will not give her a new identity. In order to get a new identity Maggie would need an *old* identity. And right now, she has *no* identity. When the D.O.J. is done with her, Maggie would be thrown to the wolves.

She unlocks the door and thanks the detective for walking her home.

"Promise me you'll sit tight on this F.B.I. business. Don't make a move until you hear from me."

"Why?"

"Because I'm the good *Policía.* That's why. "Promise?"

"I promise."

"Now, remember what I said about Roberto."

"Yes, Roberto is *loco* in the *coco* for Maggie. But I don't think so. He tell me all the time we are a big mistake."

The detective picks up his cell. For the second time that night, he calls Detective Milagros Santiago. "Talk to me."

"It's a toss-up as to who was more surprised," she says. "Special Agents Dumb and Dumber who probably shit their pants or the clique of fifteen who showed up with assault weapons, not exactly expecting an F.B.I. greeting."

"Everyone in one piece?"

"Yeah. Thanks for the heads up. We booked them on gun possession. Wanna tell me what the hell this is about?"

"When I know, you'll know."

Zarro is sitting in the dark, when Maggie walks in. "Are they still at it downstairs?" he asks.

"Do you want me to put the light on?"

"No, leave it dark and sit down next to me."

Maggie sits down on the opposite side of the denim pullout couch. "Miss Rose is pushing a snake. S-enay-A-K-E. That is what she say. And then she say don't put on the water because she shut the main. She say Robert Zarro can take his cold shower in the morning after the plumber come."

"How in all hell does Rose know that I take cold showers?" he asks, picking up his head and resting it against the back of the sofa.

"She say when the old tenant live here and she hear his shower, she cannot shower because the hot water all go away. But when Robert Zarro turn on the shower, Miss Rose can take a shower *no problema.* The hot water is there still. This is good, Miss Rose tell me. But she wants to know why a big, strong, Italian married man need to take only a cold shower. I don't know what to say to Miss Rose. She doesn't know nothing about the make-believe marriage in the City of New York. And she will be surprised, how you say, shock when I go away tomorrow."

"Well Maggie, the last thing in this world I want to do is shock Rose. Rose is a nice lady and an excellent cook. As it just so happens, her linguini in clam sauce brought tears to my eyes—that's how good it was. Can you see my wet face? Come closer. Give me your hand. Feel it. That's why I'm sitting here all alone in the dark. I'm thinking about Rose's linguini in clam sauce. So, give it some time and run it around in your mind. I really think you should stay."

"For Miss Rose and the clam sauce?"

"Yeah Maggie, for Miss Rose and the clam sauce. And for me."

"Why for you?'

"Because."

"Because is not an answer. You say that all the time."

"Because I love you, Maggie. And nothing I ever had with you was a mistake. The only mistake was me running scared from myself. When I sent you packing, I convinced

245

myself I could live without you. I needed you bad that night and it scared the hell out of me 'cause I didn't want to need anyone. Then I did everything I could to forget you. I spent time in a lot of beds, but every face I saw was yours. And every touch was yours. And I know you have every right being angry with me, but I want *you*, Maggie. Just you. I'm…I'm not too good at this talking thing. I used to be, before they sent me away. But not now. I'm no good at it now. When you lost the baby, I didn't know what to say. I should have held you, done something, said something. And…even now I don't have a clue what words I need to say to get you to stay here with me. But please, please Maggie, don't go."

As her eyes adjust to the darkness, she sees he is trembling and Maggie tries to calm him down. "Okay, Roberto, I understand. You don't have to say any more. I know many times it's not easy for you to talk. But your eyes tell me, and all the time I understand your eyes. And I'm sorry I say those things at work today."

"I bought you something, back when you told me about your little boy. Only I didn't know how to give it to you because I'm afraid. So it's sitting inside my room all these weeks."

"Why are you afraid to give something to me?'

"Because I'm afraid it's the wrong thing. I'm afraid you'll give it back to me. Tell me I got no right in hell giving this to you. And that would hurt. And I might look big and strong, but I really don't have the strength to go through another round of hurt."

"I would never hurt you, I promise. I love you all the time. I love you when you take me home when the house was on fire, but you keep pushing me away. Why you do this?"

"Because I really don't know how to live like a regular person. I have to learn all over again. You need to be patient

246

with me. I'm so screwed up." Guided only by the beam from the street lamp outside his window, he goes into his room and locates a small black velvet box. "I remember how you said you kept a little bit of the baby's hair. Here. This is for you."

Maggie opens the box and studies the contents. A gold heart lay on the bed of black velvet. "Oh Roberto, it's so beautiful. How you call it?"

"It's a locket. You can keep the hair inside. See, it opens."

Her eyes adjusted to darkness, Maggie gets up and opens her borrowed suitcase. She ran her hands around the bottom, locating a frayed envelope. Gently, she unfolds the brittle flap of the envelope and carefully takes out the scattered wisps of Sergio's hair. She holds the small, fine strands up to Zarro. "See, blond just like yours. Roberto, I feel when we lose our baby, I lose Sergio again, too. All I have is empty in me. And that empty make me angry sometimes. I do not mean to be angry today."

He watches as she places the baby's hair inside the locket. Then she tests the fastener and when she is satisfied, slips the gold chain around her neck.

"I could have been a father to your baby, too. I'm real sorry I didn't get the chance."

"And I'm so sorry what happened to you when you were another man that I don't know." "Oh Maggie, that other man you don't *want* to know."

Maggie reaches for Zarro's hand. "And you do some very good things. Inside of us are many different people who come out. I have other people in me too, 'berto. Not every Maggie is the sewing Maggie or the Maggie who pulls brass chevrons from the big shelf."

"Tell me about those other Maggies."

Maggie draws a deep breath. "Well, there's the Maggie who want to go to the school at night like Tommy's wife Joanna

247

because I go to school in Leon and I win the poetry award from my teachers. It is called the Ruben Dario poetry certificate. I write for you a poem, too."

"Really?"

"Yes. It's called *La Luz de Mi Alma,* The Light of My Soul. It's about *los suenos triste,* your sad dreams and how you come to me in the night. I will have to work to say it in English for you to read it. But when the baby grow inside me I stop the school and the Maggie inside me want to go again to finish. And there's the Maggie who wants to learn to drive Roberto's car so she can go to Associated Supermarket all by herself and not ever have to hear Roberto say, 'Hurry up. I hate this goddamn place. If I ran Schwab's like they are running Associated, I would be collecting unemployment.'"

"You do me very well."

"And there's the Maggie who want to be a citizen after the green card so she can go to vote in the booth and be somebody here, somebody maybe who can work to help those little children with the glue because I don't forget them. And there's the sad Maggie who has a father in Leon who think she's a *puta* because a soldier make her pregnant. And there's the Maggie who is hurt by her mother because she not say nothing to defend her." She says this softly, her husky voice beckoning Zarro into her world.

"I haven't been very fair to you," Zarro tells her. "I shut you out. I tried to forget you. I'm only hoping it's not too late, but I want us to have a real marriage 'cause when I'm with you, I can find the strength inside me to be good. So what do you say Magaly Ocampo, will you give me one more chance to make this right?"

"You know I wait so long to hear that," she says. "And sometimes I never think you will say that to me. Ooh 'berto, this

248

is as good for me as for Rosa Salmaje on the TV. Except there are no horses and no beach." Then she leans over and kisses him on his damp cheek. "Oh, I almost forget to tell you, I see in the office Dr. Adair on Wednesday and he say we can resume relations."

"Now there's an expression you won't hear on that language program."

"Do you know what this means? Resume Relations? Because he explain it to me very good."

Zarro smiles. "No, Maggie. I don't have a goddamn clue about resume relations. I think you're going to have to show me. And show me nice and slow, so I catch on."

Maggie leans over and kisses him again, this time on his mouth. She runs her fingers across Zarro's chest and his newly warmed blood begins to course through his veins fast and hard. He feels himself healing, his soul warming up, turning it from gray back to pink. They are working up to a sweat when a loud knock at the door startles the both of them.

"Hey, anybody home?" Rose's voice shoots through the closed door.

"Shh," Zarro whispers to Maggie. "Don't answer her. She'll go away."

"Oh I know you're in there. I can hear the heavy breathing. And I just want to let you know, Robert Zarro, that it's not too late. Go ahead and take your cold shower. We don't have to wait for the plumber. I ran the snake all by myself."

"I don't want a cold shower," he says, loud. "What I really want to do is make love to my wife. And you standing at my door talking pipes is very much getting in the way."

"That is not nice to say to Miss Rose," Maggie whispers to Zarro.

"Not nice? Let me dive headfirst into that front loader bra and I'll show you what's not nice."

Maggie laughs. " 'berto, stop. Please. She can hear us."

"Robert Zarro," Rose says from the hall. "I just want to say one last thing. Please do not flush the rubber down the toilet. Hector made the mistake of doing that one time and that hard circle on the top must have caught on something—"

"Rose, with all due respect, get the *hell* away from my door."

"Okay Robert Zarro. Goodnight Maggie. You two have a nice time and we'll continue our little chat in the morning. I can ab-so-lute-ly remember what it's like to be young."

"Yeah, back when copper pipes were standard," Zarro mutters.

Chapter Twenty-Six

When Zarro exits his very hot shower Saturday morning, he finds Maggie at the stove over a frying pan about to crack some eggs. She has a small saucepan of broccoli on a low boil next to the frying pan and she is cutting pieces off a wedge of mozzarella cheese.

"I make you the eggs this morning. Just like your mother show me. You fold the cheese into the scrambled eggs. Next to the eggs go the broccoli and then you squeeze the juice of the lemon onto the broccoli."

Zarro sits down at the kitchen table. "Poetry, a night of good, sweet loving and a plate of eggs too. Who could have it better than me?"

Then Maggie leaves the stove for a minute and approaches Zarro with a pair of scissors. "Hold yourself still. I want to take a little piece of your hair and put it in the locket you buy for me. And I will take a little piece of my hair and put it in the locket, too. We will always be together next to my heart."

Zarro lets her snip a bit of his hair, still damp from the shower. Maggie can see he is moved beyond words, as the muscles in his jaw tense and his eyes turn crystalline. Finally he

251

says in a voice that is no more than a whisper, "Come on, we were talking eggs here, Maggie. Eggs."

"You sound just like Mr. Rick Schwabs. Remember when I was sewing on his sleeve. And he make me talk to his housekeeper without the name." Then Maggie goes back to the stove and returns with two plates.

Zarro tears into his eggs and broccoli. "Mmm. Once in a great while the boss is right. Darlin', you sure know your eggs."

Their new phone rings and Zarro picks it up. He likes having a landline. It gave him a sense of stability, a sense of home.

"Hey how did it go there, pally?" the voice on the other end asks.

"Real good Thomas," Zarro says washing a mouthful of eggs down with a swallow of hot coffee. "Beyond good. Incredibly good. I even got a plate of eggs and mozzarella out of the deal."

"Never mind your stomach. I'm looking for a wedding date, Zarro. A September wedding in Boston with Father Guido at St.Vinny's. And you know why September?"

"September's when I get vacation."

"To quote Oscar the Grouch, 'Ding dong you're wrong.'" September is when my wife gets the green light from Dr. Adair to resume relations. You know what that means?"

"As it just so happens, I had my own up close and personal demonstration last night. It's now my all time favorite phrase in the entire English language."

"Way to go Zarro, glad to see at least *you're* getting some. September. Picture it. Just me and Jo. A long weekend in a hotel with my two girls parked at Grandma Trudy's. No, eighty-six Grandma Trudy's. She wouldn't miss your wedding. For some strange reason my mother thinks you're the greatest thing since

252

sliced bread. Okay. September. Me and Jo. A long weekend in a hotel with my two girls parked at my know-it-all sister-in-law Arlene's. Me holding back a little so's not to pop Dr. Adair's last stitch. And by the way Zarro, I find that holding back a little can give you one sweet bang of a release."

"Thomas, you're getting me all hot and bothered."

"I love the way you say that, all hawt and bah-thered. Jesus, I could listen to you talk for days on end. Hang on a sec." Tommy sounds like he's got a hand over the receiver, and says to someone, "What are you blushing for? It's only Zarro on the line. There's no need for embarrassment. For Christ's sake Jo, the guy's family. Better than family on account he don't hit me up for cash every ten minutes."

Now Tommy's back on the line, loud and clear. "Oh yeah, Zarro, just one more thing before my wife throws a bowl of Frosted Flakes at my head. Don't make the wedding on the 18th because that's the Jewish New Year and we're hosting my family and Jo's for a brisket extravaganza."

"We live in a great country, don't we?" says Zarro. "Who would ever believe that Southy *baccala* brother of yours actually celebrates the Jewish New Year?"

"He celebrates the brisket, Zarro. The brisket."

"September. Any weekend but the 18th. Don't even say it. A plate of fried guinea rubber bands and an open bar." Zarro pauses and then says, "Be my best man, Thomas?"

"Come on Zarro, do the right thing. Give your little brother a chance to step up to the plate. What's his name? Elbow?"

"Nee."

"I knew it was one of them connective joints. I'm sure he'd love to be your best man. I'll usher for you though, no extra charge. Listen, many happy returns. Me and Jo were rooting for

253

you. And on that other situation, I'm pretty sure I figured out what you were thinking. Time will tell on that. But no way in hell it excuses what you did."

"It just might," he says and they say their goodbyes.

"That was Tommy McClellan, yes?" Maggie asks.

"None other. He wants us to have a real wedding in September. A real wedding up in Revere. What do you say, Maggie? Want to do it right this time?"

"Yes, Roberto. I like very much. Can I invite my friends from work? Suzie Q, Shirley Wong and Lygia?"

"Anyone you want."

"Louise and Hector? And even Miss Rose upstairs?"

"Especially Miss Rose. Just say the word and she'll be in Revere with His and Hers monogrammed plungers. You know, for the young couple who has everything, except decent plumbing."

"I always love you, Roberto."

Then Zarro leans back in his chair and put his legs up on the kitchen table. "Eggs, Maggie. Eggs. Tell the girl I like them runny. Mushy. Her name? I don't know her name. Just talk eggs."

Maggie laughs. "You do that so very good."

"Scary, isn't it?"

Chapter Twenty-Seven

The last two weeks in August are brutal. Zarro keeps the fans going non-stop but all they do is circulate thick, stifling air. Schwab's is busy and tempers all around are short. Zarro is nervous about his upcoming wedding. He's on his phone to his mother at least twice a day. For although he has insisted on footing the bill, the majority of the details fall into the lap of an overjoyed but overwhelmed Marie Zarro, who luckily has found a catering hall at the last second.

On a hot, humid Thursday evening after work, Zarro and Maggie take a stroll up Queen's Boulevard to Lester Gold Jewelers. Mr. Gold was long retired, having sold the store and its contents to a Korean couple who approached him one Saturday afternoon with a shopping bag brimming with hundred dollar bills. This enterprising couple has owned the store for years now, but decided from the very beginning to keep the original name, mistakenly thinking that Lester Gold meant a finer quality gold, perhaps confusing Lester with the word luster.

Maggie is very familiar to the husband and wife jewelers. They had replaced the battery on her watch once, and since that time she likes to browse in the small storefront whenever she takes a walk. If the owners happened to glance at her outside, they would always buzz her into the tiny store and she'd admire the various pieces on display. Maggie pockets her last two paychecks, less the amount she'd sent her mother, and to this she adds her latest windfall from the Bullshit Club as well as her earnings from the money she earns sewing. She presents this rubber-banded stack of bills to Zarro who is quite impressed. He hasn't seen such a neat wad of cash like that since his dope slinging days. "Jesus, Maggie, you didn't rob Citibank did you?" he asks.

"No, I save up the moneys so we can buy the wedding rings."

"I wish you would let me pay for them."

"No, you pay for everything else," Maggie insists. "I want to do this."

The young couple heads toward the jeweler's hand in hand. They walk east, passing the pool hall and the Corner Luncheonette where Trudy works her two shifts. Zarro approaches Gallagher's cautiously, quickening his step without even realizing it. It is still light outside when a tall, nearly naked woman flies out the door, almost knocking the young couple off the sidewalk. "Sorry," she says, not even looking at them. "Damn. Where did he go?"

Matty McClellan follows her up with a man's sports jacket, which she drapes around her shoulders without even bothering to button it closed. "Well, if it ain't Mr. and Mrs. Z out on the town," Matty says, returning to the doorway of the club.

256

"Howdy stranger," Dawn Costello addresses Zarro after she realizes just whom it is she has bumped into. "I plowed right into you, didn't I?"

"How's it going, Dawn?" Zarro asks, forcing his eyes away from those huge glimmering breasts that refused to be restrained by anything as unstructured as a jacket.

"Can't complain except for this last guy who—" She cuts herself off when she sees Maggie at Zarro's side. "Well, don't just stand there. Aren't you going to introduce me?"

"Sorry. Dawn, I'd like you to meet my wife Magaly."

At this point, Dawn clasps the two ends of the jacket together with her fingers to cover that which shimmers. "I would bet my take tonight that everyone calls you Maggie."

"That is right. How do you know this?" Maggie asks, altogether fascinated by the entire presence of Dawn Costello. In five-inch stiletto heels, she towers over Maggie. And the tips of the sunset reflecting off the coppery tones of Dawn's tresses is as blinding as the burning bush Moses encountered in his travels. The jacket Matty found, a jacket that a very slender patron had left in the club last winter just about covers enormous chest, likely leaving very little to Maggie's, or anyone's imagination. Zarro can't help but figure Maggie sees Dawn Costello as a sewing project in the making, darts to be let out, panels to be added. He hides his smile.

"Oh, there was this one night where your husband talked up a storm about you," Dawn says good-naturedly, elbowing Zarro in the ribs.

Maggie looks way up into Dawn's eyes. Zarro is looking too, and he can see that Dawn's eyes are kind. He glances at Maggie and thinks she sees it too.

Maggie says, "If you need someone to make for you the blouses bigger, I can sew. I do not live too far from this place. I

257

am not too much moneys." From the depths of her purse, she produces one of the business cards her Roberto had made up for her on the computer. "Maggie's Expert Alterations, All Sewing Done On Premesis."

"Thanks. You know I do need a few adjustments, now and then. A lot of the girls sew their own outfits, but I'm all thumbs."

Matty leans against the doorway and twists his grin around a fresh toothpick. "Man, you're *awfully* quiet tonight, boss," he says to Zarro who stands in front of Gallagher's, hands in his pockets, positively dumfounded.

"You dance in there?" Maggie asks Dawn. Just then, the door swings open, and the pulse of the music and an undercurrent of conversation flows out to the street.

"Yes. Exotic dancing. Would you like to come inside, check it out for yourself? You'd be surprised how many women enjoy the show."

"No," Matty and Zarro say simultaneously.

"Maybe some other time, then. I really should get back, anyway. Great meeting you, Maggie. I hope you realize you got yourself one nice guy there," she says, looking at Zarro. "And he's real sweet on you."

They walk on without talking, until they reach the door of Lester Diamond Jewelers. Maggie asks, " 'berto, you dance with this naked girl with the big shining chests?"

With the back of his hand, Zarro wipes a bead of sweat off his brow. "Dawn and I did the horizontal mambo once. But that was *way* before we were make-believe married. Oh look," he says changing the subject. "Lester Jewelers is having a CLARENCE Sale. We should stock up. Everyone can use a 'Clarence' or two, right Maggie?"

* * * * *

Before they go upstairs to their apartment, Zarro and
Maggie knock on Rose's door. Maggie is eager to show Miss
Rose, Hector and Louise the wedding bands. Hector and Frankie
are on the couch watching the Mets and Zarro joins them. Louise
and Rose stand under the kitchen light to examine the wedding
bands. "Be careful," Rose warns Maggie. "I once lost a wedding
band down the sink and I had to take the pipes apart."

"For my mother, it always comes down to pipes," Louise
says. "The rings are beautiful."

An insistent knocking at the front door interrupts their
conversation. Hector jumps up and peers out the window.
"Looks like cops."

Zarro joins Hector at the window. "Shit. It's the F.B.I.
They're after Maggie."

"Keep your mouth shut and let me take care of this,"
Rose says, going to the door. "Louise, hide Maggie in the closet.
You know the drill."

Maggie hesitates a minute. She would like nothing more
than to help put Rafael Guzman in jail, but she did promise
Tommy McClellan that she would wait for his instructions.
Reluctantly, she follows Louise to the hall closet.

The blood drains from Zarro's face. This is it. They're
done. His plan has not worked. Guzman is still out there and
Maggie will be taken from him. His heart pounds in his chest
and he is helpless.

Rose answers the door and looks up at the two men
through her thick, black glasses. "Whatever it is youse are
selling, I don't want none of it. I'm on a fixed income."

259

"I'm Special Agent Saunders," the heavier one says. This is Special Agent Whittaker from the F.B.I. We have a warrant to search these premises."

"Special agents want to search *my* premises?" Rose asks. "Like in the movies?"

"We're looking for a woman named Nancy Ayolla. It may be an alias."

Rose squints. "There must be some confusion. My sister-in-law is named Nancy. She used to live here, but she don't live here anymore."

"Where does she live now?'

"St. Charles cemetery on Long Island. She died two years ago."

"Then that's not the Nancy we're looking for." Special Agent Saunders takes out a picture of Maggie. Zarro remains paralyzed on the sofa. The ballgame drones on in the background.

The two agents walk into Rose's kitchen and begin opening cupboards. "Oh, why didn't you say she's a dwarf?" Rose asks. "I did see a dwarf on Roosevelt Avenue on Wednesday afternoon."

"She's not a dwarf, ma'am."

"If she can fit in the cabinet with my dishes, she must be a dwarf." And then Rose's tone changes. "I see you have a little eczema," she says to Officer Whittaker. "Roll up your sleeve. I'll put a little olive oil on it."

"No ma'am. That won't be necessary. Just let us execute the warrant."

"Oh, I insist," Rose says, ignoring the agent. She takes his arm and dabs a few drops of extra virgin olive oil on it. "It helped my late husband. You should tell your wife about this."

"Yes ma'am. Thank you." The agents go into the bedrooms and Rose follows them. Zarro looks at Hector and Hector mouths a "Don't worry."

"Who's in the apartment upstairs?" Agent Saunders asks, after they are finished in the bedrooms.

"Right now, no one," Rose answers, winking at Zarro.

"Unlock the door, please."

Rose frowns. "I have a bad ankle, you know. The stairs might be easy for you, but they're not easy for me. Come on Louise. Let's show him around. Louise has a baby who's asleep in their apartment. If you're quiet, I'll let you see him. And, we have a fig tree in the backyard. You wouldn't want to miss that. It came all the way from Italy."

When the four of them are on the way to Zarro's apartment, Zarro jumps off the sofa. "Hector, we got to get her out of here. She can hide in the backyard."

"No. They'll search the backyard. Let her stay where she is. They're finished down here."

Zarro hears their footsteps on the staircase. Apparently, there aren't any Nancys in his apartment or in the yard. They are back. Almost as an afterthought, Officer Whitaker flings open Rose's hall closet and starts moving coats around. Zarro springs up from the sofa, expecting the worst. But the closet is empty. Maggie has disappeared.

"Would the two of youse care for some biscotti?" Rose asks. "I like to dunk mine in a little red wine."

"No ma'am," Officer Saunders replies. "Thank you. We'll be on our way."

No one says a word until the agents' car pulls away.

"You were great, Ma," Louise says. "No one does crazy better than you."

"Now what's that supposed to mean?"

261

"Rose," Zarro interrupts. "Where the hell is Maggie?"

"There is ab-so-lute-ly no need for that language, Robert Zarro."

"What did you cast a Sicilian spell on her and make her invisible?"

"Louise, show him."

Louise lifts a frayed mat from the bottom of the hall closet. She picks up the floorboards and turns a crank, causing a narrow staircase to drop down to the cellar. "The cellar leads to a tunnel that goes under 39th Street and into the garage of Schwab's Uniform," Louise explains. "I gave Maggie a flashlight so she could see where she was going."

Zarro looks from Louise to Rose. The color slowly returns to his face. "Rose, why is there a tunnel to Schwab's Uniform?"

"When you moved in, remember I told you my grandfather built this house with his own two hands?"

"I remember."

"I never told you *who* my grandfather was, though."

"No, you didn't."

"He was a bootlegger. Partner of Izzy Einstein and Moe Smith from Astoria."

"Never heard of them."

"Well, trust me. They were big time back then," Rose says. "Made an ab-so-lute fortune."

"Why would they need to get into Schwab's?"

"Robert Zarro. Schwab's wasn't always Schwab's, you know. We're talking the nineteen twenties. It was a plain old warehouse. They had to store the booze somewhere, didn't they? Now go get Maggie and bring her home."

"If you don't mind, I'll get there by way of sidewalk. And by the way, thank you. I'll never forget what you did for me. For us."

"Don't mention it. You're *paysan*."

Zarro crosses the street and unlocks the warehouse. He follows the beam of light from Maggie's flashlight. "It's okay. They're gone."

"Oh 'berto, I have to crawl in the dark," Maggie says, falling into his arms. "It is wet and I see black bugs."

"I'm sorry. It must have been scary as all hell, but you're safe now."

"I come up from the floor."

"Show me."

Maggie walks to the very back of the warehouse where the old file cabinets are. She points to the circular drain cover on the floor. "This is where I come up."

"And here I thought I knew every inch of the place," Zarro says, amazed at this new discovery. "You had me worried to death, Nancy."

Chapter Twenty-Eight

Their wedding is less than a month away. And Zarro has taken it upon himself to deal with the complex logistics of transporting his staff, and hammering out the best price for the sleeping arrangements at a local motel. And then there's the matter of Maggie's safety. Guzman, in jail awaiting trial for a number of charges, including gun possession and racketeering, is still alive and Maggie is still very much at risk. With good reason, the F.B.I. would like nothing more than to put him away for arson and murder.

Somewhat oblivious to her own safety, Maggie's sewing machine drones on until eleven o'clock each night, because she is very insistent on sewing her own wedding dress and the bridesmaids' dresses, as well. The apartment bustles with Maggie's friends from Schwab's and the survivors from her old apartment, women who arrive and depart throughout the evenings, all but oblivious to Zarro's presence. Some nights, he runs downstairs to Hector and Louise's place, just to escape the din.

"I can't believe you come to our house for quiet," Hector says, puffing on a fat-looking hand-rolled Cuban cigar.

"Between the baby crying and Frankie blasting that stupid Nintendo, it's not exactly a library in here."

"There's no sewing machine that's aching for a muffler and there's no women from Schwab's traipsing around in their underwear. I can't find a goddamn place for myself there any more. And Maggie's using my set of weights to hang stuff on. I went to work out last night and this pink feathery thing landed on my face from out of nowhere, nearly scared the piss out of me. Hector my friend, you don't realize this but compared to my place, your apartment is like a retreat."

"Are you serious? They walk around in their bras and panties, upstairs?"

"I swear. And the craziest thing is, they don't even notice me, your wife included. It's like I'm invisible."

"Nice."

"This might sound great to you, but you don't understand. I work with most of these women every day. I really *don't* want to know what's going on under their clothes. Now I don't know where to put my eyes. I just don't get it. Here I thought women of a certain age are supposed to be somewhat shy about their bodies. Not these ladies from Schwab's. And some of them are old enough to be my mother. But there they are, strutting around upstairs like it's some high school locker room. I walked through the kitchen to get a drink half expecting any one of them to snap a towel at my ass."

"You know something Zarro, I would like to investigate this situation for myself," Hector says, going for the door. "So lead the way, *Primo*."

"I'm not going anywhere. I'll keep my man Frankie company. I'll be more than happy to kick his scrawny ass in Nintendo. You know what to do if your baby brother gets up, right?"

"Yep," Frankie answers without looking up from the screen. "Stick a bottle in his mouth. And if that don't work, check his diaper. If it's even remotely shitty, I'm handing the baby off to you, Zarro."

"Oh you think so? Fair is fair, Frankie. Where I come from loser always changes the shitty diaper. It's a Massachusetts State law, goes all the way back to colonial days."

"We're in New York, in case you didn't notice."

"Shut up and hand me a control. Lucky you, this fall I'm going to make it my business to teach you to play hockey."

"You like the Rangers, Zarro?" Frankie asks.

"No, I *hate* the Rangers. And when I get through with you, you're going to hate the Rangers, too."

"I am on my own, then," Hector says. "I keep the cigars in the refrigerator, Zarro, so you help yourself. These smokes are the real deal, all the way from *Habana*, courtesy of my Uncle Tirso. A hand-rolled cigar from *Habana*, a glass of rum, and you are good for the night, *Primo*."

Hector walks into the hallway toward Zarro's noisy apartment. "Open the door, sweetheart. Lou-Lou, you in there? Ho--ney, I'm ho--me!"

Chapter Twenty-Nine

Zarro isn't the only man on edge at Schwab's Uniform. Rick Schwab is also jumpy because that afternoon two high ranking officers from the Arab Maritime Academy of Alexandria, Egypt will arrive by limo in order to talk about a contract for jacket emblems and baseball caps for their school. Visions of dollar signs dance in Rick's head as he waits in his air-conditioned office, a pair of barely broken in Bali mocs gracing the top of the carved mahogany desk. He can taste this deal—that's how badly he wants it. All he needs are their signatures. True, they seemed amicable enough on the phone. But who could really know what these people are really thinking. They said they would arrive at one and here it was already two-thirty and still no Egyptians. But time mattered only in the western world, Rick reminds himself. One o'clock could mean five o'clock.

Meanwhile, Matty and his boys aren't ready for the UPS driver once again and side-by-side, they're all working fast and furious in shipping. It is so oppressively hot that Matty strips off his T-shirt, runs it under cold water and rubber bands it still dripping, to his sweaty head.

Zarro, a damp sweatband stretched across his own head, is so engrossed in his work he doesn't even look up when the garage door lifts and a sleek, white stretch limo with tinted windows pulls in, just missing Rick Schwab's silver Porsche. In mufti, the two Egyptian officers exit the limo, stretch their cramped limbs and square their posture. They are dressed in expensive western style suits, a silken *caffia* atop each head, the civilian clothing doing little to disguise their military bearing. One of the officers taps Matty on the shoulder and asks him in heavily accented English to speak to the venerable proprietor, a Mr. Rick Schwab.

Matty, looking up from his carton shouts, "Hey Weeds, get a load of these two towel heads." Then he turns his attention to the two perplexed men standing before him. "Well here's hoping the two of youse didn't block the UPS truck with your caravan of spittin' camels. Let me tell you, that UPS driver is a hump as it is."

With this Zarro quickly escorts the two men into Schwab's office. He is livid by the time he's back in shipping and physically pulls Matty away from a box. "Have you lost your fuckin' mind? Schwab's been waiting on the edge of his chair for these two. These guys have money jingling out of their butt cracks from what he told me. And now you go ahead and insult them? You don't think they might mention the loudmouth overly obnoxious hairy-chested pug nosed Irish ape with the wet shirt on his skull?"

"Sorry Zarro."

"To hell with sorry. Rick's already ripped me a new asshole today 'cause a couple of days ago one of you geniuses thought it would be great fun to blister pack a couple of dead

270

cockroaches alongside the general's cap devices and send them off to Fort Polk, no extra charge. It was *not* so funny when the store failed its inspection this morning because some visiting four-star tried to buy a cap device *without* a dead cockroach and couldn't find any for sale."

"Why are you blaming me? That was Spacious, excuse me, Roman done that. He's not exactly the brightest bulb, you know."

"Roman, huh? And tell me, just who put him up to it?" Matty grins.

"Jesus, Matty. I'm *still* on Rick's shit list for getting the illegals into the union. What are you out on some IRA mission to lose me my job?"

"It make me sick us doin' business with Arabs."

"Whether you like it or not, we participate in a global economy, Matty."

"What the fuck does that really mean?"

"It means we put a phony smile on our faces and do business with people we wouldn't normally sit down and have a beer with. We take their money graciously without insulting the piss out of them."

"I'm sorry, Zarro. You're right. It's been hot as hell back here for weeks. We're all half-dead, and I was trying to be funny. I didn't mean to get you in trouble. Chill out, okay?"

"I'll chill out the day you start using the brains God gave you."

Zarro returns to another carton and tapes it shut. Then he looks up at Matty and says, "Fuck it. I'm sitting down up front where it's air-conditioned. Get Manuel, Junior and Israel and come with me. Weeds, too. We'll all take a break. Only Matty, for the love of Christ, get that goddamned shirt off your head."

271

"Wait up. There's a carton here with your name on it." Matty wheels the huge carton over with a hand truck and deposits it at Zarro's feet.

"Screw it. There's *always* a carton here with my name on it. Leave it. I'll deal with it later."

"No, Zarro. Take a look, this is weird. The label says: Mel Lieb, in care of Robert Zarro, Warehouse King. No return address."

"I swear to God, there's no rest here. Mel Lieb, dead since Christmas and the poor old guy is *still* getting shipments. How about Elmo? Is there a package for him too? Dead or alive, you still have to pull your load. Jesus Matty, don't just stand there waiting for an engraved invitation. Open the goddamn thing already."

Matty slices open the box. It is topped with crumpled newspapers. Under the layers of paper is a large Styrofoam carton. "Damn, it's packed with dry ice. You don't know how I hate that stuff. It burns like a mother."

"Did you even *look* at the damned packing slip you thickheaded donkey?"

"Here we go. Hood Dairy. It's ice cream. Ten dozen Dixie cups. Look at that. They even packed the wooden sticks."

A slow grin begins spreading on Zarro's face. "I don't believe this. Your big brother is some piece of change. Those aren't Dixie cups, you idiot. Those are Hoodsies. God love the crazy bastard, Tommy sent us a carton of Hoodsies. He said he was sending a wedding gift. Toss one over, Matty boy."

Matty twirls the toothpick in his mouth. "Not so fast, boss. Don't you want me to inventory it on that state of the art piece of shit inventory control program of yours?"

"I got a better idea, wiseass."

272

Zarro picks up the phone and presses the button marked Intercom. "Attention ladies and gentlemen. Due to the incredible heat, for the next fifteen minutes, Schwab's Uniform will be having its first-ever Hoodsie break. Everyone report down to the packing tables. I repeat, we will be having a fifteen-minute Hoodsie break, courtesy of Matty's brother, Detective Thomas Patrick McClellan. Thank you and have a nice day."

Zarro wheels the carton down the hill and stands on a packing table. He hands out a hundred ice cream cups and sticks. Even Rick Schwab comes out of his office when he hears the commotion and joins his workers on the factory floor. The two Egyptians follow him and they too enjoy their Hoodsies very much. They even take two extras for the limo ride back to their hotel.

"You're completely out of your mind, Zarro," Rick Schwab says, "but I'm telling you these Hoodsies really hit the spot. Take a look. You've even made Marilyn Friedman smile for the first time since World War Two."

"Hey, it's great to be king."

"That's my line."

"You may be royalty up front, but this here is *my* kingdom out back."

Maggie joins her husband who is standing next to Rick Schwab. When she finishes her ice cream she says, "I like the Hood-sie very much, Roberto. It is very good."

Zarro bends down, lifts the gold chain from Maggie's locket, and tenderly kisses the part of her neck that is exposed by her ponytail. And as he watches her return to work, Zarro's mind goes on a journey. An image of him and Maggie in the claw-footed bathtub edges into a corner of his head and it remains there in all its glory until Rick Schwab breaks through

273

his reverie. "Wipe those evil thoughts away. On your very first day I warned you to keep your hands off the merchandise."

"Can't help myself. A native New Yorker like you wouldn't know this but these Hoodsies are packed with powerful aphrodisiacs. You better warn Mrs. Schwab what she's in for tonight. I'll go out on a limb here, Rick, and say you could probably squeak by without the Viagra."

"I don't need Viagra, you obnoxious prick. Besides, Mrs. Schwab has been on automatic pilot since I can't remember when." Then Rick lowers his voice, "Zarro, rumor has it you mentioned to the people on the floor during yesterday's lunch break that you served time? Is that rumor correct?"

Yes, he did mention it. Yesterday, they had all gathered during lunch to celebrate an embroiderer's upcoming retirement. The woman had embroidered at Schwab's Uniform for fifty-two years. At seventy-two years old, Despina Sarapopolus decided to pack in her needles and thread. Zarro had Marilyn Friedman buy a couple of sheet cakes from Lowery Bakery, and the entire warehouse gave her a fond farewell. Despina was a small, frail woman. Her back was hunched over and she could see not more than two feet in front of her. Fifty-two years of handling the wiry bullion thread had left the skin on her fingers shredded and her eyes nearly blind. Schwab's Uniform had used her up, ate away at her youth, sucked down her vitality, and left her a dry, brittle husk.

Zarro had placed a chair on a packing table and with one swift motion he lifted the tiny, old lady up so she could make a speech. He even coaxed Rick Schwab out of his office to hear Despina talk.

"I remember when you were a little boy," Despina said to Rick in a voice that crackled like a balled sheet of aluminum foil. "You used to sit on my lap and I taught you how to sew.

274

And even before that I worked for your grandfather," Despina told him. "Long, long time ago when Schwab's was on 28th and Lexington Avenue in the City. Do you remember your grandpa, Rick? He was a Jewish tailor. A lot of them from the needle trades were back then. And his name started out as long as mine, Adolph Schvartzenloch. He shortened it to Al Schwab before he died. Your grandpa taught me how to embroider. I started out on the machines, and then he tried me out hand-sewing. We worked piecework then, got paid for each item we sewed. But that made too many fights. Too much jealousy. One lady stabbed another lady in the neck with a pair of scissors. You don't know how lucky we all are the union put an end to it. Isn't it funny what you remember after so many years? But most of all I remember the friends I made, the ones who share this day with me and the ones who are here no more." The old lady pulled a tissue from her sleeve and dabbed at her eyes. "So many gone that I know. I'm the last one here, the last Greek sewer. My daughter works in a bank. And my granddaughter is studying to be a math teacher. So it ends with me. Your grandpa Mr. Schvartzenloch started for me a life in America with the needles and thread and now that life is coming to an end. And new people will have the opportunity to make America their home."

Rick's face reddened at the first mention of Adolph Schvartzenloch and scarlet it stayed for the remainder of Despina's speech. "The old woman has obviously lost her marbles along with her eyesight," he said, glowering at Zarro. "My grandfather was an entrepreneur, not a two-bit mockie tailor. Schvartzenloch? Where did she come up with that one? Maybe the old crone inhaled a little too much Benzine when she was cleaning the shoulder boards."

275

"Come on, Rick," Zarro whispered to his boss. "She's an old lady. Say something to her. After four o'clock you'll never have to see her again."

"Zarro, I'm late for an appointment," Rick told him. "And my appointment doesn't care to be kept waiting, if you catch my drift."

"Be a sport and take two minutes out of your life and thank her for her fifty-two years of faithful service," Zarro insisted. "She's been punching a clock here since they switched over from the sundial."

Rick managed to mumble a couple of words in the direction of the old woman before he headed toward the garage. He looked so incensed to have been put in this awkward position, that he seemed to take no notice of Matty on his way down lugging two industrial size jugs and a sleeve of paper cups. Marilyn Friedman began slicing the cake in small, rectangular pieces, handing the first piece to Despina.

"Yo, just what in God's name do you think you're doing?" Zarro asked Matty when the two huge jugs of some sort of hooch came into his line of sight.

"It's a celebration, boss," Matty said. "I keep some gin in one of the old file cabinets, just for festive occasions like this."

"Matty, for the love of Christ, do you really think at a seventy-eight year old Greek grandmother of seven wants to throw down a belt with her slice of devil's food cake?"

"She might Zarro, she might. I know *I* would if this was my last day."

Zarro considers this. "All right do your thing—but not more than an inch in each cup, Southy."

"So Despina," Matty said handing the old lady a paper cup with a thimbleful of gin at the bottom. "What are you gonna do with all that free time on your hands? Run down to Atlantic

276

City on the bus and park yourself at the nickel slots, with the rest of them senior citizens?"

"No Matthew, I am going to sleep until nine o'clock every morning."

"That's the life," Suzie Q said. "You go for it, girl. You stay snug in that bed of yours 'til nine-fifteen."

As people ate their cake and drank their gin, Zarro took the opportunity to inform the staff of the new orders coming in. He thanked them for working the extra hours. He said it in English and in his Revere version of Spanish that always brought a smile to everyone's face. For after a year at Schwab's he was able to speak a rudimentary version of Spanish. Between living with Maggie, the Telemundo, and the lyrics coming out of the radio eight hours a day, he had picked it up. He told them they should be proud of themselves for what they had accomplished. Many of them had sacrificed the hours they normally spent with their families to put in overtime at Schwab's. And then his eyes scanned the floor until he found Maggie's face, and while he was focusing on her, absorbing her strength, the words, 'I want all of you to know I spent some time in jail' ran from his mouth. The place became uncharacteristically quiet for a moment and extra talkative in the next.

He hadn't planned to divulge his past, but he felt a sense of relief after he said it, a sense of peace that he had nothing left to hide from the people he spent his days with.

The old lady, still seated up on the table exclaimed, "Jail you say? Robert, did you *kill* somebody?"

Zarro took a look over at Matty McClellan, now pouring great, overflowing cups of gin, sighed and said, "Not yet, Despina. Not yet."

*   *   *   *   *

277

Zarro tucks the memory away and looks at his boss. "Yeah, that rumor is true, about me being in jail." Zarro says to Rick. "It kind of came up in passing when I was assuring the staff that no one is perfect and everyone makes mistakes and that as long as we work as a team, the job would get done. But this is cutting edge management stuff, Rick. It's all over the web. And it kind of floors me you're not familiar with it. Besides, Mel Lieb once told me to always respect your past. And Old Bay Correctional Institute in Massachusetts *is* my past."

Schwab shakes his head. "You mean to tell me some out-of-state, ex-con, bleeding-heart nut-job is running my treasured family business?"

"And doing one wicked fine job of it too," Zarro adds. "Here, have yourself another Hoodsie. Go ahead, it's on the McClellan family."

"You know if I never heard that name again, I'd be a happier king."

Zarro tosses his empty Hoodsie cup into the trash. "Well, back to work. My sauna is calling me. You think it's hot down here, Rick? Why don't you remove your jacket and tie and join us upstairs in shipping for a stretch? We're wiping sweat off our sweat. See?" Zarro asks, pulling the sweatband off his head and tossing it Rick Schwab's way.

"Oh you don't sweat, Zarro, you positively glow. Now get back here and take this overripe, saturated sweatband with you. And I hear you invited half the place up to that town of yours for a wedding reception next weekend."

"Yeah, I'm sorry you and your wife couldn't join us."

"You're wedding happens to coincide with my theater tickets. Theater is class entertainment, but you wouldn't know

278

class if it bit you in your soft spot Zarro. But never mind that, I'm about to ask a couple of favors of you."

Zarro looks at his boss. "Yeah? What can I do for you, oh king of mine?"

"I want you to make sure every last one of these people are on the train to New York by Sunday night. And I don't care if you have to hogtie them into their seats."

"What are you worried about? They'll all be back by Monday morning, bright-eyed and bushy-tailed, singing the company song. And even if they're not, you said so yourself, they're all easily replaceable. Remember? It was you who referred to them sarcastically as the great brain trust in the back, wasn't it?"

"Oh, you're on a roll today, Zarro. I take it you haven't come to the realization that no one likes their words flung back in their face, especially when the words are used to drive home a point contrary to the opinion of the individual in charge. This certain individual might even infer that it's a tad disrespectful."

"I assure you no disrespect is intended."

"Good. I wouldn't want this certain individual to jump to the wrong conclusion. And as long as the sacred employer-employee relationship is back to sunshine and lollipops, I am making a request of you, Zarro. Now I say request, but actually I'm using it as a euphemism for demand. The king would like you to call in from your honeymoon in Cape Cod once a day."

"Are you out of your fuckin' mind? You want me to call in from my *honeymoon*? For Christ's sake, Bill Gates didn't call in from *his* honeymoon!"

"Bill Gates doesn't have the privilege of working for yours truly. Just think about it Zarro, you will be away for a week. How the hell is this tower of Babel going to run?"

279

"Don't give it a second thought. The place will run itself. Jesus, you're always shooting me looks. Okay. I'll call in two times. Twice, get it? Even I have to come up for air now and then. But as long as we're on the subject of favors, I have one."

"What now?"

"Hear me out. I want you to seriously think about insulating the warehouse before winter. Too many people were out sick last winter because of the drafts. Those space heaters we have scattered around really don't do the trick. I think everyone would appreciate a temperate environment to work in. In the scheme of life, it's not too much to ask now, is it?"

"Do me a colossal favor and don't quote me your favorite saying now. You know the one; a happy worker is a productive worker. I positively gag on that warm and fuzzy stuff you're always trying to shove sideways down my throat."

Zarro laughs. "Warm and fuzzies, my sweet guinea ass. It's good business. You'll have to hide those massive profits from Uncle Sam somehow, right? Why don't I get some bids out as soon as I return?"

"Anything else, Zarro? Maybe we should get a fund going to buy that kid they call Spacious, two front teeth."

"Don't think I'm not going to hold you to it. As it is, Matty McClellan, great benefactor that he is, has already started a collection to buy Roman man's best friend."

"Matty wants to buy Spacious a *dog*?"

"Who said anything about a dog?" Zarro asks, with the most innocent of looks plastered on his face. "Matty was thinking more on the lines of a decent blow job."

"Matty could probably take *that* act of charity as a tax write off."

280

Zarro stretches, realizing just how drained he is. "Say, how did it go with the two from the Arab Maritime Academy? They weren't here more than a half an hour."

"It went well. Basically the deal was sewed up on the phone, but they wanted to meet yours truly in person, see what kind of honorable gentleman I am, as they put it. And because I *am* an honorable gentleman, we now have ourselves a nice, big contract to work on. The king is pleased. We might even have to go on overtime again next month, between this and that costume gig."

"You know, we could always hire a couple of more workers."

"Kiss my ass, Zarro."

"That's just your way of saying I did a great job and apart from Mel Lieb, hiring me was the best thing that ever happened to this company."

Zarro heads back up the hill. He stops when he reaches his back office. Weeds is holding the ladder while Matty is busy attaching a stenciled sign right next to the MEL LIEB LANE sign Zarro had put up in January. ZARRO ROADE, the new sign proclaims.

"Watcha think, boss?" Matty asks him proudly as he descends from the ladder.

"Thanks guys," Zarro says with a big grin. "That means a lot to me, especially since, well, you know. What I'm trying to say, is that I appreciate it that none of you back here gave me an ounce of grief over yesterday's lunchtime confession. That sign is positively sweet. And Road looks even better than usual with

281

an 'e' on the end. I really think the two of you are onto something here."

And as Weeds goes to put the ladder away, Zarro turns to Matty and says, "Do me a big favor and you lock up for me tonight."

"Be my pleasure, boss. I'll get your keys back to you on Monday."

"These are *your* keys. You keep them now, you earned them," Zarro says, tossing the set at Matty. "And the new alarm code is really easy to remember, five-ten-seventy."

"What's so easy about that?"

"Ah come on Matty, everybody and his grandmother knows that's the date Bobby Orr brought the cup home to Boston after a twenty-nine year absence."

"Five-ten-seventy," Matty repeats. "I'm gonna write that down."

"Listen Southy, I'm counting on you and Weeds to take care of things out back when I'm away, *capisce?*"

"Don't worry, Zarro. We won't make you look bad."

Zarro nods. "Just a couple of tokes at lunch, that's it. Under no, and I mean *no* circumstances does that three-dollar a gallon bottle of gin makes its way out of that file cabinet. You hear me? And another thing, I want you to go easy on Roman. You know, take care of him."

"I already told you what I'm doing for Roman."

"I don't mean take care of him *that* way. I want you to make sure no one hassles him when I'm not here. And that goes double for Sgt. Custard. If I hear so much as a whisper that you and Weeds made him march around the factory like some Ecuadorian Continental soldier, I'll wipe the place with both your asses."

282

"God, that would be funny, huh? Little Sgt. Custard, his mop perched on his shoulder like a rifle, playing toy soldier up and down the aisles. Left, right, left, right. A-bout face. Forward march. That would be a rip, Zarro. A rip. I'm pissing my pants just thinking about it."

"So *don't* think about it. Get the thought right out of your head, Matty."

"Okay, I hear you. Hey boss, aren't you jumping the gun a little? Don't we got most of next week to go over this?"

"I'm falling apart at the seams *now*, Matty. By next week you'll be sweeping me up in a fuckin' dustpan."

"You're nervous about walking down that aisle in front of all those people, huh Zarro?"

"Nervous doesn't quite describe it. Scared shitless comes a little closer. Anyway, have a good weekend. You really put in quite a day today, and don't think I didn't notice."

Matty beams. "Thanks. And thanks for inviting me, Weeds, and the Spanish boys, to that wedding of yours next week. You *will* have Heineken at the party, right?"

"I'm going to have to call the caterer on that one. Get back at you on Monday. And Matty?"

"Yeah?"

"I don't want to be anywhere close to those Battling McClellan Brothers in the near future, especially when I have to return the tux in one piece."

"You got nothin' to worry about. We're driving up separate. I'm riding up in the limo with Billy and my mother Friday after work. We're gonna make a little vacation out of it, see the sights and all. My mother got a cousin up your way, over in South Boston."

"A Southy."

283

"No, she don't box. Anyway, this cousin of hers told her all about Suffolk Downs."

"The racetrack?"

"Yeah, so me and Billy figured we'd see *that* sight first."

Zarro clenches his fist into a pretend microphone. "Ladies and gentlemen, the window is open, place your bets. Place your bets."

"Zarro, I'm gonna love Boston."

Zarro takes a few minutes and knocks down the empty boxes that are left on the shipping table. He picks up the box that the Hoodsies came in and is about to dump the crumpled newspapers into the trash before a bold headline catches his eye. He smoothes out the paper, and it reads, "'Gang Leader Dead at Rikers.'"

Zarro reads on. *"According to Detective Milagros Santiago, head of Brooklyn's gang unit, a power struggle may have broken out between rival cliques within the notorious MS gang after the F.B.I. arrested three high-level gang members in July. Rafael (The Knife) Guzman terrorized area residents and was known to be involved in the distribution of heroin and cocaine, prostitution, and human trafficking. Guzman was a suspect in the Christmas Eve arson that left three women dead and others injured. He was also linked to the recent slashing death of Myrna Cedeno who had been held captive by Guzman. The diminutive Detective Santiago stated at a press conference at One Police Plaza, 'This is an obvious power struggle within the gang. Guzman's body was discovered by guards during a routine bed check. His throat was slashed from ear to ear.' At present, there are no suspects in custody."*

He reads the article again. And again. Happiness washes over him. Maggie would be free of all of this. She could get on with her life and not be haunted by this bastard. It took a while, but his plan had worked. The clique thought Guzman had purposely turned them over to the F.B.I. They thought he was a rat and they disposed of him, accordingly. Suddenly, Zarro realizes he has killed a man. Indirectly speaking. And he feels good about it. Damn good. Not a drop of remorse. What does that say about him? Zarro wonders. Who cares? Let the ethicists of the world debate that one. Let them wring their soft, white hands over right and wrong when it comes to the people *they* love, he thinks. He crosses the street to his apartment and shows the newspaper article to Maggie. "Justice is served," he says happily.

Zarro watches as Maggie squints and frowns as she slowly makes out the words. Suddenly she looks up, beaming. "This is such good news," she says. "But there is a mistake, I think. Detective Millie is not Dominican. She is Puerto Rican.'

"Diminutive. Not Dominican. It means short."

"Dim-in-u-tive" she repeats. Then Maggie looks at him, her olive eyes probing deeply. She has a feeling that he had something to do with this good news. But this time she cannot decipher anything but joy in Zarro's expression.

Chapter Thirty

Zarro and Maggie have an appointment with Father Michael of St. John Vianney the day before the wedding. According to his mother, Father Sebastian's gastrointestinal problems had worsened and he had to retire from many of his priestly duties.

"Robbie, I hope you and Maggie have as happy a life as your father and I have had."

"Are you for real? After everything you've been through, you can actually stand there with a straight face and tell me you two are happy?"

"Every marriage has its peaks and valleys, but your father and I have gotten over them without too much wear and tear." Then his mother is drawn to their kitchen window. A blue jay seems to catch her eye and she follows it as it visits the azaleas, finally perching on the branch of an evergreen. She continues to look out at their small garden for the longest time.

He is unaccustomed to his mother's pensiveness. It surprises him, makes him uneasy. "Well, then I want what you and Daddy have."

She turns from the window. "You'll have to *earn* what your father and I have. Earn it over the years. You and Maggie will have to pay your dues just like everybody else in the world. And you can start by fulfilling the obligation to your parents."

"I know, I know. I owe you money for the lawyers. Give me some time to recoup from the wedding, okay?"

"You think I'm looking for *money*? I'm looking for you and Maggie to be here. For weekends now and then. For holidays. Especially for holidays. My God, Robbie, even eighty-year-old Mrs. Feinberg noticed your absence this past Christmas Eve. And don't think she didn't say anything about you not showing up for Easter. You know how old people are. They sit by the front window watching everything that goes on around them. What else do they have but other people's lives? And their world gets so small so fast. One minute Mrs. Feinberg has a job and a husband to come home to, and boom, she's a widow in an empty house planning the next visit to the doctors. She's coming to your wedding, by the way. Wouldn't miss her little Robbie getting married for all the world."

"Good old Mrs. Feinberg," he says, reminiscing. "Does she still bake those crescent cookies with the jam inside? A couple of those with a glass of milk, I can still taste them."

"Robbie, do you think people stop baking just because you don't show up to eat?"

"All right, Ma. I get the message. Maggie and I will be here for every major holiday. We certainly wouldn't want to disrupt Mrs. Feinberg's routine now, would we?"

"You try to turn everything into a joke. But you can't even begin to imagine how you turned our lives completely upside down. And those years of not knowing what was doing with you and how you were holding up were no joke."

Marie Zarro turns back to the window. Zarros sees that the blue jay has flown away. And, although her back is to him,

Zarro also sees how upset his mother is by her trembling shoulders.

"Take it easy, Ma. I know what I did. God help me, I know what I did and…and I know I can't go back and undo it. But for whatever little it's worth, I'm sorry for all the pain I caused you and Daddy. You're good parents. No way you deserved to have a son like me. But I suffered too, you know. I was hurting all the time. When you're locked up, you hurt every single hour of every single day. Ah, please don't cry, Ma. Please. We can't go back. We can't ever go back."

Still shaking, his mother nods her head. "I'll be okay," she sniffs. "Just give me a minute. I didn't want to get into this again, really I didn't. Not when there's such a happy occasion tomorrow. My little boy is getting married. I just missed you, that's all."

He watches his mother take a deep breath and smooth her blonde hair. "Ma, do you think there's time after Maggie and I go to church, to run by Pearle and get me fitted for glasses? I'm not sure, but I think I need a pair for reading."

Actually, he doesn't think *anything* is wrong with his eyes, but Zarro realizes he owes her one. And he knows it will bring his mother immense joy to parade him around the aisles of Pearle Vision, Marie Zarro's prodigal but possibly near-sighted son, returned.

"Of course. Everyone would love to meet you," she says, her expression immediately brightening. "I talk about you all the time. They constantly hear about my eldest son who runs a warehouse in New York. You never said anything before. Since when are your eyes giving you trouble?"

"Since I started reading to Maggie. And she's reading to me to help with her English. Did I tell you she writes poetry? Spanish poetry."

"Poetry, that's something. From the first day I met her I knew she was a real special girl. And isn't that nice, you two reading together? What a good idea. And thank God you came to me about your eyes. We'll get you all fixed up with a set of designer frames, the featherweight lenses, whatever the doc recommends. He's very honest, too. If you don't need a prescription, he'll be the first one to tell you. Not all of them are honest like that. Ooh Robbie, look at the time! You'd better get Maggie or you'll be late for your appointment at church."

Father Michael calls Maggie into a small office that is adjacent to the rectory. And Zarro is able to get a very brief glance. He is a young priest with dark, curly hair and an olive complexion and what either looked to be the beginnings of a beard or a very heavy five o'clock shadow. His mother had been quick to tell him he was a local boy, grew up right here in Boston. He's Italian too, she had mentioned. A *Calabrese*, but nice anyway. Didn't have that typical *Calabrese* attitude like his Aunt Carmella, the sister-in-law from hell, as his mother referred to her.

The Father spends fifteen minutes with Maggie before he calls the groom in. She emerges smiling and takes the seat outside the door that her 'berto had been occupying. Zarro is somewhat taken aback when he sees the young priest up close. True, his mother had said young. But this priest looks to be *his* age. And other than the clothing, he doesn't look anything at all like the Holy Roller Zarro is expecting. He looks like a regular unshaven guy you could sit down with in front of the Celts and have a cold one. Maybe he's twenty-eight, thirty tops. The archdiocese must be hurting for priests big time if they had to bring this lightweight in, Zarro thinks.

"I am glad we finally get to meet," the priest begins. "Your mother has told me a little bit about you. And I will speak to you and Maggie as a couple, but I'd like to try to get to know you as individuals in the little time we have. So why don't we begin by you telling me just who is Robert Zarro."

"Who am I? Is this some kind of a joke? This church has plenty of paperwork on me. I was baptized here, did my CCD. Received First Holy Communion, Confirmation, the whole works. I was an altar boy for godsakes. Sorry, I didn't mean that. It just blows my mind that you have not a clue who I am." Calm down, Kicker, and play nice. The last thing we need is Jesus doing laps around the cross.

"Paperwork doesn't tell me who you are," the priest says.

"You know you look very familiar to me. I've seen you before, maybe in the neighborhood. Were you into sports as a kid?"

"I played soccer on and off. Hockey. That's about it, and that was a long time ago. By the time I got into high school, I gave up sports for drama. My parish did a little local version of Godspell, but I don't think anyone other than a handful of parents and grandparents saw that one. After that I did do a little community theater in Danvers. Is it possible you caught me in Fiddler on the Roof? It wasn't a big role, but my Moetel the tailor received favorable reviews in the local papers."

Zarro stares at the priest, trying his best to gauge whether or not the cleric is pulling his leg about Fiddler on the Roof. "I don't think so," he says when he cannot detect the slightest bit of guile in the priest's countenance. "It must be the sports where I know you. Your hockey playing, was it travel or rec?"

291

"I played travel for a couple of years. For Newton. That's where I grew up."

"Ah Newton, that figures. Bunch of ice skating *fanooks* there. No wonder you became a priest."

"Never mind why I became a priest. We're talking about *you* here. So my son," he asks in a voice just a little too loud for the room, "just who is this Robert Zarro sitting here before me?"

Zarro shifts in the uncomfortable wooden chair. Well, the new priest certainly has a flair for drama. He probably did pull off Moetel the tailor in Danvers. Just what we need in Revere, a goddamn singing and dancing thespian priest! "I'm just an ordinary guy looking to get married."

"It states here that you *are* married. You were married in a civil ceremony in New York."

"That's right. And now we'd like to tie the knot in church."

"Before our Almighty God?"

"Bingo."

The priest gets up from behind his desk and raises a window. "It's warm in here, isn't it?" And then without so much as a breath, "Do you believe in God, Robert?"

Zarro shrugs. "In answer to question one, yes it's warm in here. And as for question two, I know if I say 'yes Father, I believe in God,' you'll marry us. And if I say 'no Father, I see no evidence of God,' me and my one hundred and twenty-three guests won't be chowing down on prime rib tomorrow afternoon. So let's play it safe and go with 'yes' for both questions one and two."

The priest continues, his voice having modulated down into conversational tone. "Robert, your mother touched on the adversity you've experienced in your life."

292

"So my mother took it upon herself to tell you I was locked up? That's rich. What else did she tell you about me?"

"Your mother was and is very concerned about your mental state. She said you spent time in prison and basically had no contact with the family for nearly three years. Did you abandon your faith when you were in prison?"

"My faith abandoned me," he states coldly, knowing his answer would raise some ire. All bets are off now, Father.

"God was with you at all times."

"Well, that's the party line they've been feeding us since kindergarten."

"There was never an act of kindness, never a moment of decency in the entire time you were incarcerated?"

Zarro thinks back, making the new priest wait for his answer. He clears his throat when he is ready to speak, thinking two could play at this dramatic stuff just as easily as one. "Well, there was this inmate who they transferred over from Walpole. He reached out to me once. He didn't have to, either. See, his boyfriend on the outside slipped him some smack on a visit. I won't tell you how he smuggled the stuff in, 'cause you'd probably lose your lunch."

"And you tried to stop him? Tried to help him with his addiction?" the priest interjects.

"Try to keep in mind I did my time at Old Bay Correctional—not on Sesame Street. It was *him* who did the reaching out. Get it? He shared his dope with me. Not your run of the mill oblation, right Father? And he didn't have to do that, either, you know. The man didn't owe me jack. And you better believe I was very suspicious at first, him being openly gay and all. But he was a perfect gentleman. He didn't want anything from me, even let me go first being there was only one needle between us and he couldn't swear if he was positive or not.

293

That's the one act of Christian decency I can remember, and this guy they sent over from Shirley wasn't even a Christian. He must have been some kind of lapsed Muslim, Muhammad something or other his name was."

"I see."

"I doubt it. The drugs, they blot the time out, and he took it upon himself to share that with me. The heroin grabbed an evil, ugly place by the balls and painted this warm, pink gauze around it. It really is the mother of all highs, just like they say it is. This gay Muhammad something from Walpole eased my pain when there was nothing in it for him, nothing. Not exactly the testament to faith you were hoping for, huh?"

The priest continues to look at Zarro. "And your family? Why wouldn't you let *them* comfort you, ease your suffering with their love? Why did you choose to do your time alone?"

"Oh, I think I'm getting where you're coming from now. You're saying, because I was an *antisocial* convict I can't receive the rite of marriage."

"No, not at all. But I'd still like to understand why you pulled away from everybody."

"Because I didn't want them to see me there, okay? Not like that. Not *ever* like that. And that's all I'm saying on this topic. Now either you're going to marry me and Maggie or you're not, but don't go looking for me to churn out fairytales so you can feel all cozy and rosy about your calling."

"Look, I didn't mean to upset you. And I'm not looking for fairytales. I'm sort of new at all this. Not that I didn't do my share of role playing in the family counseling class at the seminary, but they can't begin to prepare you for all the different scenarios you're going to encounter on a day-to-day basis. I'm sure I would've remembered if something like this heroin predicament came up. So have a little patience, please.

Understand that before I begin counseling Robert Zarro, I need to figure out who Robert Zarro is."

"And which Robert Zarro do you have in mind? The hockey player that more than likely checked you and your Newton buddies headfirst into the rail? The altar boy? The prisoner at Old Bay? The guy who runs a warehouse in Queens? The social media wizard who increased sales off the charts? Give me a clue, Father. You know something, even *calling* you Father is bizarre."

"You can call me Michael if you're more comfortable with that, even Mike. I don't mind."

"I don't know what I'm comfortable with. Maybe it's not the title. Maybe it's the third degree you're giving me. I'm not used to priests doing the asking. Priests are supposed to give you the answers, not get you all stirred up with out-of-the-blue questions. But I'll play along. I have nothing to lose. So, which Robert Zarro is it that you're looking for now?"

"I want to get to know the *other* Robert Zarro. The Robert Zarro who finds it hard to admit he is here seeking God's blessing, despite his very understandable and hopefully temporary disillusionment with the Church."

Zarro shakes his head. "This is unbelievable. Father Sebastian might have broken wind one time too many, but he never tortured me like this. Maybe he let me have it good once when I showed up ten minutes late one Sunday, but that's it. He never tied me to the rack."

"I'm not here to torture you Robert. I'm here to make sure you are aware of what marriage in our church means. A nuptial union merges two spirits. It is said where the flesh is one; one also is the spirit. When you marry within the Roman Catholic Church, Robert, your very home becomes an extension

295

of the Church. Marriage is a very sacred rite. It binds you spiritually to another person, forever."

"I get it. A life sentence with no time off for good behavior."

The priest tries to keep a serious face. "Well, Robert you are certainly blessed with a sense of humor. In fact you remind me of someone I met at the seminary, my good friend Brother Tim. He's very funny. Everyone likes him. Plays the guitar, too."

"And it's just my great luck that Brother Tim, the funny guitar playing priest, didn't end up at St. John Vianney."

"Brother Tim is now Father Tim, at a parish church in Staten Island New York nicknamed St. Rock's, if you can believe it—although the name of the saint is obviously R-O-C-H not R-O-C-K."

"Obviously," Zarro agrees sarcastically.

"But even Father Tim, the funny guitar-playing priest, would still be obligated to counsel you. I see you're wearing a gold chain around your neck. Does your chain happen to have a cross on it?"

Zarro pulls the long chain out from under his T-shirt, exposing the small gold cross. "Very impressive. After five o'clock mass you can board Amtrak to New York and get yourself a guest spot on The Late Show. Let's give a warm welcome, as he's all the way from that great hockey-playing town of *Newton*, Massachusetts. Ladies and gentlemen, please put your hands together for Father Michael, the clairvoyant priest. The town of Danvers loved him as Moetel the tailor in Fiddler on the Roof. Now let's check out is powers of ESP."

"You must hold *some* beliefs if you wear the cross," the priest says, smiling and trying his utmost not to actually laugh.

"My sponsor bought it for me when I got confirmed. And that's only because the one I got for my first Communion got busted apart at a hockey game, and believe me it wasn't the game where Revere was up against *Newton*. But don't get your rosaries all tangled. It's a piece of jewelry Father. That's all it is. Nothing more than a fourteen karat addition sign."

"Bullshit."

"Whoa. Back up there. Did you say what I think you said? How do you like that? I've been away so long they're letting priests swear like sailors now," Zarro says, grinning from ear to ear.

"Forgive me. It slipped. I told you I'm a rookie."

"Well, better it slips out with me in the room than with one of those senior citizens from the Holy Name Society. You slip up with that gang and you're likely to give any one of them a heart attack. And those old people got connections all the way up to the Vatican, Father. Open up a mouth like that and they'll see you out the door and banished to some ten-member parish in the middle of Ass-wipe, Kentucky."

"Good point. I'll be more careful," the young priest says. "And although I expressed it in the wrong way, I doubt you just the same. Whether you know it or not that *other* Robert Zarro within you wants to go before the altar of Christ. Just by coming here you are on the right path. And you chose the right path once before when you and Maggie decided to cherish the life that grew within her. It is the path *you* have chosen, whether you admit it or not."

Zarro sighs. "Maggie told you about our baby, our baby that didn't live?"

"Yes, and her other baby too."

Zarro cast his eyes downward. He pictures Maggie burying Sergio in Mexico. He takes a breath and tries to compose himself. "She's been through hell and back. And I

297

haven't really been there for her. Unfortunately, the right words don't always come to the top when I need them."

"From our brief meeting, I can see Maggie has a deep faith and a real commitment to good works. In fact, I gave her the name and address of Casa Alianza, a safe house affiliated with Covenant House in New York. They do work with the street children in Guatemala City. But before we got onto that topic, she told me what a fine man she thinks you are. Your words may desert you now and then, but Maggie understands you and it's obvious she loves you, the way God intended a woman to love a man. So, cleave to her Robert and love her, love her as Christ loved the Church."

"Look, I don't mean to rush you but my tux came in wrong," Zarro says. "The sleeves need to be shortened and the pants need to be lengthened. Other than that, it's perfect. And when I'm through with the tux, I got a dozen other last minute errands to run, including a statewide manhunt for a couple of cases of Heinekens. Seems the clueless caterer my mother dug up at the last minute doesn't normally carry the brand and I have a guest who's *quite* the connoisseur."

"We're almost finished. So who is the *other* Robert Zarro?"

"That *other* Robert Zarro fell in love with Maggie Ocampo. And this Maggie Ocampo touched that *other* Robert Zarro's soul like you wouldn't believe. And that *other* Robert Zarro is here to ask for God's blessing *not* for himself, but for the family he came close to destroying, and for the very special girl who sees some good in him and who he wants to spend the rest of his life with. The rest of his life, *capisce*?"

"What kind of life do you want to lead, Robert?"

"Do you really think that after being locked up for three years with a bunch of junkies, thieves, and sex offenders, I want

298

to lead a bad life? You're really pushing my patience to the max today. I don't know what kind of training they're giving you people these days, but this replay of the Inquisition won't go over big with the parishioners here in Revere. Maybe it would have worked in *Newton*, but that's fancy Green Line territory so who's to say?"

"Don't stop now," the Father says. "Look at us. We're actually having a conversation here! We're talking about the life you want to lead. Well, go on."

"Here goes nothing, Father Michael. I want to take Maggie ice-skating and show her the swan boats in the Public Garden. And I want to sit on the beach with her every summer. And I want to take her to the movies and to concerts, and she really wants to see the Statue of Liberty. I want to buy her new things, expensive things, because she's a girl who deserves the best. I don't want to ever see her walk into Good Wheel again, that's Spanish for Good Will in case you think it's some automotive place. And I want to dance with her, real slow. And I want to spend my nights making love to her. Oh my God, I cannot believe I just said this to a priest. Erase that last thought. Okay, I want to have kids with her Father, lots of kids. And I will try to be the best father I can. I'm still all shook up inside from Maggie's miscarriage. You might find it hard to believe listening to me now, sounding like some off the wall freak, but I really wanted that baby."

"I believe you."

"And I'm willing to sacrifice for my children. I'll even suffer through that yawn-a–minute Freedom Trail again. And once we get back from that hokey reenactment of the Tea Party, I want to sit these kids down at the kitchen table and make sure they know their fractions before Friday's math test. And I want to make sure they know how to throw a curveball and how to slide into third, especially the girls. And after they bring home their report cards, I want to take all these kids out for Chinese food. By the way, they don't put a loaf of bread on the table in the Chinese restaurants in New York."

"They *don't*?" the young priest asks with some disbelief. "Hasn't anyone there read their Bible? Go thy way, eat thy bread with joy,"

"What can I tell you? New York's one crazy place. But like I said to you, I'm running short of time here. So, can we please bring Maggie in here for our joint session?"

"Yes my son."

Zarro says, "Not for nothing Father, as they say in New York, but I'd go easy on that 'my son' stuff, at least until you hit forty, or until you clean up your act. Whichever comes first."

"Thanks Robert," he says warmly. "I'll keep that in mind. You're full of good advice."

"I'm full of something all right. Um, just one more thing Father Michael. Do me a favor. When you run into my mother, please don't mention the way I spoke to you today. It's just you really don't look like any priest I ever knew. You look like a regular guy from Newton. You even *swear* like a regular guy from Newton. And I wasn't raised to talk to a priest or to anyone for that matter, with any kind of disrespect. Look, I'm on short sleep and I'm more than a little *stonare* with this wedding business. I really don't want to mess this up, and your line of questioning just got me a little hot under the collar, that's all."

The young priest chuckles. "Listen up, you hockey playing *scocci*, *I'm* the only one in the room with a collar. And with this big mouth, I'll consider myself one extremely lucky priest if that Latin-spouting bishop of ours lets me keep it around my neck."

And with that, Father Michael opens the door and ushers Maggie in.

Chapter Thirty-One

On Saturday, as he stands at the back of the church, a long, golden circle appears around Robert Zarro. A flock of dust motes stray serendipitously into the path of stained glass, surrounding him in warm drizzles of yellow light. A clarinet begins to play, his old clarinet from high school, the reedy sound piercing through the muffled echo of the nave. His eyes are drawn to his paternal grandparents seated up front, and for a few seconds a sea of tiny gray dots float in front of his eyes, and he is a young boy in the park. The gray dots connect into an image, an image of his dead grandparents. Now all four grandparents are before him, the Zarros and the Scioffos. And he hears his Nanny Scioffo singing along with the notes of the clarinet. *Ninna-nanna, ninna-oh.* He is four years old and she is pushing him on a metal safety swing in Della Russo Park, back and forth, back and forth. *Questo bimbo a chi lo do?*

And then he appears a little older and his father is shaking him, waking him up for hockey practice. Robbie, Rob? You hear me? Get moving. We're going to be late. Clem's slobbery tongue on his face, his brother Anthony tagging after him in faded blue Doctor Dentins as he gathers up his gear. His mother, already downstairs when dark is still out the window,

303

busy packing him a thermos of cocoa. Older still and he is at his locker in Revere High School rummaging around for his chemistry homework. And there he is in college, quick with the smile, and flush with cash, no problem. Then there is a break in the golden circle, a nadir where he is at Old Bay and time ticks backwards, painfully deducting seconds from a carrion soul, and days are subtracted until zero is reached. The golden illumination picks up again in New York as his eyes gaze upon the kindly face of Mel Lieb, the people he works with, the people he counts on, the people who count on him. And suddenly he is back at the park with his four grandparents again, only his grandparents are seated on a bench and now it is Zarro pushing the swing, only the swing is empty and Maggie is standing before him. And then a child appears on the swing. And the circle continues on and on, reaching way beyond the reach of Zarro's vision.

"Rob, are you okay?"

"Nee?"

"Jesus Rob, you look like you're ready to pass out cold."

"Nee, I just saw pieces of my life in this golden circle of light. You know something? It kind of looks like olive oil. And then these little gray dots came and Nanny Scioffo was singing this Italian song. You know the *Ninna-nanna* song. And then I was late for hockey practice and you were running around in your pajamas. Then I saw myself in high school and college. And then the circle broke and I was at Old Bay. I get it now. I should really have another sit-down with Father Michael. Oh Anthony, you can't imagine how I busted his chops yesterday. I made him swear at me, that's how crazy I got him. I feel bad about it, too. But I've been in this mood lately."

"You, in a mood? You're joking, right?"

304

"We'll see what you're about when you're ready to get married. But hear me out, Nee. All along it must be God who's working to keep us in the circle. I have to tell the Father it's *not* a path, it's a circle. And there are certain people who hold us in the circle. I get it now. By the way, Father Michael played hockey. For Newton, of all places."

"Hockey? Ask me to sing 'O Canada' for you."

"Look where you are, Nee. It would be sacrilegious to sing 'O Canada' when you're standing in a church before God Almighty smack in the heart of Bruin country."

"Ask me."

"Fine, go ahead. Knock yourself out, Anthony. Just the French singing virgins now."

A momentary silence sits between them. Zarro looks up at the marble statue of the Blessed Mother, expecting her to belt out the anthem at any second. "So sing it already."

"I can't do it."

"Are you trying to tell me you lost your *French*?" Zarro asks with a smile.

"Guess again."

"Well, it's about time. I'm happy for you Nee, I really am. Be careful though, okay?"

"The way you were?"

"No, *never* the way I was. You know I live my life to set an example of what *not* to do."

"I appreciate that. But seriously Rob, you're having visions of golden circles of olive oil? You're hearing the *Ninna-Nanna* song? You really should have forced yourself to have that bowl of Cheerios before church, brother. You never were much good on an empty stomach."

"Look, I know I haven't been around too much but I'd like you to come to New York when you got time off from

305

school. We'll hang together. Catch a ballgame. It's okay to like the Mets and the Sox, because both teams would like nothing better than to wipe the floor with the Yankees. If you don't believe me, ask my friend the detective who took his time to explain his McClellan logic to me. And maybe you can come work for me over the summer, stay with me and Maggie. I'd really like that. The buzz on the street is that I'm not such a son of a bitch to work for. I…I don't know…I owe you so much, Nee. I left you all alone when I went to jail. All alone to hear the fights. You had to deal with it all by yourself…when you were no more than a kid. I can never make that up to you. But I'd really like to be there—"

"Hold that thought, I think I'm supposed to walk that girl Lygia down the aisle now."

"Promise me you'll be good, Anthony. For them. I put them through hell. I put you—"

"Shh, all right, all right, I promise. Rob, get a grip. The organ's playing. It's my cue."

"You have the rings?"

"Ah shit, *I* was supposed to bring the rings?"

"Not funny, Nee. I'm dying here. I'm trying so hard—"

Anthony taps his breast pocket. "Don't worry. I'm the responsible one, remember?"

And then it is Zarro's turn to walk down the aisle. His friends and co-workers from New York help propel him down to the altar with various words of encouragement, words such as "Go get her, Zarro" and, "It's too late to turn back." He stops and hugs his parents. And then the beautiful bride, escorted by a grinning Tommy McClellan is before him. His Maggie. His strength.

When the conversation from the pews quiets down, Father Michael begins the service. The yellow circle swirls around just the two of them now. And then the young priest has them kneel as he raises his hands to bless the couple before him. At the altar of St. John Vianney in Revere, Massachusetts, humbled before his beloved mysterious God, Father Michael joins Magaly Ocampo to Robert Zarro.

And around this, in his widening, golden circle, he, his beautiful Maggie, and everyone else, seen and unseen, whispers, "Amen."

Acknowledgements

I am blessed with a wonderful family: my husband Jeff, and my grown children Michael, Jason, and Nicole. They are my inspiration. I would like to thank Kitty Kladstrup, the Senior Acquisitions Editor at Champlain Avenue Books for her invaluable editorial suggestions and support.

Donna Cantor is also the author of the novel **Sunnyside**. She is an Assistant Teaching Professor for the Writing Program at Rutgers University.

*Visit her website at **www.donnacantor.com***

Made in the USA
Charleston, SC
24 June 2016